IN A RIGHT STATE

BY

BEN ELLIS

COPYRIGHT

CHAPTER 1

The hand of a lady, aged by time and paled by death, had been stood up on its own severed wrist, hermetically sealed within the vacuum of a bell jar. Cradled in the grip of an assistant, the hand was raised above the watching audience as though it were trying to attract someone's attention with a wave.

"£18,000!" A bidder's voice sternly announced from the bank of phones situated to one side of the auction hall.

The lifeless hand was succeeding; it was holding everyone's attention.

"Do I hear £19,000?" demanded the auctioneer from behind his rostrum. "£18,000 is the current bid from outside the room. Do I hear £19,000 from someone with the common decency to appear in person for such an item?" In one sweep, the auctioneer scrutinised the entire room. Everyone kept entirely still, ignoring itches and suppressing ticks, one rookie bidder allowing a tear to form through fear of blinking.

A bid leapfrogged from the back of the room: "£20,000!"

"£20,000 in the room, £20,000 is the current bid and I'm going to move things along, as we've got a lot to get through, by calling 'Going once'." The auctioneer looked toward the phones; a man shakes his head. "'Going twice.' Do I hear £21,000?" The auctioneer gave one final sweep before bringing the gavel down onto the rostrum. "Sold to the gentleman at the back! That concludes the introductory 'handshake' sale of Lot 230; let's get on with the introductions proper. A female, aged sixty-three, mother to one healthy son and grandmother to one healthy granddaughter. The deceased died from a brain haemorrhage two weeks ago. Obviously, being of a certain age, she was born before genetic screening, but the best of us usually are." The auctioneer surveyed the room again over the half-rimmed glasses perched on the end of his nose – a monument to such pre-screening times and a symbol of resistance to medical advancements. "Our medical examiners have determined she was in fine health and, apart from the brain, all other body parts are in very good condition and up for sale. A synopsis of the autopsy report is in your programme notes whilst the full report has been available online for the past five days. The usual caveats and terms apply. All items sold will conform to UK regulations and are grouped together in standard units."

Closing his notes and removing his glasses, he picked up his gavel to begin the new auction. "That's the legal jargon out the way; let's get down to business ladies and gentlemen. The next item on our list: Lot 230b, the full set of phalanges from the left foot. We already have a pre-auction bid of £5,000. Do I hear £5,500?"

Duncan felt compelled to attend the auction of his wife's body parts for two reasons. Firstly, it was a way of saying goodbye for the last time. He wanted to see who was going to bid for her; was she going to a good home? Duncan knew these were childish and naive emotions but he felt it would help him say goodbye. The only people authorised to purchase body parts were professional bidders from pharmaceutical corporations, insurance companies and private research organisations, so even if Duncan had put in the highest bid for his wife's heart or liver, he wouldn't have had the clearance to actually walk out the building with them. The checks may not have been watertight coming in, but actually getting his hands on his wife would've been as hard as their first date.

The second reason was he needed to see what type of companies purchased the remains. Duncan's wife, Nicole, didn't leave behind an average body constructed of norms, unexceptional and hidden safe within the bell-curve. Nicole's body may have looked normal to the untrained eye and within the broad synopsis of the programme notes, but a deeper look into the online report would've highlighted a few key anomalies. Duncan knew this and he was here to see if anyone else did.

The pre-auction bid of £5,000 for the left phalanges remained without anyone else bidding, and the auctioneer quickly ended the auction. The bones in his wife's left foot were worth £5,000. Was that a good price? Duncan had no idea. Next up were the phalanges from the right foot. The product may have appeared the same, but the auction hall came alive. The bidding opened at £5,000, as with the left phalanges, but after four bids it was up to £7,000. Someone then shouted £10,000. There was some more frantic bidding before the auctioneer sold the item for a final price of £13,500.

Once the bidding had finished, Duncan turned to the man on his right, who had not put in a bid but had been especially attentive. "Excuse me, could you tell me why the bones from the right foot sold for more than the left?"

The man turned to look at Duncan with a degree of suspicion, looked around the hall and then leaned in without taking his eyes from the front. "Are you serious?"

"Yes. I, er … I'm on a job swap with someone. Apparently he's having a nightmare down in the labs." Duncan hid the lie within a smile.

The man closed his auction programme and placed his coffee on the floor with an exaggerated effort. "Shoe manufacturers have to take into account biomechanics, ergonomics and, of course, marketing. After the computer modelling and the dummy testing, the right shoe is tested with human parts before going to the final stage of live human testing. Only the right shoe is fully tested in order to cut costs."

"All this for a shoe?"

"All this to *sell* the shoe. How effective the human parts testing is, is anyone's guess. Not much, if you ask me, but the marketing people love it." The man looked down at Duncan's own out-dated and worn footwear. "The right phalanges will do well in this lot, whereas something like her heart won't fetch nearly as much."

Duncan didn't thank him for that last piece of information as he turned back to watch the auctioneer continue with the next item; the left tibia. As the bidding started, Duncan's mind drifted back into the past. Whenever his wife Nicole had come home from work stressed and tired, Duncan would tell her to sit down and relax. He would drape a blanket over her, puff up a few cushions and dim the lights. After putting on some music or an old 2D film on the media console, he'd then go and prepare dinner. Those evenings alone together were often spent sitting facing each other on the sofa, legs entwined under the blanket, drinking wine, massaging each other's feet and talking into the night. Duncan's analytical, scientific mind took over as the thought of his right-hand's superiority in strength and dexterity meant Nicole's left foot had actually received a lifetime of better massages than the right. Whoever bought the phalanges, muscles or tendons from her left foot was going to get the better deal.

Feeling a little claustrophobic and self-conscious sitting in a small chair surrounded by such vigorous enterprise and interest in his wife's body, an irrational pang of jealousy ripped through Duncan. This place was playing tricks on him; he needed to snap out of it.

Duncan deemed the terror and risk of interacting with a stranger would help keep his senses on high alert and less susceptible to sinking into bouts of nostalgia. He turned back to the man sitting next to him. "My name is Duncan Hartley, nice to meet you." He tried to sound relaxed, using his coffee as a conversation starter. "Did you know they serve coffee with rat's milk here?"

The man scrutinised Duncan, his eyes flicking over him too quickly for examination. Maybe he was wearing computerised contact lenses, cross-referencing the name Duncan Hartley with a multitude of databases. Duncan decided not to give away any more personal information.

The man finally focused on Duncan's eyes and answered, "It's not bad."

"My wife uses goat's milk. A bit more palatable, I think." Duncan smiled in an attempt to crowbar his way through this man's austere demeanour. "Well, she used to. She passed away recently, but I don't think she's gone far." Duncan cursed himself as the auctioneer continued the redistribution of his other half; he'd just told the man he'd been married and she'd recently passed away. Now he realised why Nicole would secretly nudge him at a dinner table or during a party or a work event, warning him of his latest faux pas. Every moment without Nicole served to remind him how much he had relied on her and how much he had taken for granted. As he hid himself in the labs at work or down in the garden during retirement, how had the rest of his life functioned? God's guiding hand? Close. Nicole's omnipresence was everywhere he looked.

The auctioneer continued to sell Nicole off, bit by bit, every part reminding him of the whole. Every limb held a story, every organ a characteristic. The longer the auction went on, the more Nicole began to surround him, all the different parts of her taking on a life of their own, advancing on Duncan. In death, Nicole was a product, everything being sold, apart from her soul; each hand, ear, eye, femur, bicep – a vengeful zombie shadowed by a poisonous ghost, demanding penance for Nicole's struggle. Insisting on recompense for wasting her life with Duncan, a debt only repayable with own demise.

A woman's hand rested on Duncan's shoulder. A whisper in his ear. "Excuse me ..."

Duncan jumped, awoken from the nightmares revelling in his grief, and turned around.

"Hi, sorry if I scared you, I was just wondering if you'd finished with that programme?"

"Yes." Duncan wanted rid of it, rid of the whole place. "Have it."

"Thank you."

Duncan was here for a reason: to know who was buying his wife. But, more, specifically, to know who was going to buy his wife's stomach.

"Sold! £2,500 for the left lung. Next item is the right lung ..."

The auction was moving on, the digestive system would be next.

It's not compulsory for the deceased to be auctioned off in the UK but, fourteen years ago in 2052, a national referendum was successful, allowing this previously underground, illegal activity to become legal, public and taxed. It apparently made sense; it solved the problem of the lack of space to bury people, the waiting list for organ donors had virtually been eradicated, the illegal body part trade in the UK ended, there was an increase in exports, and it was also a financial benefit to the deceased's family as it enabled debts to be paid off and, in most cases, gave the deceased the opportunity to pass on some inheritance to those left behind, a rarity nowadays.

A small religious minority objected to this new legislation, but the public had voted and all religious groups were still free to carry on their traditional burial and cremation practices. Of course, the public had voted mainly on financial grounds; selling your body parts made a profit whilst buying a plot of land for burial or paying for carbon offsetting a cremation cost a small fortune. This fact further added to religion's demise in the UK and to the piety of the religious rich who were the only ones able to afford to be disposed of as their various deities demanded.

Another unforeseen benefit of this practice was that people looked after themselves better, especially if they were parents. Children took more notice of their parents' health, each generation taking an active interest in the health of the other. Financial institutions placed physical health above personal assets and projected income when taking on long-term risks. Banks lent money based on how much you were worth, every last piece of you.

Duncan listened to the auctioneer's enticing, rhythmic voice as it skipped and danced up the financial scale until the hammer fell and the process began again with the start of Nicole's digestive system. Her right lung had just sold for £32,000.

Duncan looked around the auction hall to see what kind of people were bidding. How could he know what company a buyer represented? Duncan was no stranger to this arena. Twenty years previous he was a key researcher for a pharmaceutical company, attending a few body part auctions himself to acquire testing material. Back then there had only been fellow researchers and insurance company representatives buying replacement parts for their customers. Now, looking around, he could tell the client base had expanded just by studying the dress code and body language of the people in the room. This place looked more like an old fashion stock market trading floor than the fairly refined and respectable place he remembered. There was no inkling of an inner moral conflict or solemn respect. These people were dealing with products.

Duncan could feel his own moral compass flickering amidst the powerful forces of love and money. £32,000 would comfortably pay off one of their many credit card bills; try as hard as he might, he couldn't ignore the slight weight this lifted from his financial burden.

The auction of your wife's body parts was not the ideal place to grieve. Duncan couldn't believe the obviousness of this statement, or the depths of idiocy he must have plummeted to believe that it might have been a good idea to attend the auction.

Unfortunately, Nicole's body contained clues to a crime Duncan committed. Duncan was here, hoping that Nicole's stomach was bought by an insurance group and used in a simple transplant for someone. The last thing he wanted was an over-zealous food manufacturer or a pharmaceutical company winning the bid and examining it too closely. Duncan hadn't planned for such an eventuality, which was foolish of him, but bureaucracy (and the human cogs turning the wheels of the machine) had a habit of missing the obvious.

Duncan thought he'd begin researching the background of the bidders in the room with the man next to him. "Who do you work for?"

The man turned with a raised eyebrow; asking which side he dressed would've been a less invasive question. "You ask a lot of questions."

"I don't know very much."

The man sat up in his seat, angling himself towards Duncan. "You've gone freelance, right? Foreign government? Corporate reconnaissance? Whatever it is, I'm giving you nothing for free, you understand me? I'll give you this, though: you're good. Your ID checked out; Duncan Hartley has a UK passport, tax record, credit score, school records, DNA – I even found a photo of you winning a young scientists prize at Wigthorn High School back in the 1990s. Impressive background work, very thorough. There's just one thing slightly puzzling me ..."

Duncan froze in fear, attempting to pass off this total shutdown of his nervous system as measured calm. It was illegal for him to be here. It was illegal for him to know where the auction of his wife was taking place. Prison was not one of the dying requests Nicole had whispered to Duncan on her deathbed.

"... and it's not the perfection of the back story, though rare. It's how I would've played it, so I respect that. Not so much the bumbling fool on a job swap act, I would've gone for a more subtle approach. No, what stands out for me, is this: your son shares the same DNA as the woman whose body parts we are currently bidding on."

The man locked eyes with Duncan, grabbing his arm and holding it firm against the arm of the seat.

"Don't move, Duncan, and please, don't panic. There's no advantage in me informing the authorities ... yet. I need to explore all avenues first."

"How do you know all this?"

"The same way you know the time and location of your wife's auction. Information is the world's most precious commodity and all commodities have a price, am I right? You paid someone to tell you about the time and location in the same way I pay organisations to let me peruse their databases every now and again." The man let go of Duncan's arm. "Now let's not get too excited, we're both intelligent people. A few questions if I may be so bold, Duncan? My people have been analysing the autopsy report for the past few days and we've found some unexpected results, especially with regards to the digestive system. Tell me about these abnormalities."

Duncan feigned surprise. He'd been foolish to think there would be no consequences for what he'd been doing for the past twenty years and that supposed box-ticking bureaucrats would miss such an irregularity. Nicole had obviously been affected to a greater degree than he'd realised, her remains leading prying eyes straight to his door. This wasn't dead and buried; this thing had only just started.

"I don't know what you mean." Duncan continued the bumbling fool act. It came naturally.

The man turns to Duncan once again, this time with a false joviality. "Come on Duncan, that's why you're here, right? You don't strike me as the kind of freak who would come here to say '*goodbye*', hardly the place to get closure on all those years of marriage, is it? I know you're not a religious nut with a bomb under your jacket protesting against the so-called inhumane act of buying body parts to save lives, so stop stalling and tell me what you know."

"I thought all information has a price?"

"It does. Your freedom. If you don't give me anything."

The auctioneer's hammer slammed down once again onto the rostrum as Nicole Hartley was making her way, bit by bit, all over the UK helping out researchers, patients and product engineers. "Next up we have the stomach, ladies and gentlemen." The auctioneer moved the auction on; both Duncan and the man turned at the sound of the keyword they were both attuned to. "We've already seen parts of this fine digestive system sell above common expectations, so I'm going to open up the bidding accordingly: £25,000. Do I hear £25,000?"

A hand went up. Someone else nodded. A face on one of the large media displays at the front nodded as a green light switched on above it. The light then went out as another hand went up at the back of the hall. The man watched the bidding intensely; Duncan watched the man.

"The bid is £47,000. Do I hear £48,000?"

Whilst the opening bids were being made, the man spoke to Duncan, keeping his eyes fixed on the auctioneer. "Did she have any problems with her stomach?"

"I thought you said your team had been analysing her medical and autopsy reports?"

The man quickly acknowledged Duncan with a sideways glance. "Just testing, old man."

A shout from the back of the room entered the bidding, "£49,000!"

The man remained cool. The bid was immediately overtaken by someone on a media display. "Her stomach is small, why is that?"

"It's healthy, in excellent condition." Duncan tried avoidance – something else that came naturally.

"I know it's healthy, but it's small."

"She wasn't a drinker, only the odd glass of wine every now and then."

"Duncan!" the man forcefully whispered. "The stomach is very healthy, I know. The stomach is small and has an unusual chemical makeup and yet appeared to operate so effectively? How?"

The bidding slowed down to a point where the auctioneer gave his first indication he was ready to sell. The man kept the bid alive by declaring a bid of £55,000. This short period gave Duncan an opportunity to think of a legitimate reason for his wife's apparently miraculous stomach. He didn't know it was small or had an unusual chemical makeup; she had never had any digestive problems that he knew about. One of the advantages of being old and born before a time of genetic screening was there was always a grey area in which you could hide abnormalities.

Duncan eventually responded. "Sorry. Look, you know how they never bothered screening us old people properly because they're just waiting for us all to die out? She must have had a rare, genetic pre-condition that meant her stomach never grew to full size."

"No health insurance check-ups brought it up?" The man asked quietly out the side of his mouth.

"Why would they? They only check for the obvious and the not-so-obvious. They don't check for the billion-to-one shots.

They haven't got the time nor do they want to spend the money. You still get the odd person dying from extremely rare conditions because it's cheaper to pay out on it than to check the whole population for yet another human frailty."

The auctioneer confirmed the highest bid was currently standing at £62,000 and asked for any further increases. The man looked at Duncan for a moment: an evaluation. Duncan returned his stare, emptying his mind of all thoughts and memories. The auctioneer asked for one last bid.

The man stuck his hand up. "£63,000!"

"Why are you so interested in a defective stomach?" Duncan asked.

"I wasn't that interested until you turned up, but now a small curiosity has grown into a very large question – one I want to answer." The man imperceptibly moved closer to Duncan, filling his vision with determination. "I'm going to examine this organ to within an inch of its life."

"That's if you win it."

"Oh, I'll win it, don't worry about that." The man sat back in his chair. "Do you know what we do with the parts once we've finished with them?"

Duncan ignored the bait.

"Feed them to the rats." The man leaned towards Duncan, whispering, trying to suppress immense satisfaction. "I mean, why do we even have rats? People think it's part of the testing, but why test on rats when we have human remains to test on, right? Makes no sense. The rats are part of the disposal process, nothing to do with the research."

"Government agencies and international standards would say you're just trying to scare me."

The man scooted forward in his chair, leaning right into Duncan's field of vision. "Oh, you mean that one bloke down in some long forgotten, underfunded government department in London who comes to our facility once every five years and sees only what we allow him to see? Yeah, I wouldn't trust that bloke to evaluate my dishwasher at home, let alone audit one of the biggest scientific labs in the country."

Duncan nodded a small acknowledgement and turned to face the auctioneer as though he were preparing for a duel to defend Nicole's honour. His warning was not *en garde*, but, "£99,000!"

"£99,000 bid in the room. Do I hear £100,000?"

The man placed the auction programme over his mouth. "What are you doing?"

"Stopping you from winning."

"You haven't got the money."

"Well, in this auction I'd only be paying myself, so technically, I guess I can go as high as I want."

The auctioneer interrupted a whole room of secret, side conversations. "Do I hear £100,000?"

The man held his programme up to confirm his bid.

"£100,000! In the room. Going once!"

The man lowered his programme to his mouth. "Keep bidding, old man, I dare you."

Nicole was always telling him how much of a frugal, stick-in-the-mud he was, never letting his hair down, living a life so closely guarded that no fun or spontaneity could ever flourish. Now he was spending so loosely on his wife (in the most literal sense) was yet another twisted irony he was getting himself tangled up in.

"£101,000!" Duncan raised his hand, the whole room watching the two bidders neatly sitting side by side battle it out against each other. A most polite and genial affair to any onlooker.

"Can I see your bidder's number please, sir?"

Now the whole room *and* the man next to him turned to look at Duncan.

The man's granite face cracked a jagged smile. "I warned you."

The auctioneer continued, "I'm so sorry, sir, but I don't know you and I have yet to see a bidder's number. All bids over £100,000 have to be backed up with a deposit account. Occasionally we get some weirdos in here who think this is a fun day out."

A light fluttering of laughter rippled through the crowd. Duncan felt he was losing the pieces of his broken heart.

"I'll save your blushes, old man. £102,000!" The man raised the bid, before facing Duncan with the programme shielding the lower part of his face from prying eyes. Duncan noticed a large '74' in black ink on white paper stapled to the cover. "I'm going to take this stomach and get my boffins to analyse the shit out of it, you understand? And when they find something, which they will, I'm coming after you, Duncan Hartley. This conversation has been recorded, I know where you live, your DNA, your name, which wasn't hard considering you gave it to me freely. Do you really think you're equipped to fight me? Go home, have a cup of tea and wait for me like a good little boy."

"Sold to *Number 74*. Next we have the pancreas ..."

"Now scram, Duncan. There's more of your wife I want to get my hands on."

Duncan stared blankly back at the man, processing the ever changing tide rapidly rising up and lapping against his chin. Only a buoyant conundrum was keeping him afloat; his hunger for answers outfighting his will to live. "You've just paid over the odds for a sixy-three-year-old's stomach – why? There's plenty more out there, healthy ones you can infect and manipulate however you wish. Why Nicole's?"

"You wouldn't be able to stomach it." The man spat out a laugh. "It would make you sick!" More laughter, like an old-fashioned petrol car engine starting up on a cold morning. "Now stop thinking, Duncan. Go home before I call security just for the fun of it."

Duncan left the auction hall in a daze and walked back to his car for the long drive south to Wigthorn. He'd come to say a final goodbye to Nicole, but it now felt as though this was the start of a longer goodbye to life itself. The best thing that had ever happened to him was gone, the best years of his life were behind him – what future was there to look forward to now? He had no future, but his granddaughter had her whole life ahead of her. If there was one thing that could bring a smile to his face now, it was she. The only reason he had to live was for her future. If he could secure something positive for her then he could say goodbye, not to Nicole but to everyone else.

CHAPTER 2

The immense sprawling office complex of The Pharmara Corporation stretched across the entire fifteen-mile brow of the hills overlooking Wigthorn. Deemed an 'Area of Outstanding Natural Beauty' by The World Heritage Foundation in the past, the trees and hedgerows once lining this landscape had been replaced by pure white buildings sealed with black solar panels, with no windows or doors. This was the view a Wigthornian would see if he or she looked northwards. If one were to look south across the sea towards France, the horizon would be filled with the tops of wind turbines like rows of runaway wagon wheels careering through the English Channel out towards the Atlantic Ocean. Wigthorn was a town cannibalising its natural assets in order to survive, as all towns were.

The Pharmara Corporation headquarters up on the hills of Wigthorn were only on one floor and designed to have no right angles or curves, every corner irregular and every surface flat like a stealth fighter plane. Each department had its own building, the biggest being 'Statistical Acquirement and Analysis', responsible for tracking every single item leaving the factory floor, from products and packaging to pallets and people. Every item contained its very own CBID tag (Constant Broadcast Identification) transmitting, via satellites, its vital statistics ten times every second. Temperature, location, direction, speed, altitude, humidity, human DNA in vicinity, other items in vicinity, the speed, temperature, location of those nearby humans and other items ... and so it went on, every statistic vital.

Amy sat at her ergonomically perfected desk watching live graphs and numbers reflecting the reality outside as The Pharmara Corporation products moved about the country, changing hands, changing temperature, changing altitude, appearing and disappearing. All desks were communal and free of personal identity as employees were always being moved around to discourage the establishment of friendships and other time wasting activities. The desk surface was a flat media display recreating an electronic version of a keyboard and navigation to operate the computer. The display continued to slope upwards until it was vertical, and showed the necessary documents, files and video. Each desk was part of a hexagonal unit housing its six workers like a hive, each unit a finely engineered cog, each office ordered by rank, each department born into a caste.

Amy's face was lit up by all the information dancing in front of her, her eyes hypnotised by the constant manufacture, distribution, consumption and disposing of The Pharmara Corporation's output. Where others saw charts and figures, Amy saw people and relationships. Amy didn't feel like a God, she felt like a voyeur.

Amy leaned back in her chair, pulling her brunette hair back into a ponytail. She always felt more comfortable tying it up and hiding it away at the back somewhere. She made an effort for a Christmas party one year, spending an obscene amount of money at one of the best hair salons in Wigthorn. The overwhelmingly positive response put her in a place she didn't want to be: the centre of attention. Being brought up by a single father, along with three older brothers, meant her feminine instincts lacked any acute honing – but this was how she liked it. There was something to be said for keeping things simple – the wardrobe, the bedroom, the social life. Jeans, t-shirts, occasional flings and toasted sandwiches were enough sustenance. That's what she told herself, anyway.

Amy was putting together a report detailing a sudden up-surge of 'Giant Bolster', a muscle building chocolate bar, when a holographic representation of her supervisor appeared in the centre of the hexagonal desk overlooking the six media displays of the hive. He first appeared with his back towards Amy and looked down upon each of his charges until he found the one he wished to speak to. Amy kept her head down and focused on the display in front of her when all of a sudden it shut down. She slowly raised her head up to face her supervisor.

"Miss Jay, I have been sent a request that you should meet with the Head of Statistical Acquirement and Analysis in precisely one hour."

Amy felt a knot tighten in the pit of her stomach. Those employees located in the corporations that manufactured her clothes, mobile device and shoes with the same job as Amy would now be detecting a sudden change in physical disposition of a female, approximately thirty years old, located in an air-conditioned Pharmara office on the hills of Wigthorn. Heart rate had just gained a few beats per minute, body temperature had just dropped a few degrees, and body was slightly shaking due to frenetic foot tapping. All this would be lost within the masses of aggregated, anonymous information passing from customer to seller via satellite, but it was still recorded and available for analysis all the same. In quiet moments, Amy liked to drill down to an individual and watch them via their vital statistics and imagine what they were actually like, as a person. She was not immune from such scrutiny; trackers were tracked, too. The trackers who tracked the trackers were tracked as well. No one, it seemed, tracked the trackers who tracked the trackers though; that was the career aspiration Amy secretly harboured.

"Do you know why?" Amy asked.

The supervisor looked down at Amy. "Her PA did not specify. Report back to me when you return." With that, the hologram flickered for a split second before disappearing in a puff of smoke, an amusing touch added by a new employee with time on his hands. Tiny giggles rippled around the desk unit, breaking the deafening silence of the office.

Once the quiet was quickly restored, Amy racked her brains to find a reason why the Head of Statistical Acquirement and Analysis would want to see her. Amy had never met Estelle Hawthorne, only glimpsed her on the odd occasion when she had breezed through the office on her way somewhere else far more important. Being the head of the department seemed to mean you rarely spent any time there or interacted with your own staff.

A co-worker sitting at a desk directly behind whispered to Amy, "Are you OK?" A Pharmara subsidiary manufactured the jeans Amy was currently wearing and this co-worker had quickly drilled down to track Amy as soon as she heard the supervisor talking to her. Amy dismissed the concern by ignoring her co-worker. There was no such thing as privacy in the tracking department of any corporation.

Whilst the hour dragged, all Amy could do was try to think of a reason why she was being summoned. Promotion? Transfer? A promotion that meant transferring over to the stats department? In Hawaii?

No chance. Who'd ever heard of a member of staff at a large organisation getting promoted purely through exceptional talent and hard work? Amy knew too much, and because she knew too much, and because she was exceptional and talented, she knew promotion was a fantasy. Imprisoned by her knowledge, she was both a threat to her superiors as well as a reliable crutch for them to lean on. They would delegate to her mercilessly and take credit for her ideas. After over a decade of hard work, maybe today was the magical day her skills would be recognised and she'd be nurtured into fulfilling a high flying executive role, translating all those statistics into company strategy.

Amy wrote a resignation letter in the undigitised format of pen and paper four months ago after a particularly depressing week at work where no one pats you on the back or even acknowledges your existence and the sheer monotony lulls you into an amoeba-like state where you make a slight, inconsequential error and suddenly everyone comes out of their hiding places to jump down your throat. The thought of finding another job, learning the office politics of a different employer, losing the perks, probably a longer commute and then reminiscing over those pitifully few special moments she'd experienced, soon broke her and got her marching back in step.

Amy pulled a lighter out from a drawer in the kitchen, the letter quickly going up in flames, the orange embers floating down into the sink: unrecoverable, unreadable, unrealised. Like the seven before.

Amy could see patterns humans and computers could not. The pattern she could see at the moment wasn't hard to spot or even hard to predict, but when it was your own life in the spotlight, it could be hard to accept. Amy was going nowhere, slowly.

A pre-set alert startled her, signalling the waiting was over. Amy arose from her exquisitely styled chair and exited her department towards Estelle Hawthorne's office.

As Amy walked through a myriad of offices and corridors, she gave herself an internal pep-talk, demanding she stay strong, confident, in control, a winner, not one of life's victims. Then the disturbingly improbable, but nonetheless true, thought pierced her one-woman motivational seminar: she didn't know anyone who had actually spoken to Estelle Hawthorne or had been in her office.

Oh my God! thought Amy. *What if Estelle has a stupidly high pitched voice or a lisp and I start laughing?* These thoughts weren't the kind she needed so she returned to the motivational seminar in her mind.

Amy approached the receptionist, who sat outside the office like a Grenadier Guard with matching hairstyle and as dutifully detached. "Hello, I'm Amy Jay and I have a meeting with Miss Hawthorne."

"Yes, go on through," the black beehive said without deviating from her work or posture.

A pair of large double doors automatically slid open as Amy approached and she walked through. Immediately opposite were another pair of double doors but they didn't slide open as she approached. Amy tried to push them but they were not to be budged. The first doors shut behind her so she was enclosed in a fairly small space. Then she felt the whole room begin to descend. This elevator was unexpected but non-threatening; there was light and barely audible, soulless music. A few seconds passed, the elevator ceased its descent and the doors in front of Amy opened to reveal the office of Estelle Hawthorne.

The first thing to hit Amy was the size and shape of it – an extremely large circular room covered on all sides by glass. As Amy stepped in, she glanced at the floor to check her footing and was taken aback by the sight of tropical fish swimming in the crystal blue waters beneath the glass floor. Estelle was sitting at a large round table in the centre of the room, beckoning Amy over. Amy walked towards the chair with some trepidation due to the transparent floor. The equally transparent walls appeared to be holding back a potential avalanche of soil from below the South Downs. As she focused on certain areas, she could see cross-sections of burrows and warrens occupied with their architects and inhabitants. Claustrophobia wasn't Amy's concern down here. She felt abandoned by the satellites, like a child who had deliberately disobeyed their parents and roamed beyond their reach, out of sight. Anything could happen down here and no one would ever know.

Amy turned to focus her mind back on the meeting and sat herself in one of the chairs at the end of the grand, circular table. At the other end sat Estelle Hawthorne, dressed in a figure-hugging, charcoal coloured suit with her smoky grey hair elegantly blowing out the top. Her face was intriguingly beautiful: smooth tanned skin, rejuvenated lips, rehoused cheek bones, an inviting smile like a good deal, and intense blue eyes like the small print.

Seated next to Estelle was a middle-aged man in a suit who knew his place and sat in it comfortably, waiting for Estelle to get the meeting started. Estelle stood up from her chair and walked to Amy's side of the desk. "Welcome Amy, I'm Estelle Hawthorne." She shook Amy's hand as she took a seat facing her.

Her voice was normal, thankfully. Amy imperceptibly relaxed.

"Call me Estelle. I'm glad you could come, it's always nice to meet fellow employees."

Being this close to Estelle and sitting face-to-face was unnerving, especially with the other man looking at her from across the table. What was even more unnerving was Estelle's apparent friendliness.

"Amy, let me introduce you to Gerard Abbot."

Amy looked over at Gerard as he nodded his acknowledgement.

"Gerard is one of our managers from the purchasing department; more specifically, he purchases body parts for Research and Development. A recent purchase has resulted in a few irregularities and Gerard has asked us for assistance."

Amy, keen to show she belonged in such elevated company but even more keenly aware she shouldn't say anything idiotic, cautiously replied. "OK."

"Gerard, could you go into further detail about our predicament?"

"Yes, of course. I recently purchased a stomach and our research scientists have been taking a closer look at it. It turns out minute remains of illegal plant DNA have been found within the stomach lining. Further investigations have revealed that the genetic code is that of a tomato but not a patented version manufactured by an approved source. This is evidence of a patent violation. If an emerging black market of illegal produce were to take a foothold, it could threaten the future of The Pharmara Corporation and the market as a whole. We need to end this production not only to end the proliferation of an illegal industry but, more importantly, illegal seeds being released into the natural environment would threaten food crops up and down the country, resulting in economic instability."

Estelle took over the conversation. "As you can see, Amy, we cannot let this happen."

Amy, feeling the focus of unwanted attention, entered the conversation with more certainty and confidence. "I'm not sure where I fit into all this. This isn't the first patent violation of fruit and vegetables and I'm sure it won't be the last. Why don't you go back to the auction house and ask them where the stomach came from?"

Gerard answered, "They are not legally obliged to release that information."

"So you've come to a dead end?"

"Not exactly," replied Estelle, regaining Amy's attention. "We've managed to identify the stomach's owner via DNA records."

"How can anonymous DNA records have any identifying information that could trace the owner of a stomach? Only the government has personally identifying records of people."

"Mostly true, however we are allowed to personally track employees via their DNA."

"If you already know who this Pharmara employee is, how do I fit into the equation? This person is dead, I hope, for their sake." Amy's improvised wisecrack made her heart sink. A dead Pharmara employee – Amy knew of one.

"We need you to help track down the origin of the illegally grown plant, a tomato. We need to find out where this person lived, the places she frequented, the friends she kept, family, etc. Any one of these trails could lead us to the perpetrator."

"You must already know most of this if you'd been tracking this employee when they were alive. Why me though? There are more qualified members of your department further up the pay scale than me for this kind of work, why me specifically?" Amy let some concern spill into her voice.

Estelle leaned back in her chair, turning down the intensity in her eyes.

Gerard leaned forward in his chair across the table and spoke with a sickly smile. "Because you knew her."

"Who?"

"The owner of the stomach."

Amy knew only of one person who it could possibly be. Only one person she knew had died in the past year. "Who is it?" replied Amy, focusing every sinew of her mind to think of absolutely anything except …

"Nicole Hartley." Estelle stole Gerard's thunder.

"Nicole?"

"You did know Nicole Hartley, right?" continued Gerard.

"Yes, yes, of course." Amy knew immediately there was no point lying. There would have been reams of tracking data showing Nicole and Amy socialising. It was undeniable they were friends; they had lunch together a few times every week, did yoga every Tuesday evening at the local gym, bought birthday presents for each other and also communicated via email and mobile device. Despite the age gap of about thirty years, Amy considered Nicole a close friend, someone she had grown very fond of over the years – not quite a mother figure, more of an older sister. She admired her vitality, her knowledge, her enthusiasm and the way she was always friendly and nice to everyone, always willing to take time out to selflessly help people – a dying art like crocheting or wiring a plug. Amy had missed her so much over the past few weeks since she had passed away, not only losing a friend but a mentor and a role model. Amy was slightly confused, though. Nicole and Amy shared many alternative views on the world but she had never mentioned anything about being a 'Mother Naturist'.

"Did she ever talk about growing or buying illegal produce?" asked Gerard.

"No, she didn't. This is a bit of a shock to me, as you can imagine. I never knew she would take part in anything like that. Are you sure it's definitely her?"

"Oh yes, there's no doubt," answered Gerard. "Her husband confirmed it himself."

"He's seen the stomach?"

"No, he was at the auction."

"What the hell was he doing there?"

"I'm not sure, but he's an avenue we plan to look into further."

"Do you know Duncan Hartley, Amy?" Estelle asked, relaxed in her chair, comfortably at home during an interrogation.

"No I don't. I've never met him. Nicole said he was very involved in his work, only mixing with family and one or two very close friends."

"What is this very involving work?"

"He worked in the garden a lot."

"How involved can gardening get?"

"I'm not sure, I've never had a garden. He was retired and worked in his garden, how suspicious can one get about that?"

"If he's growing illegal tomatoes in his garden, then very suspicious." Estelle leaned forward to closely examine Amy's response. "Don't you think it strange that a friend of yours never spoke to you about her husband's work?"

"Stranger than meeting the head of my department for the first time after ten years? Stranger than being asked questions you already know the answer to? Stranger than this office? What's with all the fish and the rabbits?" Amy's outburst took her by surprise but somehow it had enabled her to convincingly change the subject.

Estelle leaned back, smiled and raised her hands to show off her office. "Yes, yes, you are right. The world's a strange place, isn't it?" Estelle stood, releasing the tension in the room. "So, what do you think of it?"

"It's big."

"I'm important – it has to be big. You can't be in my position, have a small office and earn respect. It doesn't work."

"Why the fish and all the soil? Do they earn you respect, too?"

Estelle started walking around the perimeter of her office. "They don't know we're here. The glass is one-sided so we can see the fish below and the rabbits and moles in the soil, but they can't see us. They have no idea we're here watching them. It's important to observe the observed without them knowing they are being observed."

"Spying."

"'Naturalistic observation' is the official term." She turned to look at Amy. "It's important in our line of work that we make ourselves invisible."

"But everyone knows everything is tracked. We're hardly invisible."

"If we remain out of sight and out of mind then we become forgettable. That is virtually the same as being invisible."

Amy looked around the office, shuffling a little in her chair. "I'm not sure I'm following you, Miss Hawthorne."

"Estelle, please." Estelle advanced towards Amy. "Our work is to measure. We don't need to watch everyone all the time. We can observe by numbers. We track, we measure, we analyse and we make changes to improve efficiency and increase profit. The division between the observed and the observer is paramount." Estelle placed her hand lightly on Amy's shoulder as she passed her on her way to the other side of the office. "We should be forgettable and remain forgettable. The way in which our methods of tracking are woven into the fabric of everything around us allowing us to see a complete and true picture of the world. If this changes, the information we gather becomes diluted and diseased. The picture we see becomes a distortion of the truth. You know how important this is, and you also know there are people, groups, who want to change this. Regress into a Neanderthal lifestyle without measurement or monitoring and leave our futures in the proven unreliable hands of serendipity. They don't seem to appreciate information has a price; intellectual property is protected because new products aren't freely given to us. Statistics and probabilities are gathered and analysed – they don't fall from trees. If we ignored such threats, where would that leave us?"

Amy remained silent and straight faced as a defence against not knowing what the truth of her words were beneath the hyperbole.

"Inefficiency and less profit, that's where, which would lead into unknown depths of inhumanity."

"Am I under suspicion?" Amy asked, for some clarity.

"For what?" Estelle replied with forced joviality.

"For somehow being involved in this situation, however remote."

"Oh, I know you're not involved directly. The short elevator ride down here confirmed you are clear of any evidence. I believe only circumstance has brought you here, so please do not feel under any pressure. I only wish to make it clear to one of my most valued employees that matters of patent violations and genetic sabotage are taken very seriously. I only hope that you will help us solve and eradicate such crimes."

"Of course. I've given my whole working life to this company and my intentions are to work harder for more responsibility."

"Good, I'm glad to hear of such determination. Gerard and I like to thoroughly grill potential new recruits, please forgive us. I've heard nothing but good things about your performance. That's why I've decided to help your advancement by transferring you to a special security team, headed up by Gerard, who will work with our legal department to track down the perpetrators and bring them to justice. I'd like you to start immediately as the special liaison between 'security' and 'analysis' and be their dedicated 'eye in the sky', if you'd like the position?"

"Thank you. I'm not sure what to say." Amy manufactured a smile for Estelle and Gerard. "I would love to take this opportunity, thanks."

"OK, good." Estelle returned to her seat next to Gerard. "Take the rest of the day off. Your old team will have to get used to life without you. Details of your new job will be sent to you later this afternoon along with the not insubstantial pay rise. Go home, get some rest and come in refreshed ready for tomorrow."

"Yes. Thanks again." Amy turned and made her way back to the elevator. As the doors started to close, Amy turned and stole a look at Estelle and Gerard. They had remained in their seats, silently watching Amy. Amy returned their gaze unblinkingly until it was broken by the closing doors.

Estelle turned to Gerard. "Well, I think that's set the cat amongst the pigeons."

Amy knew she was walking out of The Pharmara Corporation offices for the last time. The sense of being used was almost palpable. The first time she meets her head of department, she's offered a plum job with a healthy pay rise and given the afternoon off? She'd never heard of such things happening before in her decade of service at Pharmara.

After years of inaction and boredom, Amy now faced a stark choice between her job and the faith she had in her friend, Nicole. There was no real choice to be made. She would have to walk out ... now. This very second. As soon as the elevator doors opened, she'd turn left towards the car park and not right, back towards her office. Her chicken soup would have to remain in the refrigerator until basic hygiene overruled office etiquette and it got chucked away, probably in about three months' time. Amy had a black mark next to her name – no matter how little input she'd had in receiving it, it was there nonetheless. Any kind of promotion or career path were fantasies. The thought dawned on Amy that maybe they always had been.

Patent violations were only ever committed by rival corporations, foreign governments, terrorists, environmental activists and the like, not by the delightfully friendly lady down the road. What had Nicole been up to? Had looking at the world through graphs and patterns obscured something that was right in front of her?

Amy would have to turn to Nicole's husband, Duncan, warn him, and ask him what he knew. Pharmara were clearly keeping their cards close and saw Amy as an expendable resource in closing this matter, which only added to Amy's curiosity. She would have to work quickly to get Duncan hidden from prying eyes and find out what he had to say before deciding on either giving him up or helping him further.

Walking out of your employment for the last time increased the average heartbeat of thirty-one year old women in Wigthorn by twenty-seven per cent. A ten second video advertisement for a heart tablet to be taken twice daily was triggered and sent to Amy's mobile device.

Amy hoped Nicole didn't have bad taste in men. She had to find Duncan before they did.

CHAPTER 3

Duncan was sitting in his favourite lazy boy chair with a cup of tea and an old paper book, one he had read once before in his early twenties. It was one of the few paper books he still had and was reading it more for the sensation of the pages against his fingertips than for the story itself, although the wildly optimistic predictions of a future he was now living in did raise a few smiles.

One of the few accurate predictions interrupted him now, the house central computer. "Sugarpops, I have an urgent message from Brit Roads Ltd."

Duncan laughed reluctantly. Nicole sometimes called Duncan 'Sugarpops', as well as other similarly embarrassing terms of endearment in their more intimate moments. She liked to update the central computer to refer to Duncan in the same way.

"Sissy, please can you change my name from Sugarpops to Duncan?"

"Yes, Sugarpops."

Sissy was actually C.I.C.S.I., Centrally Integrated Computer Systems Intelligence, the central computer that controlled every function in the house, from answering the door and cooking a roast chicken, to recycling water and redirecting excess energy back to the national grid. Every household had one and most programmed the personality settings to resemble a woman in her thirties with the same accent as the household owners. Women feel safer with a woman in control, and men like the dominance. Of course, there are exceptions – when students get their first house, these generalities go out the window. The amount of computer hacks for personalities such as superhero, pornographic model, extremely effeminate gay man, strict sergeant major and a fictional Igor-type dogsbody, was immense and sustained a highly lucrative industry.

Via Sissy, a male advertising voice speaks. "Brit Roads Ltd would like to thank you for being a regular customer of Mordinges Drive and all our roads in Wigthorn, and have debited your account for this month's tolls."

"I live on Mordinges Drive, I had no choice but to drive down Mordinges Drive to get to my house," Duncan pleaded in vain.

Duncan finished his tea and read on to finish the chapter before making himself another cup. Sissy, again, interrupted. "Duncan, there is an urgent message from Channel 84."

"Go away," answered Duncan without breaking the typewriter movement of his eyeline.

Another male advertising voice is patched through the lounge speaker system by Sissy. "Hello, Mr Hartley. We at Channel 84 would like to offer you an exclusive discount on future programming for next month as we have noticed you haven't watched any of our output for the past two weeks."

Duncan looked around the room, addressing all the speakers and computerised equipment attempting to catch Sissy's eye. "Sissy, can you turn all this crap off? I don't want to hear any messages."

"Channel 84 is part of the premium plan, Duncan. If I were not to relay premium plan messages, you would be billed extra."

Duncan slammed his book on the coffee table and got up. "I don't friggin care! Charge me! I don't want to hear anymore bullshit messages!"

"Yes, Duncan," replied Sissy.

Duncan checked his messages. He was having an end of season sale – everything must go before the man from the auction two days previously came knocking. Duncan figured that after collection, transportation, analysis and evaluation, he had seven days to dispose of his stocks of contraband and the facility he housed it all in.

One of his longest serving buyers was Julius Talent and he'd offered to buy every natural fruit and vegetable Duncan could provide him with at a special discounted rate. Duncan replied telling him to come over in an hour. The sooner he could get rid of his stock the better. Duncan grabbed a quick lunch before Julius arrived and got stuck into a cheese and tomato sandwich. A big juicy, one hundred per cent natural tomato with seeds, the self-sustaining building blocks for propagation; just add water and a little sunlight. An absentee within genetically modified fruits and vegetables due to their extreme patent voiding and non-repeat buying properties.

"Duncan, your faecal and urinal waste results have now been analysed and there's ..."

"Sissy! Sissy! Why do you always do this when I'm eating?" Duncan said throwing his hands up to the ceiling. "I'll ask you for a report later."

"OK, Sugarpops." Sissy missed Nicole, too.

Duncan didn't need to ask Sissy about the report; he knew what irregularities there were. Duncan's consumption of contraband throughout the years had taken its toll, as it had with Nicole. The one saving grace about this habit of taking illegal substances was that Duncan had managed to calibrate Sissy's external reporting so that this information was not fed to the external world and therefore alert the authorities. Duncan allowed Sissy's analysis to remain functional within the four walls of their house in case anything irregular did show itself, but the automated reporting to the outside went through one of Duncan's specially configured filters. Like a pet unknowingly eating a pill hidden in its food, Sissy was little more than a loyal dog.

Duncan stepped out of the patio doors into the back garden. It was time to get to work. He walked to the left of the garden and stuck his hand into a bush, pulling a false branch upwards. A computerised, male voice whispered.

"Please wait two minutes for a clear window."

Duncan casually stood waiting on the patio and cast an expert eye over the lawn and flowerbeds that lay before him. The manicured lawn was about the size of a tennis court, surrounded by a high wall and bordered on three sides by a flowerbed lush with many varieties he had collected over the years. At the bottom of the garden were ten tall pine trees standing grandly in front of the far wall, dressed in climbing ivy.

"Satellite gone, clear skies above confirmed."

A dark line suddenly appeared across the centre of the lawn, running from left to right. The back half of the lawn remained as it was whilst the front half lowered itself by half a metre and started receding beneath the back half. As the front disappeared, it revealed the reflective surface of many green, rectangular solar panels that slightly tilted southeast towards the sun, which made its daily arc across the front of the house.

Duncan then whispered back to the bush, "Open Sesame."

The steps that lead from the patio down to the lawn sunk further into the patio to reveal another set of steps leading further down beneath the solar panels. Duncan descended until the steps ended in front of a big, secure metal door; in the centre was a heavy wheel, like on a flood door found on a ship. He turned the wheel and pushed the door open. His face was illuminated by the strong light coming from within. He squinted as he walked in and sat at the large desk situated in the corner immediately to his left. After consulting the huge display on the wall behind the desk and taking stock of the readings, he swivelled around in his chair, leaned back with hands behind his head and surveyed the rest of the room.

The plants were lined up with military precision matching the lights above. The nursery was noticeably divided by age. Opposite Duncan's desk in the right hand corner were shelves of seedlings, each box marked with the plant name, dates, and its own little sun shining down upon it. Next, along the right side of the wall, were bigger shelves containing bigger plants, the shoots breaking through the soil and some with the odd leaf sprouting from them. On the opposite side of the room, on the left hand side, were the adolescent plants; most were about half a metre in height, others taller, standing like a regiment on parade. The rear half of the nursery was completely closed off by a wall with a door in the middle.

Duncan walked through the middle of the nursery between the rows of forbidden flora, each stage of development adding to Duncan's crime and length of incarceration should he be caught. The door was opened to reveal the star witness in an open and shut case: a hydroponic heaven illuminated by a thousand suns. Walking into this closed section of the nursery was like walking onto another planet. It was hot, so hot, yet lush with plants. Duncan took off his shirt and left it outside, shut the door behind him and activated the watering system, which sprayed a fine mist over the plants. Walking through this man-made rainforest in the middle of an ordinary English seaside town was a joy Duncan never grew tired of. Caring for his plants, inspecting every single one with tenderness and concern, he would spend hours down here.

He had spent more time caring for these plants than with Nicole, now realising what a mistake that was. He was more tactile with them than he had been with her.

Percy, the nursery C.I.C.S.I., step-brother to Sissy, spoke again. "Duncan, I have detected a satellite will be overhead in twenty minutes. Would you like to exit now or will you remain within the nursery?"

"I'll stay here. You can close it up, thank you, Percy."

"There is enough power and water for three days Duncan."

Duncan wasn't worried about lack of power or water – there was always enough to sustain the nursery, and a warmer world was a wetter world. Duncan was more interested in the personal care of his plants – his source of revenue, his sustenance and his passion. Duncan wasn't leaving for at least half an hour, so he asked Percy to activate an old gardener's trick he'd learnt from his grandfather. It had no real scientific background and was probably more for Duncan's sake than the plants, but nonetheless, Duncan saw it as a vital element of the horticulturalist's armoury. "Percy, can you continue with Mozart's 'La Finta Giardiniera' please."

The half hour passed in a moment, Duncan lost in the work of preparing an order, the smells and the music. He couldn't deny that the secretive nature and the element of risk added to the whole experience. It seemed more worthwhile. Duncan was expecting Julius soon, so he cleared things away, checked over all the plants one last time, gathered some home-grown to take back into the house and left the nursery to hide itself away again. A secret at the bottom of the garden.

Duncan didn't have many clients mainly because he didn't want to arouse suspicion but also because demand for his natural product had declined over recent years. Society now wanted man-made, genetically enhanced products reinforced by excessively gilded marketing ideals. Going underground was no longer an option for many natural idealists as it was becoming ever more expensive, time consuming and increasingly harder to achieve without arousing the suspicions of the omnipotent satellite and tracking coverage. Breaking statistical patterns was almost as dangerous as breaking copyright law.

Duncan was in the kitchen washing his hands when Sissy announced his client's arrival. "Mr Julius Talent is at the door."

Duncan examined the display within the kitchen table. "Sissy, are there any unfamiliar vehicles or people on the street?

"No."

"Good, let him in, please."

Julius entered, giving Duncan an enthusiastic handshake.

"Nice to see you again, Julius, how have you been?"

"'Jules, please!" Julius retrieved a book from the brightly coloured, well sealed courier bag hanging down from his right shoulder and handed it to Duncan. "I'm doing good, man. Here, I got you a little pressie."

Duncan read the front cover: *Unusual Jams from Unusual Fruits*. Duncan smiled like a slice of melon. "Thanks so much. How do you get your hands on these things?"

Julius tapped his nose and winked.

Duncan examined the back cover. "Look, this was printed over fifty years ago in 2011." Duncan appreciated the rarity of the printed word. "It's in good nick, too. Amazing what you 'Unrecorded' boys find lying around under the radar, isn't it?"

Julius got down to business, unconcerned about the printed word. "After we spoke yesterday about you stepping up operations, as it were, what exactly did you mean? How do I fit into this?"

"I'm selling everything. The lot. I've got these bags of fruits, which you'll have to sell quickly, but I've got all these seeds, too."

Duncan placed his hand into a bag and let the seeds fall through his fingers.

"Can you eat them?" asked Julius.

"If you want."

"A plant won't grow in my stomach, will it?"

Duncan smiled at the naivety. "No, but eating them isn't the point. You have the potential to grow an almost unlimited amount of fruits and vegetables with these different seeds."

"How am I going to grow plants with these seeds?"

"Not you, but there's a market out there. You'll have to look further afield, possibly abroad, to find it – but it's there."

"How do you know? This stuff is hot as hell. How do you know I can get rid of it for a price?"

"Are you saying you can't?"

"Duncan, my man! It's me, Jules! I can sell anything! Leave it with me, mate, I'll put the feelers out and get back to you."

"No. You'll have to take all this now and pay my regular foreign account."

"I can't afford a deposit for this much, Duncan."

"No deposit this time, Julius, I trust you." Duncan sealed up the bags he'd opened for demonstration. "It's time to go. This is a one-time deal – there's no more where this came from so get the best price you can. You can take a twenty-five per cent cut on this one."

Julius took the bags off Duncan. "Well, why didn't you say old man!"

Duncan asked Sissy to check the near vicinity again before letting Julius out and returned to his chair to enjoy the new book Julius had brought for him. He started by smelling it.

Duncan managed to read a whole chapter without interruptions until Sissy informed him of visitors. Duncan didn't have friends turning up unannounced, family knew better, and any business visitations were all pre-arranged.

"Who is it Sissy?"

"Their mobile devices state they're from Marks & Waitadsco. Would you like to address them directly?"

"No, no. Have you ordered a food delivery?"

"No. You requested I cancel all orders."

"Good. Do you recognise these delivery people?"

"No. I have no recording of their DNA or mobile devices."

With Duncan's suspicions confirmed, he viewed the front of his house via the media display. There were three men standing in the doorway with too much poise and focus to be mere delivery workers. Duncan viewed another angle of Mordinges Drive and saw the delivery van. This was either the newest and most expensive delivery van in the Marks & Waitadsco fleet or it was no delivery van at all.

Duncan allowed the reality of the situation to sink in and started to implement his escape plan. Standing just inside the patio door, Duncan addressed the external C.I.C.S.I. system controlling the underground nursery. "Emergency exit, beta, delta, delta, zeta." A row of slabs leading from the patio doors to the lawn started to rise, lifted by small arms extending out of the floor. Once the slabs reached head height, providing a roof, the patio stairs at the far end that led down to the nursery began to sink down once again.

Sissy replied, "I'm sorry Duncan, I don't understand."

"I wasn't speaking to you, Sissy."

"Shall I open the front door or would you like to meet them yourself?"

"Tell them I'm not here."

"But you are …"

Before Sissy could complete her logical conclusion, Duncan stepped out of the rear patio doors, closed them and exited down the sunken patio steps to the nursery. Sissy, able to perform unfathomable calculations per nanosecond, re-evaluated the household's number of occupants and informed the waiting delivery men that no one was home.

Gerard, uncomfortable in his delivery man uniform and impatient with lying computers, ordered Duncan's front door to be opened, to no avail. "It's lying – he's in there. Harris, get this bloody door open."

"Computers don't lie, sir."

"Thank you, Rogers. He's either hacked it or has a voice simulator. Either way, our satellite identified him standing in the kitchen not ten seconds ago."

"But he's not there now, sir."

"So where did he go, Houdini?"

"I don't know, sir."

"No, I didn't think so. Let's go in and find out shall we?" Gerard looked at Harris, a man built to get computers to open doors for him rather than barging doors open himself, and he went to work. A couple of minutes later, the front door opened and Gerard, Harris and Rogers entered the house.

"Intruder alert! Intruder alert! Exit this house now! Viciterra Ltd security has been informed. Exit now!" Sissy's security program activated.

"Shut this bloody thing up, Harris."

"Yes, sir."

"Rogers, set up the portable media system here on the kitchen table and let's find out where our Mr Hartley has disappeared to."

Rogers brought out a black object, about the size of a book, from his shoulder bag and placed it on the kitchen table. A laser shone out a light sensitive QWERTY keyboard at one end as extremely slim glass folded out in an origami fashion, extending the display screen to almost half a metre square. Rogers put a thimble-like device onto the end of his right index finger and informed Gerard he was ready to begin.

"OK. Have we got direct control of a Pharmara Satellite?"

Rogers moved his finger across the kitchen table as though he were drawing. "Yes, we do now."

"Let's get heat signatures in this house and see if we can find Mr Hartley the easy way."

Rogers' fingers danced some more on the table, his eyes glued to the display. Gerard paced around the kitchen table with his hands behind his back, looking around for any clues that may give him an edge.

"Negative heat signatures, sir, just the three of us."

"OK. I want a close-up video feed of this house so we can see if anyone exited from the back or the front."

"It's ready now, sir."

"OK, so we knew Duncan Hartley was in here when we rang the doorbell due to the satellite heat signature, but that got lost by the back door, right?"

"Yes."

"OK, I want a close up of the back patio area from the moment we rang the doorbell."

Rogers got the necessary footage on the display and ran it forward for Gerard to view. "Not much going on, is there?"

"Nothing at all, sir. The patio door opens and then about a minute later it closes again."

"Strange, huh?"

"Yes, sir."

"Continue playing that footage and look closer. Hartley can't have simply disappeared."

Gerard walked towards the patio door, opened it and walked out, examining the slabs until he reached the lawn. Gerard looked out over the grass as Duncan had for many years, scrutinising the garden for imperfections. He walked back to the patio door, and paused to look straight up into the sky for a few seconds before he proceeded through.

"Have you found anything, Rogers?"

"Nothing, sir."

"Let me take another look." Gerard walked over to the display, demanding Rogers replay the footage with even more of a close-up. "Look here." Gerard pointed at the patio being shown on the display.

"What is it sir? I can't see anything."

"The light. Look at the light on the patio slabs here, here and here. It's changing. Zoom in more, Rogers."

"Yes, I think you're right. And look at the slabs to the left and the right. The light and shadows remain the same."

Gerard slowly walked to the patio door, crouched down and gently placed the palm of his right hand on the first patio slab. "He's beneath the garden."

Duncan was in the main hydroponics section of the nursery at the far end changing into some new clothes and filling his bag with as many varieties of seeds as he could. Once he was ready to escape his underground garden, he checked with the C.I.C.S.I. system for an update on his pursuers' progress.

"There is one person on the patio and two in the kitchen. The entrance has not been violated. The house and garden is being scanned by x-ray and infra-red."

Duncan busied himself by making sure all loose objects were securely put away except the plants, vegetables and fruit. Duncan walked to the centre of the nursery, unhinged a ceiling vent, went through into the main hydroponics area and then stood by a small door in the corner at the back.

"Percy, get ready to activate 'Seed Evacuation'."

"Yes, Duncan."

Duncan opened the small door and had to get on his knees to get through it. The door only led into a box room about a metre in all dimensions. Once in, Duncan turned on a small light and shut the door.

"I'm in and door is now secure. Activate 'Seed Evacuation' as soon as the patio perimeter is broken."

"Yes, Duncan."

"I'm also going to remove your primary hard drive. After the seed evacuation has started, corrupt and delete all files." Duncan stopped what he was doing briefly. "And run the 'Compucide Virus'."

"Yes, Duncan."

"Thank you, Percy."

Duncan unlocked a small cabinet door in the wall, removed the hard drive, put it in his bag and then opened the far door, which led out to a small tunnel. Duncan climbed through the tunnel a few metres until he was at the bottom of a hole. He looked up and saw light breaking through a grill at the top, which lay in an alleyway running down the back of the houses along Mordinges Drive.

Rogers left his display on the kitchen table and rushed outside to the patio to report his latest findings to Gerard. "Sir, we have completed a full infra-red and x-ray scan of the back garden and can confirm that below us is an extensive space about the same area as the lawn. The grass and soil are only about 30cm deep. Also, the patio slabs here in the centre are lined with lead."

"Harris!" ordered Gerard. Harris immediately appeared in the patio doorway. "Harris, somehow these slabs move to reveal an entrance. Move them."

Harris went back into the house and got his equipment. After only a few minutes, the three patio steps down to the lawn were sinking even further. Rogers was standing on one and was caught off-guard before quickly stepping away. The three

Pharmara personnel watched as the steps sank further down to reveal a longer stairway that ended with a big metal door. As Harris began walking down the steps to use his talents on the door, the lawn began rolling back.

"Sir, look! The front half of the grass is rolling under the back half."

"Stay alert; we don't know what this man is capable of."

A noise began within the nursery, it sounded like a fan, a big one. It was getting increasingly faster and stronger. The further the grass receded, the more manic the turbine sound became. The solar panels were by now fully revealed but they did not spring into life following the sun. Instead, a tube about half a metre in diameter telescopically lifted itself from the centre towards the sky. It finished its ascent standing about twenty metres tall. The whirring of the fan within the nursery reached a crescendo when all of a sudden there was a manic chopping sound, like a wood chipper, as all the plants, fruits and vegetables were sucked into the fan, shredded and then shot out the top of the long tube.

The three men stood below, watching as the tube vomited out its long stream of multi-coloured exhaust. The trajectory veered off to the east with the wind, taking with it hundreds of seeds searching for new fertile ground on which to plant themselves and grow. Some seeds dripped out of the tube and fell at Gerard's feet.

"Seeds infecting the land, Rogers! Get samples for evidence and analysis so we can start scanning the surrounding area for this filth and get it cleared up. Then we'll spray it for good measure." Gerard looked up at the continuing shower of salad, soil and tools. "Harris! Get that bloody door open!"

Duncan struggled out of the tight hole, slid the grill away from the opening, took a hasty look around to make sure the coast was clear and then heaved himself out. Once the grill was re-placed and he had dusted himself down a bit, he stood up to collect his thoughts and took a deep breath before continuing his escape, when all of a sudden he felt a finger tap his shoulder.

"Mr Hartley?"

Duncan froze.

CHAPTER 4

"Mr Hartley?"

The question indicated uncertainty, uncommon in a predator catching his prey red-handed. Duncan turned around slowly, both arms at his side and hands spread open to show he was unarmed.

"I take it you're Mr Duncan Hartley, yes?"

"Who's asking?" The girl standing before him didn't look threatening. She appeared to be alone and a quick survey along the alleyway found no back-up.

"Thank your lucky stars I'm not Pharmara Security."

"I'm sorry but I've no time to chat, I'm otherwise engaged. Unless you're going to shoot or arrest me, I'll bid you good day, madam."

"I'm here to help you. My name is Amy." Amy started to exit the alley towards the road, motioning to Duncan that he should follow her. "Come with me, I have a car down here."

Duncan paused, weighing up the situation. Following a stranger didn't seem the best option. "Why should I follow you? I don't know who you are."

"I know, but we don't have time." Amy turned back towards Duncan. "I knew your wife, Nicole. We worked together at Pharmara, we were good friends, did yoga together, had lunch, you know." Amy looked over Duncan's shoulder. "We have to move. Stay under these trees, it makes it harder for the satellites to see us."

Duncan followed at a distance. "A bit convenient you turning up just as Pharmara Security knock on my door, isn't it?"

"I'd call it 'lucky' personally."

"So you just happened to be walking down this alley and thought you'd help the next person that appeared from a drain cover?"

Amy turned to face Duncan, without any congeniality. "Look, it just so happens I've been dragged into this by your little gardening hobby. In the past hour I've found out my dear friend, who recently passed away, was engaged in illegal food growth and consumption, and I've been virtually accused of doing the same. I've had to leave my safe, boring job and now I'm trying to help out the man who essentially caused all this!"

"Why? Why would you want to help me?"

Amy started walking again. "I'm here for Nicole. She'd want me to be here and I can see you need my help. What's your plan right now? Your car is in the garage. You gonna run?"

"Yes."

"You may think you can outrun younger, trained security personnel, but you can't outrun the satellites, drones and CCTV. Also," Amy looked up through the trees, blinking at the rays of sun breaking through, "curiosity has gotten the better of me. This situation has escalated far faster than I would've expected and it isn't making sense. That makes me curious. Makes me wonder if there's more to this than meets the eye."

"More to what?"

"I don't know, but I want to find out."

"Maybe you should've remained in your boring job."

"Naah." The thought of going back reeked of failure. "I'm finally moving, progressing. I haven't gone down a new path for too long. Come on, let's get out of here."

Amy and Duncan peered out from the end of the alleyway onto the adjacent street. Amy, looking up and down the road, saw the coast was clear and indicated to Duncan her car was the blue one parked across the road.

"Before we go," said Duncan, "tell me something about Nicole, something personal so I know you actually knew her and you're not going to lead me into the jaws of Pharmara Security."

Amy's eyes met Duncan's and then drifted off into thought, a subtle smile playing across her lips. She snapped back to the present and returned her line of sight to Duncan's. "She was ultra helpful, always going out of her way to help people, especially old people who didn't have much, haranguing Pharmara to donate money, drugs and host educational courses to help them socialise and get back on their feet. Oh yeah, she started to get arthritis in her left hand, hated soap operas and also said you'd be absolutely useless on your own in case of an emergency, so here I am."

Duncan seemed to remember Nicole mentioning Amy on a few occasions but realised he had always tuned out, his wife's words floating through him whenever she spoke about aspects of her life not involving himself. Unless it concerned him directly, Duncan just wasn't that interested. He would deem it unimportant, especially compared to his activities. That greenhouse at the bottom of the garden was not only growing illegal, natural fruits and vegetables, but was also nurturing Duncan's own ego and self-importance. He was glad it had been destroyed.

"You know, she'd always want to go to the old side of town in winter so she could help some of the homeless people there? She made them soup, tomato soup with original natural tomatoes. She didn't care about any potential consequences. 'Just like my gran used to make,' they'd say."

"So can we go now?"

"You know I could over-power you at any time, right? I'm no old codger."

"Nicole told me you have a dodgy right ankle from an old football injury. If you come anywhere near me, I'm giving it a good kick."

Seeing no suspicious activity, Duncan quickly walked towards the car. "Come on, we better get out of here."

As they approached the stylish family-sized car resting on its four corner stubs, the door slid upwards into the roof and they both got in. The interior of the car, as with most cars, consisted of a perimeter of seats with a media display on a window. Cars had gone through two revolutions in a relatively short space of time in the 2020s: automated driving and solar powered energy.

This massive project to change the road infrastructure was implemented as part of the country's revolutionary push for self-sustainability during the millennium's teens and twenties following the Great Recession and leading up to The Big O, the point when the country's total oxygen emissions exceeded it's total carbon emissions. The Big O was celebrated on 6th June 2035, bringing with it a sanctimonious post-coital daze the country had yet to fully wake from, especially as it was the first and still one of the only countries to boast such an achievement. A second British Empire emerged, exporting new ambassadors of solar technology and viceroys of carbon-neutral transportation across the globe to new colonies and dominions. The sun never set on this second incarnation of empire, but if it did, there was always the wind powered back-up generator.

Amy's car, as all automobiles and trains, levitated via electro-magnetism to greatly reduce drag; the base of the car floated upon a bed of opposing magnetic forces between the road and the car. The PMP (Photovoltaic Magnetic Polymer) road generated its own electro-magnetism from the sun, whilst excess energy wirelessly recharged all car batteries passing over it. Once levitated, the car was powered laterally by compressed air, jets located around the car, so the tightest of parking spaces could be conquered. Air was sucked in from grills at the front, fed into the air compressor, which then distributed the compressed air to the relevant jets directed by the onboard computer; all powered by solar energy collected by the photovoltaic paint and glass dressing the car.

During this time, road sensors were also embedded into the new PMP road surface to aid computer navigation. Purists reminisced over vintage cars because of their design; this new age of automated cars negated the need for safety and aerodynamics so space was the dominating design factor. This, coupled with the fact cars had neither wheels nor an engine, resulted in cars looking more boxy. The disadvantages included the fact that not all roads were PMP resurfaced meaning the public's movements were restricted. Roads could also have their electro-magnetism switched off depending on the whims of the roads' private owners and operators. Traffic could be controlled, speeding was impossible and road safety was almost perfect. The only accidents now involved inebriated pedestrians with no understanding that computer-controlled vehicles had no influence outside the laws of physics and could not predict the stupidity of drunks. Mass and momentum were still kings of the road.

Amy spoke to the onboard C.I.C.S.I. "Tint the windows."

"Where are we going?" Duncan enquired as the car gently rose up, a blue glow intensifying from both the underside of the car and the road surface below.

"I'm not sure yet, but we need to get moving."

"Harris!" Gerard screamed down the patio steps into the nursery. A mumbling answer ambled back up. "What did he say, Rogers?"

Rogers, who was standing at the foot of the steps in the nursery, relayed the answer. "There's no-one down here, but there's a short tunnel that leads up to an alleyway along the back of the garden."

Gerard shouted directly to Harris, ignoring Rogers as a conduit for his message. "Go through the tunnel and search the alleyway, pronto, Harris!" Quietening his voice slightly, Gerard ordered Rogers to accompany him to the kitchen to continue their search via satellite.

"Zoom out so we can see the alleyway and run it back fifteen minutes."

Rogers moved his thimbled finger around the kitchen table as they both followed events on the portable media display. Rogers broke the silence. "Nothing there, sir, I can't see anyone."

"It's those damn trees. He's hiding under there like vermin, Rogers. Zoom out again so we can see both ends of the alley-way. He'll stick his head out to smell cheese at some point."

Rogers' index finger pirouetted and twirled some more.

"There! Zoom in at this end and go back two seconds. Yes, there. He's with another person. ID them. What's the time in-dex on this footage?"

"Ten minutes ago."

They both stared at the display, intensely following their prey. They watched Duncan and Amy walking towards a car and saw the doors open. Gerard activated his mobile device. "Monty, do we have records on a car, registration R0072FRU17? ... Bugger! So what level of registration is it? ... Really? Do you know which hire company? ... Bugger! Hang on."

Gerard played with his device and phoned another number.

"Jerry! All right, mate? How's the wife and kids? Good. Look, mate, need a favour from your neck of the woods. We've got an errant employee in one of your cars and we need to track them down. If I give you the registration can you give me a heads up?" Gerard waited on Jerry's response. "Jerry, mate, come on. You remember the conference in Rome, right? Well then, I just need that favour returned." Gerard looked at Rogers and shook his head in disappointment. "Really? Bloody shits! Can you give me anything?" Gerard walked back towards Rogers, finishing off his phone conversation. "Yeah, OK, cheers for that, mate. Every little bit of info will help. See you in Prague this summer? Nice one."

Gerard hung up and spoke to Rogers. "OK, they've disen-gaged the tracking in their hire car but I've got some more information. Let's do a complete sweep of Wigthorn for this make and model with two occupants, one male and one female, and let's speed up this satellite footage so we can catch up to the live feed."

Gerard's device interrupted him just as he had put it back in his pocket. "Yes? What do you mean you're on hold? Fuck off, Monty."

Duncan sat checking through his bag as they drove aimlessly along the seafront of Wigthorn. Amy sat back watching Duncan, trying to picture him and Nicole together, chatting, eating together, being in love, but no imagined situation could convince Amy that they would've made a good couple. He looked good for his age but his personality seemed to be completely different – maybe the old adage of opposites attracting was true? Amy thought she should re-evaluate her first impressions as they hadn't met under the best circumstances, and he obviously had good reason to be guarded and on edge.

Duncan broke the silence. "Have you turned the tracking off in this car?"

"Yes, of course, but that doesn't mean we're safe from being tracked."

"We should get into another car or go by foot as they'll be looking for this one."

"It's not that – they'll be scanning all cars of this make and model for one female in her thirties and one male in his seventies. We can stop and get out to walk or change car, but Pharmara will have both their Wigthorn satellites focusing on us and it won't take them long to catch up to a live feed if we stay exposed like this. We can't out run them, we have to try and lose them."

Duncan stopped playing with the contents of his bag. "How can they tell who's in the car?"

"They can't get a DNA reading unless there's a direct line of sight from the satellite to the target but they can still measure body temperature, body mass, body position, body movement, heart rate, body shape, breathing, etc. plus ambient readings. All these factors have common patterns amongst the sexes and different age groups. For example, men over forty tend to cross their legs more in the car than men under forty."

Duncan immediately uncrossed his legs. "How do you know all this?"

"I analyse tracking information at Pharmara. Well, I used to. I know what they are all capable of. It's just a little different being the fox rather than a hound."

"We need to get out of this car; if we leave the tracking off, they'll search for the only car in Wigthorn without any tracking activated. We'll be spotted getting out the car in any car parks or tunnels from the CCTV. They'll have caught up to the live feed if we try and drive into the countryside. We don't have enough time." Duncan addressed the car's onboard C.I.C.S.I. "Activate the roof view."

The roof untinted itself to give the occupants a view of the sky.

"Damn! This must be the first unclouded sky for months. Typical!" Duncan instinctively sat back in his chair to hide from the eyes in the sky.

"That's a myth, clouds don't give you any kind of cover. We've probably got about ten minutes before they catch up to the live feed, so we need to do something now."

"You got any ideas?"

"Not just yet."

"What kind of rescue attempt is this?"

Amy looked around the car for any clues. "You'd already be caught by now if it wasn't for me. What about some kind of smoke and mirrors trick?"

"I suppose it can be done, but elaborate tricks or re-enactments take forward planning and assistance." Duncan looked around the car for any clues Amy might have missed. "There must have been situations when you were the eye in the sky and the information being presented to you wasn't as clear as you'd have liked?"

Amy thought for a second. "Lots of people in close proximity can provide problems. At first there are so many readings it takes time to separate them and answers only emerge once patterns have been established. There are only two of us though and, as you already pointed out, we've got no help."

Duncan spoke to the car's onboard C.I.C.S.I. "Take us to Meadow Acre Road."

Amy looked at Duncan in surprise. "Why are we going to the old side of town? It's a dump round there."

"Exactly. We can buy all the help we need plus CCTV coverage isn't so perfect. How much cash do you have on you?"

"About £5,000. I took out as much as I could when I hired the car."

"Good." Duncan started going through his bag, putting a few objects into his pockets: Percy's hard drive, his wallet and as many small pouches of seeds as he could fit. "If you have anything you absolutely need to keep hold of, make sure you keep it to hand. Here, take some of these seeds. It's important they get out of this, more important than me. OK?"

Amy held Duncan's eyes to ensure she'd heard him correctly. "You want me to prioritise these seeds over you?"

"Yes."

"You're nuts."

"No, they're seeds."

"Very funny. If I get these seeds out of here without you, then what?"

"Take them to Norway. There's a seed bank on an island called the 'Doomsday Vault' where they store and protect as many non-genetically modified seeds as they can. A reference library humanity can use to start again after we've manipulated Mother Nature's creations to such an irreparable state."

"A bunch of hippies collecting seeds called it the Doomsday Vault – that's a bit dramatic, innit?"

"It's actually called 'The Svalbard Global Seed Vault' but that's so undramatic it doesn't quite install the sense of importance it deserves. Getting these seeds to the Doomsday Vault is my key objective, all right? If anything happens to me, you take these seeds ..."

"... to the Doomsday Vault, I get it. They'll already have these seeds, won't they? They must have tomatoes, radishes and sweetcorn coming out of their ears. They'll want ultra rare ones."

"Maybe. If it's still there."

"*If it's still there?* You don't even know if it's still there?"

"No. I haven't read any communications from it for over a year now. Corporate interests see it as a patent violation; I fear something drastic might have happened. That's what I intend to find out. But first ..." – Duncan fastened his bag, then sat up – "... we've got more pressing matters at hand. Get ready, we're going to play a little musical chairs."

"Rogers! Have we got live footage yet?" Gerard demanded from the other side of the kitchen, not looking up from his mobile device.

"In a couple of seconds, sir."

"Good. I've got five Pharmara Security cars ready to move as soon as we locate them."

"We're live, sir!"

"Excellent." Gerard walked promptly over to the kitchen table where Rogers was watching the live feed. "Where are they?"

"They're driving down Meadow Acre Road."

"What are they doing in that God forsaken shithole?"

"They're stopping sir!"

They both leaned forward to get a better view of proceedings twelve miles below their vantage point.

"Zoom in, Rogers; I want to see the sweat on their brow as they start running." Gerard activated his mobile device and spoke to his security units on the streets. "They're down Meadow Acre Road. I want two of you to approach from the west and three from the east. Go!"

Rogers zoomed in to get a closer view of the car and surrounding area, but there was no movement from the car or its occupants. Instead, a couple of homeless people sitting against the wall of an abandoned shopfront got up from their temporary home and approached the car.

"Those tramps are talking to them ... hang on, the door's opening sir. The tramps are getting in."

"Activate the non-visual sensors, Rogers. Let's see what's going on inside."

The screen changed from regular video footage to a hybrid view consisting of many colours and shapes, all recognisable as people, cars, etc. but looking more like an ethereal cartoon. Gerard and Rogers watched the footage as the two homeless people stepped into the car and sat down before the car drove off again.

"Which ones are the tramps?" asked Gerard, inexperienced in viewing such images.

"This one here and this one."

The car stopped again only thirty metres down the street and two more homeless people got up from their insufficient doorway homes, approached the car and got in.

"You still got your eye on Duncan?"

"Yes, sir."

Once again the car stopped and three more homeless people got in.

"There's music being played, sir."

"I don't care! You still know which one is Duncan?"

"Yes. The music has stopped and now they're all moving sir."

"Just keep your eye on Duncan – forget everyone else."

"I'm trying, sir." Rogers leaned in even closer, watching like a hawk as the action played out. "They're changing clothes, sir. All of them are removing clothes and swapping them." Rogers squinted to try and get a more detailed view. "Crap!"

"What?" Gerard demanded.

"Two of them have just got on top of each other. Now another two have. I'm not sure which one is … now they're all huddled together and moving around."

Gerard roared into his mobile device. "Is anyone on Meadow Acre Road yet!" After a pause for the answer, Gerard vented his frustration as it was confirmed none of the security vehicles had yet made it to their target.

"They've stopped, sir! Two of them are getting out and one of them has the bag!"

"Is it Duncan?"

"I'm not sure." Rogers replied apologetically.

"Bugger! Get the other satellite to track them, stay with the car!"

"They're carrying on down Meadow Acre Road. They're all still moving around in there, I don't know who is who."

With his arms crossed, Gerard stood behind Rogers, listening to his running commentary. Gerard's frown was getting ever deeper, his patience ever shorter. He whispered to Rogers, "Don't lose them."

Suddenly, the screen went dark grey.

"What's happened, Rogers?"

"They've turned into the public hospital multi-storey car park, sir. We can't follow them via satellite anymore – the concrete's too thick."

"So switch to the car park CCTV," Gerard implored.

Rogers turned around with his eyes firmly focused on the floor. "Sir, the public hospital doesn't have any CCTV. They can't afford any security or surveillance."

"What!" Gerard looked at Rogers in disbelief and then looked at the screen. "You mean they put their own patients at risk by not having CCTV? Bloody public services! The sooner they shut down the last of them, the better." Gerard re-addressed the security vehicles via his mobile device. "Go in and get them!"

Almost afraid to speak, but managing to in the hope of re-demption, Rogers updated Gerard on the latest events. "Sir, there are cars leaving the car park. I can keep track of some of them but not all of them as well as all the exits." Rogers quickly turned back to look at the screen, mainly to keep away from the ensuing reaction.

Gerard, knowing that there wasn't much more Rogers or himself could do, decided to vent his frustrations on the next level down the chain of command. "Harris!"

Harris appeared at the patio door entrance. Something other than Gerard was demanding his attention. An inner feeling of being watched washed over Gerard, which, for a man in his role, immediately put him at unease. Rogers, sensing an at-mosphere descend into the room, lifted his head from the display to see why Harris and Gerard were standing in silence. Gerard turned around.

"Afternoon, gentlemen." Estelle stood in the archway di-viding the open plan kitchen and lounge, her silhouette enhanced by the late afternoon sun pouring through the lounge window. With one slender arm resting on her hip and the other removing a pair of sunglasses, Estelle awaited a response with a slight tilt of her head. "I trust everything is in hand?"

CHAPTER 5

"Duncan?" whispered Amy, disorientated in a claustrophobic blackness.

"Yes?" muttered Duncan in a pained response.

"Where are we?" Amy pushed against the roof of the space they were enclosed in and felt around for a latch or handle.

"I'm not sure, I can't see a thing." They both tried to manoeuvre themselves into more space but without much success.

Amy pulled out her mobile device, activating the torch app to get some light. "I'm not getting any reception. I can only tell it's 5pm."

Duncan blinked in the sudden light and looked at Amy. "We're moving, that's for sure. We could be in the boot of a car. Are you OK?"

"Yeah, a little groggy, like I've just woken up from a heavy night out, but apart from that, I'm OK. What about you?"

"I'm knackered, plus I've got a headache. It's 5pm? We left your car in the hospital car park around 3pm, if I remember correctly."

"Yeah, it was just after 3pm. What's the last thing you remember?" Amy asked whilst moving again to address Duncan's face rather than his knees.

"I remember entering the hospital and going into one of the abandoned wards to wait for help."

"Me too. I don't remember anything after that."

Duncan froze, remaining silent as he listened to changes in the outside world. "Turn your mobile device off – we've stopped. I think I can hear someone."

A small whirring sound came from the top of their enclosure, and a small ray of light escaped into the space followed by more as the far wall began to sink into the floor and part of the roof started to scroll back. Blinded by the sudden change, both Duncan and Amy struggled to see who was standing above them and cowered back into the darkness. Eventually the glare gave way to colour and shape.

"Duncan!" came a cheerful voice through the light. "You all right in there, old man?"

"Julius?" Duncan questioned, still unsure as his eyes continued to adjust to the light.

"Yeah, who else would it be?" Julius was sitting on one of the side seats within the car, leaning in to get a better view of his cargo. The backseat elevated slightly to better reveal the contents of the boot.

Amy, having just produced a mass of adrenalin with which to unleash on her captors, was thrown by this sudden outpouring of civility. "You know this guy?"

Julius tried to make his way closer to Amy to introduce himself but was immediately met by a kicking boot. "Who the fuck are you?" Amy demanded, ready to bring her boot back for another kick.

"Easy, Amy!" Duncan said as he tried to restrain her from doing any damage. "This is Julius Talent. He got us out of Wigthorn in one piece." Letting go of Amy, he finished the introductions. "Julius, this is Amy Jay."

Amy, in mock politeness, turned her attentions to her captor in a stunningly un-Stockholm Syndrome manner – it was the polar opposite, more like Auckland Syndrome. "Pleased to meet you, Mr Julius Talent. Thank you for your most gracious hospitality. I've never been drugged and stuck in the boot of a car with as much style as today. Pray tell, to what do I owe this great honour?"

Julius reluctantly smiled. "I apologise, but it was necessary to get you out of the hospital."

Having heard enough, Amy made her way out of the boot and into the car.

"No, no!" Julius said firmly as he fell from the seat to his knees to block Amy's path. "You have to stay in here for now; the boot is lined with lead, which will give us a bit more time."

"You're kidding me? Bloody hell Duncan, where did you find this guy? Why not line the whole car, numb nuts?"

Julius looked at Duncan apologetically before answering Amy's question. "A whole car lined in lead? An unscannable car would light up like a Christmas tree on a peeping Tom's computer. You'd notice it, wouldn't you?"

"Suppose." Amy's reticence satisfied Julius he had got the message through. "I ain't no peeping Tom, Jules."

"I wouldn't mind even if you were." Amy's immediate use of Julius' nickname unfortunately led Julius to a misjudged familiarity. Amy's unimpressed response convinced Julius to continue with more urgent matters. "There are drones all over the place at the moment and we're still on Pharmara controlled roads. We've managed to fool them into thinking we're heading east, so they're concentrating their efforts over there, but there's still some major hassle following us west."

An unmistakable warning sound came from the car's computer. "Hang on a minute, we might have company." Julius went to the media display to investigate.

Amy engaged Duncan in a hushed conference regarding their current travel arrangements. "Duncan, who the hell is this guy?"

"Amy, Amy, relax. Look, I trust Julius. I've known him for years. He's part of 'The Unrecorded'. We do business on the black market. We trust each other and neither of us have let each other down. I know this isn't an ideal introduction but Julius is a good man, and this is the only way he could get us out of Wigthorn. Drop some of the attitude and you might even like him – he's a good kid."

Julius shouted out an update. "Drones are heading our way and pretty sharpish. If we can stay clear for another couple of kilometres we'll be off this Pharmara motorway and onto someone else's road network."

"They'll never let you off; they'll shut down power to this area before you reach the border." Amy had been through this cycle of events before; trained on it and trained others, but always on the other side of the media display. Amy started to enjoy herself, the challenge of outwitting one of her work colleagues. She always thought she was the best, and now it was time to find out.

Julius lived his life averting predators. He relished the rare chance to impress a girl with the finer details of staying unrecorded. "We managed to get about twenty decoys to the hospital within ten minutes – not bad, eh? Pharmara haven't got the coverage to stop all twenty of us at such short notice. They can scan us all they want but until they've got their dirty little mitts on us, we're still on the run. Shutting off power to the motorway means their own cars can't move either."

Amy raised an eyebrow. "What do you think the drones are for, genius?"

A jolt. The car came to an immediate stop. "What was that?" Duncan said, trying to steal a glimpse out of the window.

Amy kept her eyes on Julius. "The electro-magnetic power to the motorway has been shut down, rendering the car a heap of junk."

Julius maintained Amy's stare until a clunk was heard on the roof.

"What was that?" Duncan repeated.

"A drone," Amy said as Julius looked upwards.

Julius confirmed Amy's evaluation. "A drone."

"You know what's next on the list of the drone's standard operating procedure, right?"

"Not really, these drones are quite new," Julius tentatively replied, hoping for good news.

"They crash all computer systems on board."

Julius rolled his eyes to the side and saw the media display lose all life, waving goodbye with a final white dot before complete darkness. "Crap! We're so close to our exit."

Amy added to Julius' problems, reopening an old wound. "Drugging us was essential to this escape plan?"

"I apologise, but it really was necessary." Julius was surprised at this change of tack, answering whilst he remained on the look out for any signs the drone might be trying to force an entry. "The hospital was crawling with security. No one was allowed to enter or exit without being thoroughly scanned. We had to drug you both in order to …"

"We?" Amy interrupted.

"Yeah, I couldn't get you out by myself when you were both unconscious. I brought some acquaintances along to help.

Who do you think all these decoys are? You contacted me, remember?"

"I don't actually," Duncan said, peering around Amy to get a better view of the ceiling and Julius.

"Me neither."

"The drugs must have affected your memory."

Amy crossed her arms. "So. Drugging us ... please continue."

"Yeah, we had to make you appear to be dead so we could get you past security and out the hospital. They had bio scanners on every floor and exit, so asking you to lie there with your eyes shut wouldn't have worked because your heart rate and brain activity wouldn't have changed. If anything, you would have stuck out like a sore thumb with the amount of adrenalin pumping through you."

"You *killed* us?" Duncan exclaimed.

"Shh!" Julius urged, bending down in case the drone thrust a sharp implement through the ceiling. "That thing might hear you."

"You killed us?" Duncan repeated with less accusation. His temporary death may have meant he was closer to Nicole, but he didn't remember feeling anything.

"Only for about twelve minutes. Anyway, you weren't dead – you were 'in stasis'."

A human voice with all personality removed through script and rehearsal spoke through the cars speaker system. "Attention occupant, your vehicle has been selected for a routine evaluation. Please confirm your identity and destination."

Amy continued her conversation in a whisper despite the interruption, letting curiosity rule reason once again. "Dead or alive, they can scan our DNA. How did you manage to avoid that?"

Julius prioritised the drones question first. In a high-pitched voice, he answered, "I'm Mrs Carol Ford of Wigthorn, and I'm off to Plymouth to visit my sister."

Amy glanced up at the ceiling, trying to see why Julius was speaking in a higher tone but discovering nothing. "These drones also have DNA scanners, they know who we are regardless of heart rate, brain activity or ridiculously high-pitched voices. You can't change our DNA."

Julius paused, whispering an aside to Amy. "I can."

"No you can't," Amy mouthed.

The drone spoke. "Thank you Mrs Ford. We have a few more evaluations to do in this sector but power will soon be re-established."

"Thank you, young man." Julius struggled to contain his giggling.

"How the hell did you do that?" It was all Amy could do to remain confined to the boot.

Julius could see her frustration and welcomed the opportunity to embrace his advantage. He sat on the floor next to the boot so they were both face to face. "Extreme skill, great talent, vast intelligence and rugged good looks."

Amy shoved the grinning Julius so he rocked backwards, his muffled laughter following him to the floor.

"Do not attempt to leave the vehicle!" the drone demanded. "A second occupant has been detected!"

Julius and Amy locked eyes in terror.

"Your arm!" Julius whispered, and then spoke louder in his unconvincing female voice to address the drone. "Err, that was my dog Poochie. Get back, Poochie, you bad boy."

"A human was detected. Remain in the vehicle until a security operative arrives."

Amy crawled out. "You shouldn't have been such a dumbass! What now?"

Julius opened up a compartment beneath one of the front seats on the opposite side. "I'm getting the 'Drone Detachment Device'."

Duncan crawled out behind Amy. "That's a cricket bat."

"Well spotted." Julius stood up on the front seat and reached for a handle to slide open the front section of the sunroof. Upon spying the rugby ball shaped object with rotor blades on top and a belt of blinking lights, Julius took up a rather unorthodox baseball stance and swung hard.

Duncan saw the drone propelled to the side, landing in the hedges lining the road. "Good shot, old boy."

Amy tried the media display. "It's still locked down. The drone must still be active."

"You've got great legs, Amy." Julius put away the bat whilst still admiring Amy's lower physique.

Amy screwed up her face. "You what?"

"You cycle much?"

"No."

Julius then slid open a compartment from the floor and unfolded what looked like a unicycle but without the one defining wheel. "This car has not only been registered under a false name of Mrs Carol Ford, but also has manual functions such as a sunroof." Julius gestured at the roof as he took up the alter ego of an air stewardess and then clipped the cycling contraption into place. "And forward motion."

Amy shook her head. "Oh no, no. What happened to chivalry?"

"I've got to steer this thing – you ever manually driven a car?" Amy shook her head again. "You're not going to ask – forgive me Duncan – an older gentleman to take up the strain, are you?" Amy sheepishly looked at Duncan. Julius continued, "That's settled then. I'm the brains, you're the brawn."

The seat leaned back with the pedals raised up so when Amy sat down she could get good traction with her legs. Julius took up the controls located within the front seat where the cricket bat was stored and Duncan sat up next to him.

Amy started pedalling to generate enough power for the car to produce a magnetic force to lift it and compressed air to propel it forward.

"Not far to go, Amy, just a few hundred metres."

What Amy didn't know was that steering the car was very easy – just one joystick that could also be extended to the cyclist's position so one solo operator could control and power the car. Julius kept this little morsel close to his chest.

"Come on, girl, put your back into it. We need to get out of here pronto!"

Amy grimaced, and not from the effort of pedalling.

Julius looked back over his shoulder, storing the view of Amy lying back, breathing heavily and working up a sweat. Amy got suspicious at the lack of banter and opened her eyes from the strain to find Julius keeping his eyes on another destination. "What?"

Julius quickly faced forward. "Nothing."

Duncan shuffled in his seat. "So, where are we going?"

"Shaded Vale."

Estelle calmly paced around the lounge of Duncan's house, scrolling through a media display deconstructing his reading and listening material, drawing a mental picture of his family life from photographs. She walked into the garden to go through the debris left behind by the shredder; roots, pots and mangled gardening tools lay strewn about the lawn and solar panels. Estelle picked up part of a pot that still had a thick mass of soil stuck to the inside. Dropping it onto the concrete patio, she awaited the appearance of the copyright infringement.

Brightly coloured seeds could be seen aginst the dark brown soil, still intact and damp from having been freshly watered. Estelle pulled out a handkerchief from her handbag and slowly bent down to see these rare objects for herself, having never seen one up close. Simpler than a microchip and yet able to contain so much more than mere data, Estelle held one in the palm of her hand and closed her eyes to see if she could feel any sign of life.

What she held in her hand represented DIY food production – something that could cause a huge part of Pharmara's sister companies to collapse, as well as threaten the superiority of the UK economy. The seed's miraculous simplicity to reproduce and to infect hybrid seeds was reason enough for Pharmara to hunt this agricultural terrorist down and submit him to the fullest extent of Pharmara's corporate punishment.

Estelle kept the seed in her hand to dispose of as she walked back into the house.

"Where are they, Gerard?"

Gerard looked up from the media display, where Rogers was still frantically working away. "We stopped a car and got a drone clamped to it which managed to get a brief scan before being partly disabled, but no sign of Duncan Hartley – just the car's registered owner, Carol Ford, and another unidentified female."

Estelle walked over to the oven. "Who's Carol Ford?"

"No idea. She emigrated to The Florida Isles three years ago. The thing is, though, the car has disappeared. There's no road power but it was still able to move a few hundred metres down the motorway before disappearing just here."

Estelle turned around to view Gerard's finger on the map. "Good."

"Good?"

"Yes. Good." Estelle turned back, switched on an oven hob and watched it quickly glow red-hot.

"There're only fields surrounding a restricted iPatch sector. We can't follow them."

Estelle dropped the seed onto the burning surface, watching it shrivel and char, the heat corrupting its blueprints, data and replicating processes. Then she glided out the kitchen. "Gerard, get a team down here to clean this place up. We're leaving."

"Where to?"

"Shaded Vale."

CHAPTER 6

Ten minutes later, and after some vigorous cycling by Amy, they had made it off the motorway and down a side road containing two exits: one heading right over a bridge so cars could easily do a U-turn and get on the opposing lanes of the motorway, the other leading only a few metres to a gate and, beyond that, a field of fallowed mud with woods bordering the immediate horizon.

"Keep going, Amy, only a little bit further to go," Julius encouraged as he took the former exit to the field gate.

"Where is Shaded Vale?" asked Duncan.

"It's just here."

Duncan looked out the window, appreciating the view of fields, hedgerows and woods but no obvious conurbations. "How big is it?"

"It's a fair size. About twenty thousand residents, zero unemployment, zero crime and the highest average salary per resident on the planet."

"I can't believe I've never heard of such a town." Duncan continued to survey the surrounding landscape for this metropolitan role model but couldn't see any buildings for the trees.

"Its residents like to stay under the radar."

"We're all under the radar, aren't we?"

"Not everyone. The omnipotent satellites will turn a blind eye for the right price."

"'iPatches'." Amy stopped cycling and continuing her explanation whilst catching her breath. "'Invisible Patches', there's a few of them scattered around the country, areas that are blacked out and ignored by satellites. Even if you do manage to get a satellite over one, it won't acknowledge anything is there, not even the ground. We were told they existed because of natural phenomena or were highly classified areas; I didn't know you could opt out of satellite surveillance."

"You can and they do."

Amy lifted a leg over the seat and rested her elbows on her knees with her head bowed. "Why? What have they got to hide in Shaded Vale?"

"All sorts of things. We all have, haven't we? Would you let me examine the search history on your computer? Are you happy that your employer can access your financial data and geographical whereabouts? Look where that got you with regards to Nicole: fired. If you've got nothing to hide then you ain't living." Julius manually lifted up the car door so it receded into the roof and spoke to an intercom hidden in a bush. "Pete, you on the gate tonight? Our computer system has been zapped by a drone. Give us a scan and let us in, mate."

The reply chased a small bird out of the bush. "Jules, what brings you to these parts?"

"Here to see The Colonel. He should be expecting my friends and I."

"Yeah, yeah, you're all right. Come on through, mate."

"By the way, Julius, I resigned – I didn't get fired." Amy moved to the front of the car to get a closer look at where they were meant to be going, her job of sufficiently recharging the main battery having been accomplished. The gate opened and the car progressed effortlessly over the muddy field. This intrigued Amy. "How are we driving on grass, Julius?"

"There is an enhanced electro-magnetic surface about 5cm below the mud and grass. It's enough to keep the car moving and hovering above the surface. This is the quickest way into Shaded Vale."

"Where is it though?"

"Just the other side of those trees."

Amy kept an eye on the woods coming closer to view. As they approached, a hole started to appear in the field directly in front of them with the road they were following leading down into it. The car drove down and into a well-lit tunnel; Amy looked back and saw the hole close up. Turning back to look ahead, the tunnel stretched out in front of them for about a kilometre under the woods until it started to lead back upwards as the last of the days sunlight lazily streamed in from the exit opening up ahead. As they drove back up to the surface, Amy could see a picturesque view of manicured lawns, closely cropped hedges, pampered trees and the most polished, multicoloured PMP road surface she'd ever seen. The road led to a roundabout with all four exits signposted to different locations within Shaded Vale.

Julius sat on the pedalling seat with the steering controls in hand so they could continue to their destination within Shaded Vale. Amy gave Julius a raised eyebrow upon seeing his capability of both powering and steering the car by himself, but was more concerned with the scenery of Shaded Vale. Having never been outside of Pharmara controlled territory, she wondered if everywhere else was like this.

In the half-light between night and day, the road glistened, all line markings illuminated for pedestrian use, computer guided cars not requiring such primitive assistance. The kerb side gutters were clean, with evenly spaced filtration drains, and the grass separating the colourful pavements from the road was cut and dyed like a putting green with the occasional water sprinkler. People could be seen walking along the well-lit streets, arm in arm or with their dog, one of which was barking at a sprinkler as it started to wash away its excrement before he had finished, catching him unawares.

As they turned around a corner, a group of boys on Magna-Bikes sped past in the opposite direction, clothed in football kit and muddy faces. Amy looked back at Julius and before she spoke, he answered, "They're new, too expensive for the outside world just yet."

Homes were shrouded by statuesque trees and tall, protective hedges, allowing only a brief glimpse of pedestrians and drivers as they passed by. Each house was individual and detached, not one blueprint allowed to reproduce so the copy could cheapen the original. Architectural styles spanned the centuries, from grand faux Greek and Roman to the latest modern designs of spheres and chameleons, changing their structure depending on sunlight, wind, season and current occupants. Lighting was an important element in not only providing safety and visibility during the night but, seemingly more important than that, showing off these designs to others.

Around another corner, the unmistakable sight of a security officer was seen walking briskly along the pavement towards the car. Amy and Duncan ducked down out of sight and earnestly looked to Julius for co-operation. Julius stopped his leisurely pedalling. "Don't worry, you're safe here. Relax."

The officer signalled for some assistance. Julius pulled the car over and unwound a window. "Excuse me, sir," said the officer, "you haven't seen a group of lads cycle past here, have you? About five of them, muddy little blighters."

"No, officer, I'm afraid not. Why? What have they done?"

"They managed to skid their bikes through some mud and get my trousers." The officer presented Julius with the evidence.

"We'll keep an eye out for them, officer."

As Julius pulled away, he explained his little white lie. "I've done him a favour. He's got nothing else to do around here. That'll be front page news on *Shaded Vale Gazette* this Friday."

Driving down these streets during the early evening incited Duncan's curiosity. He wanted to see more of Shaded Vale during daylight hours, but his joy was tempered by a concern of how the secrecy protecting Shaded Vale (and keeping its beauty from influencing the rest of the country) would manifest itself.

"What do you think?" Julius asked as he sat back, observing their reactions.

"It's beautiful, quite amazing actually," Amy replied, not taking her eyes off the view.

"Who's The Colonel?" Duncan asked curtly.

"He's the one who requested I bring you both to his house and offer you sanctuary."

"What does he want with us though?" Duncan asked, the lack of specifics arousing his suspicion.

"I'll let him answer for himself. He's not part of Pharmara, if that's what you're concerned about. We'll be at his house soon."

The car rounded a bend and turned into a driveway sandwiched between two large hedges that blocked any view of the house from the road. As they drove under a stone archway covered with ivy and down a short winding driveway, the large hedges finally came to an end and revealed the house hidden behind. The house was built in the Tudor style; brilliant white walls with original oak beams were highlighted by artificial lights. The solar roof tiles were tinted dark red to match the illusion, with four huge chimney stacks at each end spitting out excess steam.

The car circled a marble statue in the middle of the driveway: Sir Isaac Newton sitting cross legged with a hand stroking his chin, deep in thought with an apple magnetically hovering motionlessly above his head – that great eureka moment frozen in time. Once the car had stopped, they all got out and remained standing as the large front doors opened. The Colonel strode out of the doorway purposely, greeting his guests with a booming voice.

"Welcome Julius and friends. Come in!"

Amy, Duncan and Julius approached The Colonel as he warmly shook Julius' hand and was then introduced to Duncan and Amy. The Colonel was fairly tall, solidly built with a black moustache as straight and firm as his jaw and given greater prominence against his short grey hair. It unnecessarily underlined an already emboldened nose, slightly italicised by a youth spent on the rugby field. They followed The Colonel into the front entrance, a circular hallway containing a grand spiral staircase, and then through a minimalist lounge furnished only with three huge sofas surrounding a large, dark wooden coffee table facing the dominating yet featureless fireplace.

Amy noticed a shadowy figure watching them from behind a glass door on the other side of the lounge; the voyeur disappeared once it saw Amy lagging behind to return the observation. Once it had gone, Amy caught up with the others, who had exited the lounge onto an enormous decked balcony stretching across the whole width of the house at the back. The view was stunning. From the house's hillside vantage, it revealed the majority of Shaded Vale to be situated within a huge bowl, a valley enveloped by four hills, one of which they were perched on looking out onto an evening vista of lights; houses were lit up in the darkness and a river to the east was illuminated by small boats and riverside restaurants.

"Sit, please." They each took a seat in one of the luxurious outdoor chairs. It was the end of a long journey, and Duncan and Amy were glad to be sitting out in the open relaxing in comfort and breathing in the fresh air. "Can I get you anything to drink?"

"Coffee would be great, thanks," Julius answered. Duncan and Amy agreed. The Colonel had a fully equipped bar on the balcony and made his guests drinks whilst he introduced himself in more depth.

"Amy. Duncan. You're probably wondering why you find yourselves here."

Duncan, being the senior member of the fugitive duo and beginning their life on the run, decided he should take charge and get some kind of grip on the situation since they had been chased out of town to a secret hideaway somewhere in the countryside, all within half a day.

"Yeah!" Amy butted in without any such forethought. "Firstly, who the hell are you? Secondly, what is this place, bloody Narnia? Thirdly … err …" Amy looked at Duncan for some assistance on this third point, but he appeared shell-shocked at her outburst. "Yeah, thirdly, what kind of name is 'The Colonel'?"

The Colonel stopped making coffee. When Amy had finished, he let out a booming laugh, turned on the coffee percolator and confronted his concerned guests with arms crossed. "Amy Jay, section leader within the Statistical Acquirement and Analysis department in Pharmara headquarters in Wigthorn. Thirty-three years old, given eleven years excellent service to Pharmara and only promoted once. An unblemished record, until today, when it was discovered that you were in a possible collusion with ex-employee Nicole Hartley, recently deceased. You have my sympathies, Duncan."

Duncan didn't acknowledge The Colonel and let him continue speaking as he rotated on his heels away from Amy to face Duncan himself.

"Duncan Hartley, aged seventy-two, and in fine fettle, if I maybe so bold. Qualified from the Pharmara University in Manchester with a first in Pharmaceutical Research Science and gaining a doctorate with your thesis proposing genetically modified foods were negatively disturbing the finely honed balance of foetal development, moving to a full-time position within the Pharmara research department where you remained for twenty-three years until unexpectedly leaving due to poor health – although, as everyone here can witness, that cannot be the whole truth, can it?" The Colonel looked at Duncan, leaving an opening in his monologue for Duncan to retort.

Duncan took it. "'Artistic differences' is probably the technical term."

"Holy crap!" Amy proclaimed in her own inimitable way. "You used to work at Pharmara?"

The Colonel butted in. "Duncan's research proved vital to the growth of Pharmara's sister companies over the past three decades, as well as their competitors. After discovering exactly how the foetus was being adversely affected, Pharmara exploited this information to further enhance its own transgenetic food production."

Duncan wasn't sure The Colonel's explanation was defensive enough of his own character. "They exploited this information in a harmful way, taking all my research and flipping it on its head. Genetically modified foods at the time caused slight mental side effects such as lethargy, stress, lack of ambition, greater reliability on the senses rather than reason, and a few others. Pharmara remarketed and developed this slight side effect into a more controllable and affective product benefit. In basic terms, this ladder up in our food's evolution resulted in human development snaking its way down considerably towards more animalistic desires."

"Domesticated animals are easier to train," The Colonel said to himself as he dropped two sugar cubes into a mug.

"You never said anything." Amy wasn't used to learning new information about people; she was more accustomed to having it all at her fingertips.

"I've only just met you!"

"No, no, it's not that, I'm sorry. Nicole never mentioned it to me. She never said you had any scientific background."

It was now Julius' turn to voice surprise. "Duncan, you dark horse. Living in the shadow of the beast, dealing forbidden fruit, when all the while you were once up in that ivory tower yourself." Julius couldn't help but smile in admiration. "You don't import your fruit and vegetables, do you?"

Duncan didn't answer, but gave Julius a taste of his own medicine and winked.

With his back turned to his guests, The Colonel continued to stir the coffee and the conversation. "Duncan, why don't you tell your friends more about the 'artistic differences' you encountered?"

Duncan, in a corner, began to fight his way out. "Hang on a minute, Colonel, I think you have a few questions from Amy still hanging in the air."

"No, no, no," Amy interjected. "You can't go deflecting questions like that. The ball's in your court now."

Julius, clearly enjoying this lively bout of revelations, also urged Duncan to continue. "Duncan, you're amongst friends here – you can tell us."

"Friends? I've known Amy for about twelve hours and you, for what?" Duncan looked at The Colonel. "About twenty minutes! How do I know satellites and CCTV are not recording my every action, building up a case for my incarceration?"

The Colonel turned from the bar with two mugs of fresh coffee in his hands to save Duncan with a change of tack. Walking through the steam in the slightly chilled air, The Colonel spoke. "Duncan, relax. Here, take a mug. By allowing you into my house I am already guilty of harbouring a known criminal, so please, do not think I am holding you against your will or giving you up to the authorities. You are free to walk out of here at anytime, you have my word."

Amy noticed the shadowy figure once again at the large bay window overlooking the decked balcony as The Colonel was serving coffee. It stood by a long curtain, obviously thinking it could not been seen from the lit balcony in the dark room. But Amy could see one side of a woman's outline jut out from behind the curtain; a slender figure with one hand on her hip.

The Colonel grabbed two more mugs for Julius and himself then joined the others sat around a large round table. "I should introduce myself properly, my apologies. I can understand that this is an awkward situation for the both of you. Flung together so suddenly and then finding yourselves in a strange place shortly after."

The Colonel took a sip from his coffee and leaned back into his chair, talking whilst staring out at the view from the balcony, framed by ivy growing up the sides of the walls and the fence along the balcony's edge. The hillside fell away into a small valley only to rise again at the far side. The lights dotted around the valley floor continued up the hillside, gradually getting smaller as they receded into the horizon, where stars and planets and drones and satellites continued the quilt of speckled illuminations into the canopy of space. The moon was full and bright; closer inspection revealed tiny black spots shooting across it like ants running across a lampshade. The satellites made Amy and her generation feel safe. It gave Duncan and his generation stage fright.

The Colonel continued talking to his guests who were all enjoying the view whilst being warmed by their hot mugs and heated chairs. "My name is Billy Gold and I'm fifty-six years old, born in Plymouth, educated at a Prospero X4 school to the age of sixteen, enrolled in a Product Engineering course but dropped out. Got a job at a Prospero X4 subsidiary warehouse and eventually worked my way up to running one of their biggest UK warehouses. That was just the day job, though, to pay the bills.

"About twenty years ago, through experimentation and research at home, I invented 'PMP Resurfacing', the method for quickly and efficiently resurfacing roads with a liquid form of PMP that quickly hardened and was ready to use within forty-eight hours. After ten years licensing the patent to Prospero X4 and further developing the process, I left due to 'artistic differences' as well. They fixed an artificially high price, only allowing the most affluent towns and cities to resurface their busiest roads, creating the 'Turnpike Magnates'.

"Over the years, the price dropped slightly, allowing more minor roads to be resurfaced, but they wouldn't go any lower, meaning thousands of side streets and rural homes were left unconnected by the solar and magnetic powered transport revolution – even though petrol engines were being phased out and were eventually banned as part of the UK's push to eliminate the use of fossil fuels. This product was a licence to print money. Prospero X4 was posting record profits but still they wanted to squeeze every last penny out of poorer communities. At this point, I'd had enough. I withdrew the licensing agreement we'd had and all production stopped. After much posturing and negotiating, we agreed a deal where they would fix prices at a much lower level and resurface fifty thousand kilometres of road for free. In return, they bought an exclusive licensing agreement for twenty-five years."

The Colonel opened his arms to confirm that his house wasn't part of a rent-to-buy deal. Leaning forward onto the table, he focused on his guests one-by-one and lowered his voice to emphasise his point. "Hence my obscene wealth." The Colonel opened his palms, shrugged his shoulders and then exhaustedly sunk back into his chair. This wasn't showmanship, boasting or an alpha male confirming his social status: this was an admittance of guilt.

"So you're pretty minted then?" Amy spelled out the obvious as she stood up to add some more sugar to her coffee. As she stirred, she looked again towards the window to see if she could spot the mysterious voyeur. Amy strained her eyes to make out the interior of the dark room, which proved difficult as the balcony spotlights were reflected in the glass. Amy moved a little closer and saw someone standing by the door at the far end of the room. The person caught sight of Amy and shuffled nearer to the door. Amy silently mouthed the words 'I can see you' to the silhouetted woman, who then vanished into the doorway. Even though Amy saw very little of the figure and hardly any detail, the mannerisms of her movement felt familiar.

"And why 'The Colonel'?" asked Duncan.

"Just a nickname that's stuck with me from school. I've no military background. I was captain of the school cricket team but my teacher thought I was so ambitious he promoted me to Colonel of the cricket team as a joke one day and it stuck. I don't mind it. I seem to get the respect the title deserves without the hard work of actually earning it. That's the dream isn't it?"

"Seems that way." Duncan sat forward and tall in his chair to elevate himself to the focal point of the table. "Colonel, your hospitality has been very kind and your personal history very interesting, but can we please cut to the chase, skip all this posturing? Why have you bought Amy and me here? I appreciate your help in putting us up for the night and getting us out of Wigthorn, but I have no intentions of remaining on the run or living in Shaded Vale for the rest of my days. I have things to do."

"Your granddaughter?"

"What of her?"

"You wish to give her a better future than you gave your own children?"

"I wish the country to offer her a better future than it offered my own children."

"Too true, Duncan. I believe we are of the same opinions on many matters. I don't intend on sitting on my wealth, keeping it warm, just so I can leave it all to my daughter without actually doing anything with it." The Colonel stood up from his chair and walked over to the edge of the decked balcony to get a better view of the Shaded Vale evening. "There is something rotten out there. A corrosive force is eroding the human spirit, separating us, dividing communities, harming our children. The world has changed hasn't it, Duncan?" The Colonel turned to face his audience. "We may be carbon neutral as a country now and helping others to follow our success, we may have virtually eradicated unemployment and poverty, but is the quality of life better?"

"Oh no! We've fixed the environment, solved poverty, life is so much worse." Amy rolled her eyes towards Julius, expecting some generational camaraderie against these moaning old farts. Julius stared into his coffee.

"She doesn't see it, Duncan, does she?" The Colonel asked Duncan rhetorically. "Education has changed fundamentally – no more history, geography or civic lessons. Art is now advertising and advertising is a cancer infecting every aspect of life, the most pervasive being sponsorship and partnerships, a form of domestic violence. The most severe form being outsourcing, and before you know it, the sports brand once graciously sponsoring a school team is now setting the school curriculum. The town council who outsourced parking to cut costs now suffer from a skeletal high street, starved of commerce because of exorbitant parking costs, leading to falling tax revenues meaning they can no longer afford to bring parking back in-house to save the high street. Government has all but virtually disappeared; we don't even pay taxes anymore!"

"The humanity!" Amy butted in.

The Colonel laughed. "You get what you pay for. How can a customer have any complaint when what they are receiving has been given to them for free? Who's the customer nowadays? Who's paying for everything?"

"Colonel, quick, you better get the tin foil on your head before the satellites read your mind!" Amy turned to Julius and Duncan for some acknowledgment that this man was surfing a tirade of paranoid nonsense. "You're not buying this crap are you?"

Duncan held Amy's stare. "Things have changed."

"You mean improved."

"Only for a handful of people, like me. The rich. Those who can afford it," The Colonel interjected. "The country's financial and political structures have changed and the fact history is not taught in schools owned and run by commercial enterprises is one of the reasons why you are not aware of it." The Colonel sat back and crossed his legs. "This country, this world that exists today, is far from perfect but it's not your fault, Amy. We're not saying that your generation is screwing it up – it was us. We've screwed it up. We took a screwed up country from our parents and continued to screw it up. We had opportunity to change things but we didn't. We took the easy way out and washed our hands of all responsibility. Instead of big changes we made small compromises."

Amy, slightly taken aback, looked at Duncan with some surprise. "I didn't take you for a conspiracist, Duncan."

"I'm not."

"There's no conspiracy here, Amy." The Colonel leaned forward. "There's no grand master plan or a supreme council controlling every nuance of everyday life."

"No, Shaded Vale appears to be the model of equality." Amy crossed her arms, offering herself support

"It's only money. Wealth congregates together, that's all. Yeah, your average person can't hope to live here, but what I'm talking about goes further than any of this. I'm not talking about the drop in educational standards, media integrity, equality, public services, public spaces, the death of the creative industries and every aspect of private and public life being determined by the year-on-year profit it can generate. Quite simply, the numbers don't add up. This isn't about paranoid thoughts, feelings of inadequacy or a misguided throwback to an extreme version of socialism. I'm not interested in deluded perceptions anymore than you, Amy, but I am concerned when balance sheets don't balance.

"Business has changed since the push for self-sustainability in the UK. This change should logically not have seen the kind of growth we've seen. The government has instigated regulations and tax breaks along the way to cushion the blow but reports of the British economy weathering this seismic shift purely by businesses educating their consumers effectively doesn't bare out in the numbers. The balance sheets for each major business *do* balance, of course they do – they have to – but if you look at the balance sheets of all the major corporations, the government and subtle movements in the economy, you'll see strange things happening.

"How could a weak government command such change over global corporations unless there was a crossover, unless they let them? The 'Big Five' corporations in the UK today all stemmed from fledgling start-ups in the 2020s, a concerted government shake-up to rid the country of foreign corporations controlling affairs here was no bad thing for these guys as it gave them a home advantage. The government didn't rid the country of foreign corporate imperialism; it merely swapped it for some local faces. They'd like you to believe there are ghosts in the numbers, but I don't believe in ghosts."

Amy suddenly stood up, facing the door onto the balcony. "Now I can definitely see you." The figure had stepped out of the shadows and was watching everyone from behind the glass door.

"This is my beloved daughter, Poppy." The Colonel introduced Poppy as she stepped out onto the balcony nervously and stood next to her father, who wrapped a protective arm around her. Amy had been wary of the shadowy figure spying on them but not overly concerned as the spying seemed more like a game than anything maliciously clandestine. Poppy was awkward in her posture, her limbs having grown faster than the rest of her body, her blue eyes shining from her white freckly skin and framed by the brunette waves gently bobbing in the starlit evening breeze. She hid herself behind an intense shyness and constantly bowed her head in an attempt to achieve invisibility. Her head remained bowed as she mumbled a hello to each person as her father introduced them. Amy held out a hand to shake when she was introduced and had to virtually grab Poppy's hand from her side to complete the introduction.

"Nice to meet you, Poppy. I love your hair." Amy tactfully pointed out the only part of her not being cruelly toyed with by adolescence, keen to put her at ease. "Mine's too straight and dull to do anything with."

Poppy smiled at Amy, meeting her eyes for the first time. "Thanks. Have you come here from Wigthorn?"

"Yeah, you ever been there?"

"A few years ago. We went there for a holiday. I had a stick of rock for the first time from the Whale Café."

Amy smiled. She knew it well. "It's still there, with the blowhole on top."

Duncan, impatient at the distraction, attempted again to get a satisfactory answer as to why they were here. "Colonel, I don't believe the elephant in the room has been addressed yet?"

The Colonel took his eyes of his daughter. "Of course, Duncan. Our hand has been forced by circumstances out of our control. I'd have liked us all to spend more time together so I could fully put to you my plan for the future, my plan to start a new business. Did you know that not one new company has been formed in the last twenty years? The existing system does not allow it; the competition is too powerful and the financial service companies too enormous to want to work with fledging start-ups. This has resulted in a generation being educated and entering the workforce without being exposed to or given the option to make it on their own. We now have a generation of employees, protected by their motherly employer and watched over by the polytheistic deities above, afraid to wander out of view for fear of failure and the uncertainty of the unknown. This fear has restricted creativity and the freedom of expression; artistic inventiveness has been suppressed by this fear and replaced with formulaic reproductions of the past. Entrepreneurism has been priced out of the market."

The Colonel got up out of his chair and paced around the decking. The condensation and candlelight making it look as though he were breathing fire from the passion in his belly. "An opportunity has arisen and must be taken with both hands. No, no, in fact two opportunities have arisen. The other being the two of you. Amy, I need your expertise to analyse the tracking data I have gained access to, and to figure out how to use it to accurately misinform the competition. Duncan, your independent spirit and uncompromising beliefs coupled with your advanced years are a bridge back into the past, before people let the leash out too far and their country was placed in the hands of profiteers. To find people such as you, with unbiased and educated thinking without the confines of an employer tracking your every move, is no easy task. I'm in need of a gadfly."

"I think Amy would be better pest than me," Duncan quipped.

Julius let out more of a laugh than he'd intended.

Amy looked up from choosing a biscuit, shooting a raised eyebrow at Julius before moving things on. "And the second opportunity?"

"The Rooftech contract renewals. The first twenty-five-year contracts implemented to ensure the longevity of domestic solar power are due to expire in two months. Not surprisingly, no serious competition has entered into the bidding war for people's signatures and so Rooftech will be offering contracts with much lower rates of return for the energy produced by each household. This will mean households will receive less income. Therefore people will either have to work more or spend less to survive. The government tax breaks will also end with the new contracts, so Rooftech have negotiated with the government a new tax rate low enough to enable Rooftech to still profit but also high enough to discourage any serious competition on a national scale. There are small pockets of solar energy bought and sold by other companies, but Rooftech only allow them to exist to avoid accusations of unfair competition or claims of monopoly. So the domestic solar energy market is where I plan to start a new business, and I need your help." The Colonel crossed his arms to signal that he had stopped talking.

"Entering a market where it's impossible to make a profit against a monolith such as Rooftech seems like a poor business plan," Amy replied.

"Yes, it is! But we have a competitive advantage: we are not planning on making a profit!" The Colonel smiled like a child who had just done something for the first time, completely by accident.

"You plan on losing money?" Duncan let the echoes of his question reverberate in his mind. It felt like repeating a foreign phrase – it made no sense.

"Yes, lots of it, too."

"Why?"

"To get a foot in the door, so people can hear another point of view. Imagine a company talking to people without wanting their money or wanting to profit from it. What a change!"

"Yes, but such a company couldn't survive for very obvious reasons. Companies have to make a profit – everyone knows that. Why do you want to challenge Rooftech? Why not enter another less competitive market?" Duncan looked at Amy for any help in making sense of this but found her wanting, too.

The Colonel answered, "People with money need to be reached and everyone with money has a roof over their head. I have nothing against Rooftech in particular but they are a good target as they preach about the environment and doing good, but at the end of the day they need to make a profit for their shareholders. They may have helped bring an end to our old oil based economy, but they still want to screw people for every penny. They have no regard for loyalty or community because there's no competition challenging them and the government is so weak and subservient that companies like this can virtually do what they want."

Duncan looked painfully into thin air, trying to encapsulate a host of opposing ideas. "I know you're a rich man, but even you cannot bankroll this plan long enough to make a difference. What happens when you run out of money? Everything will go back to how it was."

"Shake it up Duncan!" The Colonel became even more animated. "Shake things up, wake people up! Plant some seeds, my man! You know about that, don't you? Yes, I'll be losing money, but the new company will still continue to sell this energy, too. It'll just be at a slight loss – a small price to pay to loosen the grip of Rooftech over every household in this country. Once there is room to breathe, other corporations will want to test the water and enter the market. I'll encourage them. Once one of the biggest markets in the country has been blown open to intense competition, it'll hopefully give the country back its hunger for innovation and creativity.

"This isn't a business plan, but a spark. The general population are no more than automatons, fitting their lives around the most profitable methods researched by the major corporations. Why do we now have the three-day working week? Homeowners can still earn a full-time wage as their income is supplemented by the energy production of their home, but they could still work five days and earn more. They don't because corporations have realised it is more profitable to ensure employees work less so they have more time to spend as consumers. Give them time off to be entertained, play games, go shopping, travel – but under no circumstances should these extra-curricular activities develop the mind or explore the arts. Give people the illusion of being set free without actually diluting the central message.

"Where are the free museums and galleries, the small music venues, the drawing classes, adult education, the public spaces, the demonstrations or the protests? Once you've been educated to become an adequate shopper and worker, that's all the requirements needed to be a modern day, effective British citizen. Social cohesion between business and citizen has become unglued by the corrosive force of distraction. There is no more feedback. There is no more consultation. Where once the political process demanded organisations get permission from the electorate, now the electorate have become so dazzled and blinded by the multitude of entertainment and opportunities to consume, freedoms and rights have slowly been dissolved behind their backs. Pockets of populations have been reorganised to fit the bill; town planners build cheap housing here, retirement homes there, whilst the survival of public services depends on voter turnout rather than necessity. Look at this cute little rabbit I just pulled out of the hat whilst performing some sleight of hand."

Amy spoke up. "What do you actually want from me?"

Poppy spoke gently to her father. "Entrance security just phoned, Father. Pharmara personnel have just arrived and are heading this way."

"OK, thanks, Poppy." The Colonel re-focused to finish his summary. "It's show time, people. Here's the rub: my idea is to rock the boat and get people to examine the current state of play. The best part is that no advertising medium will carry this message so old fashioned word-of-mouth is how people are going to hear about this. Amy, I assume you know what 'nodals' are?"

"Yeah, they're people who mix with many groups and pass on messages effectively, whether they know about it or not."

"Exactly, like the popular kid in class wearing the latest pair of trainers and sending a torrent of salivating peers to the sports shop. With your tracking and analysis experience, you can provide a list of the most effective nodals who can spread the message of our new energy company."

"How are you going to get this message out there once Amy gives you what you want?" Duncan asked, still trying to navigate his way through the jargon.

"A carnival!"

"What? Clowns and a bloody freak show?" Amy replied.

"Almost. Billboards, TV, internet and radio are all mediums that won't carry our message as they are owned by the few and would never broadcast any form of dissenting message that would affect their own business or ignite a communications war with their inbred counterparts. The only way to get a message out there is face to face. We can't cover the whole country in two months, but with Amy's help we can get to the most influential parts."

"And just how am I meant to get access to this information? My existing passwords will be long gone by now."

"Yes, that's why you're taking Poppy along with you. She has information on a few contacts that can help you along the way, plus she has access to money and communications so we can keep in contact without alerting the relevant authorities, namely Pharmara and Rooftech."

"What do we get out of this if we do decide to help you?" Duncan asked, modesty about such matters diminishing with the increasing risk.

"Firstly, you get my protection. Secondly, you've already got shares in this new venture, so the quality of information you give me directly impacts on your remuneration – levels of which will allow you to buy yourselves out of any altercations with certain corporations and enable you to live under the sheltered umbrella of an iPatch town."

"I thought this whole venture was going to result in a dramatic loss of your personal fortune? I'm no expert, but shares in this venture don't sound very attractive," Amy enquired, rather surprised.

"These shares are part of a sister company whose profits rely directly on the success of the energy company in terms of customer base rather than profits; it'll provide the necessary domestic hardware. A company that will be paying dividends, you'll be pleased to hear."

Amy looked at Duncan, not quite following the business arrangement, but his relaxed demeanour coupled with the fact she was being offered something more than a life on the run allowed her to paper over the cracks of the full arrangement.

The Colonel led Amy, Poppy and Duncan to a door leading out of the hallway. "Please, let us not get focused on minor details. We have more important things to concentrate on."

"Julius?" Duncan noticed Julius remained standing by the front door.

"I'm staying here, mate. The Colonel needs me here and too many of us out on the road will slow us down. Good luck, see you soon, Amy."

Amy put her rucksack on, giving Julius only the slightest hint of a nod.

"You must go now. Pharmara Security are here. Poppy will take you out the back. She will take you to where you need to go before you're able to leave Shaded Vale. Good luck, my friends. Look after my daughter." The Colonel and Poppy hugged. The Colonel had to unpeel Poppy's arms from his body before encouraging her to leave so he could answer the front door.

Amy took Poppy's hand so she couldn't follow her father and tried to lead her out to the back of the house to make their getaway, but Poppy was adamant she needed to see her father answer the door.

"We have to go now, Poppy."

"Wait, please wait, just one moment, please."

Poppy, hiding behind a door at the far end of the hallway could see her father open the front door. Her view was blocked by The Colonel and Julius. The only clue as to the caller's identity was a wisp of smoky grey hair protruding above.

"Poppy, let's go!" Amy whispered with restrained force.

"Please, I just need to see her ..." Poppy's voice tailed off as she struggled to listen to the conversation at the front door.

A woman's voice grated the air. "Darling! It's been too long."

"Estelle, what a pleasant surprise," The Colonel replied, convincing no one.

Julius turned back to see if the fugitives had left the hallway. As he did, he opened the view up for Poppy. She focused on the woman at the door, whispering to herself as Amy finally dragged her away, "Mother."

CHAPTER 7

"Estelle Hawthorne is your mother!" Amy immediately tried to reel in her initial reaction to ease Poppy's already fragile state.

"Yes," Poppy replied between shuffled steps.

Duncan, Amy and Poppy walked through a small shopping area in a picture postcard suburb of Shaded Vale – a clutch of faux-cottage shops topped with thatched roofs. They had left The Colonel's house through the back on bikes down a make-shift cycle path through trees and undergrowth shaped by adventuring kids through the years. It was a shortcut to the nearest shops and a quick getaway from both parents and security officers alike.

After dumping their bikes at the bottom of the hill, Amy bought a bottle of water from one of the small shops, resuming their journey by foot. Amy could still not completely wrap her head around the Shaded Vale social system. "So the guy serving in that shop, is he a multi-millionaire moonlighting as a shop assistant?"

Poppy covered her mouth as she quietly chuckled. "He lives on the outskirts in the non-members district. Non-members do not pay any membership fees or council taxes. They are employed by the council and remunerated via free housing, food and an expense account so they can travel outside Shaded Vale."

"Sounds like a cushy number to me."

"It is. Every non-member is head hunted by the council and then invited to work in Shaded Vale. Every level of non-member is the very best in the country, from barista, maid and dustman to chef, fireman and teacher. You know that Shaded Vale is not under any kind of surveillance?"

"Yeah, Julius told us on the way here, but what is there to hide?"

"Everything. It's a beautiful place. Imagine if every barista, dustman, maid, chef and teacher in the country knew about Shaded Vale? We'd be overrun by every out-of-work opportunist in the UK. Unless you're a guest or a new employee then outsiders are not welcome here.

"That's beautiful!" Duncan proclaimed out of the blue.

"What is?" Amy asked.

"Don't you see? The best of the best end up here. The richest can afford to live here regardless of whether they're good at anything, but the workers can work their way here. There's middle management all over the country earning ten times as much as the workers but they can't afford to live here. They're caught in the middle and left out in the cold!"

Duncan speeded up his walk with an added spring in his step as he imagined the barista's children living an idyllic childhood, mixing with the offspring of the great and the good whilst the administrators, bankers, doctors and other professionals not at the very top of their profession had to hide their own families away in the gated communities of towns like Wigthorn across the country whilst the poor and the vagrant roamed around just outside.

"How long have your parents been divorced?" asked Amy as the two girls continued in Duncan's wake.

"They never married. My mother left when I was about five and my father brought me up alone."

"Do you see your mother much?"

"Not really. Maybe once every few years when she's passing this way."

"You poor girl." Amy put an arm around Poppy to offer some comfort and friendship as they walked down the tree-lined street. There was no breeze and the sound of tropical birdsong could be heard in the distance, a product of numerous detailed surveys to determine the ingredients of the ideal community. Tropical birdsong increased morale, which helped contribute to higher productivity, increasing employee and resident satisfaction. There were no birds, just speakers hidden in the trees.

"My mother's a successful woman, you know. Excellent job, beautiful house, expensive car and her wardrobe is amazing. She tells me all the famous designers she's worn."

Poppy's defence of a woman she hardly knew was heartfelt, as though she had to justify half of her genetic makeup. Poppy wanted to show she understood her mother's lack of connection, and being a mere tick in a lifestyle checklist was enough for her. Her mother was important, with many responsibilities. Expecting to be the main focus in her mother's life was selfish and probably undeserving. To be included in this particular checklist was an achievement in itself.

"Yes, your mother is a very successful woman, but has she been as successful in other areas of her life?"

Duncan, overhearing the conversation behind him, turned around and immediately played his diplomatic hand. "So, where are we going, Poppy?" Estelle may not win Mother of the Year but highlighting this to Poppy, who probably already realised this fact, was not something Duncan thought Amy should be getting into right now. The three of them were still not safe from detection, plus good relations and camaraderie were important elements to their own success.

"We're going to see Leroy Merlin."

"Who's Leroy Merlin?"

"A master of disguise."

"We're here." Poppy declared after a twenty-minute walk through the visually and aurally pleasing suburbs of Shaded Vale.

The three of them stood at the entrance of yet another beautiful house in yet another stunning street in Shaded Vale. Poppy pressed a button on the front gate and waited for a reply.

"Hello, Poppy, your father told me to expect a visit."

"Your house looks very nice today."

"Thanks, come in."

The gates opened and they walked down the metallic driveway, stepped onto the porch and waited for the front door to open. They waited a little longer, and still the door remained shut. Duncan looked at Poppy; Poppy looked back with a poorly hidden grin and averted her eyes from Duncan's. "Maybe you should knock?"

Duncan stepped forward and raised his hand to knock on the door. As he struck the door, his hand disappeared straight through it. Duncan withdrew his hand immediately and looked at Poppy, whose grin came fully out of hiding. Amy walked up to Duncan and stood next to him, stretching out a hand, palm first, so it went through the door. Where the hand passed the plane of the door, the wooden façade went slightly fuzzy and distorted, but soon settled so all that could be seen was the end of Amy's wrist.

"It's a projection."

Poppy squeezed between Duncan and Amy. "We need to walk through the door." Disappearing through the door, Amy and Duncan looked at each other with raised eyebrows.

"Cool." Amy walked through followed by Duncan.

Through the door was a fountain, in the centre of which was a large statue of a strand of DNA, twisting its familiar pattern up to the height of the house projection, which was still visible, albeit faintly, from inside. The fountain refilled itself with the water spraying out of the top of the two parallel strings of DNA into a large, eye-shaped pool. Poppy walked around it with Duncan and Amy in tow, heading for the far end where a small entrance came into view. The light spray from the water hit their faces as they walked around. Leroy Merlin was leaning against the door, a shock of spiky red hair bunched up by the safety goggles resting on top of his head, a grey tuft of hair on his chin pointing downwards. His baggy blue overalls kept a record of his research – and today's lunch.

"What do you think, huh?" Leroy shouted across the pool.

"If short blokes did it for me, I'd let you know!" Amy replied.

"Yeah, sorry, no disguise here." Leroy removed the goggles. He always thought wearing them like that made him appear taller. "Please, come inside and let me show you around."

The three guests walked through the door, followed by Leroy, and down a spiral staircase. Amy occasionally touched the wall and grabbed the banister to double check they were real. They emerged into a large underground lab. The walls were lined with shelves containing electronics, computers and various tools. In the middle of the room was a large desk, at waist height, with a roller-coaster ride of tubes, bottles, Bunsen burners, jars and funnels with different coloured liquids boiling, dripping, swirling, spiralling and running around the tracks. In the middle were two large tubes that led straight up into the ceiling, fuelling the fountain lying above.

Amy took the initiative in her own way: skipping any introductions and bypassing the small talk. "So, what's all this crap?"

"This is where the magic happens!" Leroy said, hoping to inspire some amazement from his guests.

"No such thing." Amy was already looking around elsewhere in the lab.

"OK, I see I have a tough crowd here ..."

"Only her," Duncan pointed out with a tinge of apology on behalf of his companion.

"You must be the surveillance person?" Leroy asked Amy.

"Yes."

"No way you can fool the satellites, right?"

"Well, turns out you can lose them, as Duncan proved in getting us out of Wigthorn, but you can't fool them."

"Let me shatter another belief I'm sure you hold dear. Here, take this scanning device. I'm sure you know how to use one." Leroy handed Amy an electronic handset.

"Yeah." Amy looked it over and, never one to shy away from improving her own stock, listed a few key characteristics of the device in her hand. "A Sonjitsonic Hunter 445 mobile tracking device. Twenty mile max distance, two week battery life, can track up to twenty subjects at once with full DNA, body and environmental stats."

"Using the device, tell me what you see in this room."

Amy switched it on and set up the device to scan the interior of the room. "OK, here I am, one elderly gentleman who seems a little warm, which is Duncan. One girl in her early twenties whose heart rate has increased somewhat and ..." Amy looked up at Leroy who had remained motionless throughout. Amy took a closer look at the device and pressed a few buttons. "I, errr ... I don't understand." Amy pointed the device at Leroy and hit it firmly with the side of her hand out of frustration, a pointless yet ancient habit.

"What do you see, Amy?" Leroy clearly relished Amy's agitation.

"This can't be right."

Duncan was intrigued with what had finally caught her tongue. "What do you see?"

Amy looked up at Duncan. "I see a hyena."

Leroy started laughing.

"So you've hooked up the device to read your DNA as a hyena, very funny." Amy remained humourless.

"*Au contraire*, the device has not been tampered with. I have simply covered myself with a specially created liquid that, when scanned, recreates the DNA signature of my choosing. Go ahead and run a diagnostic on the device, reset the default settings, anything – the result will be the same."

Duncan walked over to Leroy and examined him closer. "The Colonel told us the satellites could be fooled with a fake DNA reading, but how? I've heard of previous attempts failing with body suits, gels and other more bizarre ideas. The main problem seems to be providing a DNA signature for a sustained period and in a good enough quality to fool the system."

"It's true, in the past other gels and liquids have either dried out, dripped off the body or are not robust enough to provide a good quality DNA reading. Body suits and the like don't work because they don't fool the satellites into thinking they're part of the skin. I've managed to overcome this with a gel that can not only be programmed to give any kind of DNA reading you want, but can also be applied with a simple spray lasting up to twenty-four hours. Technically, it's more of an adhesive than a conventional liquid. It sticks to the skin and creates a thin layer that won't get melted by the satellite lasers, a common problem with the old liquid solutions." Leroy stroked the side of his face. "It's also very good for your skin. A few friends of mine came up with the name, 'D 'n' Away' – what do you think?"

"Yeah …" Duncan filled the pause by staring at Poppy.

"I love it," Poppy reassured Leroy. "My friend said he'd design you a logo."

"Great. Living in a town of business gurus, you have to make sure the branding is up to scratch, even when it's a black market product like this."

"How come I've never heard of it?" Amy protested while still running a diagnostic on the device and double-checking the settings.

"I don't exactly go around mass marketing this product. I have a few select clients keeping this operation … well, operational."

Duncan, wanting to understand this new development further, asked Leroy about the spray. "Do you have to shower in this spray every morning? And how do you program the DNA it will represent?"

"Here, look." Leroy picked up what looked like a thermos flask with a computer panel on the side and showed Duncan. Amy reluctantly looked over Duncan's shoulder, suppressing every curious bone in her body from appearing over-enthusiastic. "The liquid solution is stored in here. The computer panel allows you to select up to twenty pre-set DNA signatures, or you can enter hair, skin or saliva into this slot and the DNA will be sequenced, ready to be programmed into the liquid within just a few minutes. This container holds enough liquid to be used up to ten times. When you select a DNA signature, all the liquid gets changed, selecting another DNA signature changes the liquid again."

Amy, wanting to know the answer to the first part of Duncan's question, but feigning disinterest, nudged Duncan. Duncan took up the slack. "And how is it applied?"

"Just spray skin and hair that is going to be exposed to the satellites so they have some DNA to analyse. The worse thing you can do, which I'm sure Amy will clarify, is to completely cover yourself up. An object that moves like a human but has no DNA to analyse is just asking for trouble."

Amy smiled, more to herself than for anyone else's benefit. "It's true. We call them 'ghosts'. Nothing gets as analysed and tracked more than a ghost. 'Ghost hunting' was the only thing that made your day interesting."

Leroy continued his lesson. "To apply the liquid, simply remove this lid to reveal the spray nozzle and just spray it like a deodorant. A couple of things to remember. First, spray every part of your skin that is exposed, because it's not just the satellites that scan you – there are tracking facilities on buildings and on the ground undressing you with their spies. One person I gave this to didn't cover under his chin or on the palm of his hands; he's now disappeared off the face of the planet. The second thing to remember is that you can only fake the DNA signature; you can't fake your mass or movement. The satellites will track you without going into too much analysis, so if you're disguised as a hyena, there's no need to walk on four legs and hunt antelope in packs. But, if you disguise yourself as a hamster then the satellites will not be able to match your DNA to your mass. If you do need to use the DNA from another animal or human, only pick those that are roughly the same mass as you and not unusually situated. An obese human will trigger an alert for any of you guys. A leopard on the streets of England would also trigger an alert. I managed to get away with a cactus once, but that's another story. There's a bunch of pre-sets on here that are all fine to use. Mostly they're faked or deceased humans. Here try it."

Amy took up the offer and began spraying her face and arms. "Why would you want to be a cactus?"

"True, there's not much call for it here, but in Mexico I was backed into a corner and couldn't escape. If I'd become a human or an animal, I'd either have to be on the move or they'd come hunting for me, no matter what I was. Surrounding me was a great open space populated only by dust and cacti. I'd never tried synthesising any plant life before but I had no other choice. I fed in a small cactus needle into the D 'n' Away sequencer and a few minutes later, sprayed myself. The drones tracked me down to where they last saw me and then saw nothing. I just sat there in a vast dusty expanse. They passed over, suspecting nothing."

"They can't have been good trackers. Why didn't they narrow down the point where you changed from human to cactus?" Amy sprayed a little on her arm. It smelt good enough to taste.

"Yeah, true, but this was a few years ago before continuous satellite monitoring. Plus Mexico isn't as far advanced as us, so here you'd have to make the change undercover. I wouldn't do that if I were ..."

"Urgh!" It didn't taste as good as it smelt. "It feels weird, like I've just covered myself in lip balm."

Duncan and Poppy examined Amy closer. She looked fairly normal, just having a slight sheen to her like a newly polished mantelpiece.

Poppy, conscious they had to stay on the move, asked Leroy for his help. "Leroy, we need to leave Shaded Vale as Pharmara Security are searching for us and may track us down here."

"Of course, I have prepared one D 'n' Away sequencer each for you. Use them sparingly. The liquid will last as long as you don't wash, and obviously it doesn't work in the rain for very long." Leroy turned to Amy. "You might as well keep the DNA scanner. You never know, it may come in handy."

"How are we going to leave town?" asked Duncan.

"Well, conveniently, I live on the outskirts of town and keep sheep. Unfortunately, I'm not very good at it and sheep regularly go missing from my flock so we'll get you sprayed up and then you can simply walk out of here. Luckily for you, it's a pleasant night out there."

Estelle made herself at home in The Colonel's minimalist lounge, perching herself on the edge of a sofa, legs crossed and back straightened with her hands together, resting on her knees. She could've been bronzed and mounted upon a plinth as a symbol of poise.

Estelle never conversed, she interviewed. And this was never more apparent than when addressing the father of her only child. "So, William, how long has it been?"

"It's been a while since anyone called me William, that's for sure." The Colonel was sitting on the sofa opposite, manifesting his feelings of imposition as much as possible whilst trying to keep an eye on Gerard as he walked around behind him in deep consultation with a mobile device. Julius sat beside The Colonel, too out of his depth to sit anywhere else.

Estelle utilised her strict yoga regime by positioning herself even more forward without visibly moving her lower half. "We have avoided each other for so long, let me get a closer look at you."

"I see you've had more work done, Estelle." The Colonel attempted to deflect any closer analysis of himself.

"Public perception is a cruel mistress."

"You look younger than when we first met."

"Why, thank you William." Julius thought he saw the briefest sign of blushing flush across Estelle's face.

"What brings you down to Shaded Vale? It surely can't be your daughter."

"How very traditional of you, William. No, I think you are more than aware that our presence here is strictly business."

"I have no idea what you're talking about." The Colonel launched his lame duck reply into the ether to test the water.

Estelle smiled, looking up at Gerard who was still roaming behind The Colonel and Julius, keeping watch over them rather than focusing on his mobile device. The subtlest of looks from Estelle missed the attentions of The Colonel and Julius, making it's way successfully to Gerard who reached into his pocket and slowly brought out another device.

"What? You're not going to tell me the location of my own daughter?" Estelle revelled in her mock surprise, letting out an uncharacteristic little laugh that revealed the true shallowness of her concern. "I'm not here to get information on Poppy, Duncan or Amy, even though I know they were here earlier today and I could have you locked up for crimes against Pharmara."

"You know I have the best defence against threats you may lay at my door: a ton of money."

"Not in this case, William. Times have moved on, you're no longer protected against the rigours of corporate law because you have no leverage, there's nothing you have that we want. Putting you away does not adversely affect any of our business concerns, so you really don't have a friend in the world."

"And …?"

"I know you, William. You forget that. We have detected anomalies in Shaded Vale and elsewhere across the country and they all lead back to you. I came here to look you in the eye and your face has given you away, like it always did. I've seen this look twice before: when you first developed PMP Resurfacing, and when you dumped me."

"Hell hath no fury, eh?"

"Don't flatter yourself, dear old Billy boy. You were a business deal I milked before it went sour. My more pressing concern is the future well-being of Pharmara."

"Never heard of them."

"Ohh, you're so much fun, Billy! We should get together more often." In between the giddy schoolgirl impression, Estelle flashed Gerard another look. Gerard activated his second device and slowly glided behind Julius like an evening shadow.

"William, I don't want you getting involved in things you can't handle. If you continue to play games with forces out of your league, people will get hurt." Gerard was in position behind Julius as Estelle continued, "Your money can not protect everyone and it cannot buy you out of any dark hole you might find yourself in, you understand me? We will stop at nothing to protect our assets, regardless of whom or what lies in our way."

Estelle sent one final look Gerard's way and the device was raised to the back of Julius' head. Just as Julius felt a slight draught against his hair, Gerard's other device came to life with a beep and halted him. Gerard withdrew and answered the call.

Silence suffocated the room. Julius observed the chemistry being exchanged in front of his eyes; how many adversaries were actually soul mates in the wrong light?

Gerard depressurised the lounge. "It seems this town has very intelligent sheep. We have tracked everything coming in and out of Shaded Vale and we've uncovered three sheep walking across a few fields and then getting into a car. Not everyday you see that, is it?"

"Indeed," Estelle replied, changing tack and ending her interview. "It seems events have caught up with us. We will have to thank you for your hospitality and leave for more urgent matters." Estelle stood up, straightening her skirt. "You should be careful, William, living in this town. Hiding from surveillance may satisfy your prudish need for privacy but anything could happen to you here and no one would know."

CHAPTER 8

The satellites drifted overhead like gods in the heavens, the drones angelic messengers, collecting prayers and delivering vengeance. The flock sat in their pews keenly confessing every little detail to those on high to keep them safe. Gods required faith, satellites needed secrets; without them the good citizens of the United Kingdom would be orphaned. A flock without shepherds, lost and vulnerable.

The satellites and drones followed the melodies of the people and the people followed the rhythm of the sun. A cockerel was heard, the tapping baton bringing to attention the instruments of the day.

Duncan lazily rolled his head onto his shoulder, resting on the rear seat to enjoy the view from the back window of an empty road growing with the sunrise. Armadas of glinting silver satellites fell into the rising sun as though it were collecting the fistful of diamonds it had tossed eastward into the sky the previous evening.

After driving overnight, the small group of fugitives arrived at the River Thames and crossed through Battersea Bridge Tunnel, a thoroughfare built using the old bridge, which was now submerged beneath the Thames.

"We've crossed through the river, now can you tell us where we're going?" Amy asked, impatient at being kept in the dark by a daddy's girl.

"Yes," replied Poppy. "Parliament."

Duncan's ears pricked up.

"Parliament? What's that?" Amy questioned, unfamiliar with the word.

"The House of Commons," Poppy confirmed.

Duncan offered more clues. "You know 'Westminster Mall'?"

"Yeah."

"It's in there."

As the car turned into the King's Road and headed towards Westminster, Poppy's mobile device alerted her to an incoming message. Poppy answered it. "Father." Poppy frowned as she listened intently to the small device buried in her ear.

"OK ... We're not far. We'll go to the rendezvous in the Green Park industrial complex ... Bye."

Poppy turned to Duncan and Amy to relay the information. "My father says we've been tracked down by Pharmara Security. Apparently Leroy didn't tell us a fundamental rule of DNA disguise: do not perform actions your DNA signature could not perform, e.g. sheep do not get into cars and head for London."

"Good point." Amy looked at Poppy. "So, what's at Green Park?"

"There's a contact there with facilities for us to get out the car and lose anyone following us."

"How are they going to do that?" Duncan asked.

"There are three people waiting who are not only similar to us in terms of gender and mass but have also applied a sheep DNA signature to themselves. We'll get out the car and they'll get in, taking the car out of London and drive around aimlessly until they get stopped ..."

Amy took over from Poppy: "... where their DNA signatures will be analysed in more depth and found to be a different match to the sheep that left Dorset. Eventually, it will be discovered that the DNA signatures changed in Green Park ..."

Duncan closed the final act: "... by which point they'll be too late and we'll be long gone."

"Man! I didn't realise how easy it was to fool the satellites with a little bit of teamwork." Amy was both conflicted and impressed that human ingenuity could erase the certainties she had worked with for over a decade.

"It's not the satellites that are getting fooled though, is it?" Duncan replied, reversing Amy's glimpse through a new window and reflecting back a contorted image.

Poppy ended any further analysis. "OK, we're here."

After a quick change and applying a new human-based D 'n' Away disguise, Duncan, Amy and Poppy walked towards Westminster Mall, which was famous for having the most historical landmarks underneath one roof.

Walking alongside the River Thames was a new experience for Amy as she had never been to London before and never seen the famous River Thames Aquarium either. The surface of the River Thames had risen about ten metres above ground level due to the increased sea levels over the years. The city had protected its old landmarks by building huge glass walls to contain the river so now walking beside its banks was comparable to walking alongside an immense fish tank.

This feature was not unique within the world's river-based cities. Many had built similar glass walls to protect themselves from the rising sea levels of the past sixty years and, with most cities, the river water had to be crystal clear if tourism, and indeed the native population, were to view any sea life. The rising sea levels stemmed from rising temperatures, so the Thames could now sustain much more colourful, tropical sea life; this was accomplished both naturally and accidentally, most notably from the record breaking flash floods of 2032 which claimed over two thousand lives, one zoo, and its tropical fish centre. The result meant a sizeable colony of sea mammals (including seals) and tropical fish thrived within the river, especially due to shopping malls up and down the riverbank building viewing platforms as attractions so customers could feed them. After only thirty years, different species of dolphin had emigrated to the warmer waters of London and all inter-bred, quickly evolving into a new sub-species commonly known as 'London's politest residents'. They had a ravenous appetite for fish and chips, a distinctive accent and rarely travelled outside Zone 2.

Lambeth Bridge was renamed Lambeth Tunnel, providing one of the many entrances into Westminster Mall. It gave an uninterrupted view to the other side, the appearance of a lost underwater world where ghostly figures could be seen walking amongst shimmering buildings. People bustled as they each hunted out their own little bits of treasure lying hidden among the junk. Travelators moved people, signs moved people, bargains moved people, and people moved people. There were no windows, no clocks, no exit signs and no hiding places – once you were in, it was only a matter of time before you spent your money, hard earned or otherwise. If you had no money then you wouldn't be able to get through the entrance toll. 'Window shopping' was a crime worse than shoplifting. At least shoplifting was a form of viral marketing and could be claimed on insurance.

Poppy scanned her device at the entrance toll. Reborn IDs resurrected from the past.

Duncan had not been in a mall for over ten years, not since he discovered that his wife was more than happy with theatre tickets for birthdays and Christmases, so his bi-annual torture quest through these self-contained retail hells had been gladly swapped for tickets purchased online. Malls had not only gotten bigger and more advanced since Duncan's last trip, but they had also got more invasive. Holographic sprites and whispering voices invaded his head with messages to get fit, enjoy a breakfast cereal and look cool with the latest watch.

Duncan squinted through the neon messages and found the two girls walking ahead of him, seemingly undisturbed.

"Aren't you two hearing all this?" Duncan swiped at a small singing projection fluttering just out of reach.

"All what?" Poppy replied, undistracted.

"These advertising messages! It sounds like someone is whispering them to me just behind my back."

"Oh them." Poppy stuck a finger in her ear and twisted it. "You say you've never had a mobile device, right?"

"No, never."

Poppy fished out the wireless receiver from her ear and told Duncan to stick it in his. She then handed him the mobile device to hold. Duncan's near-perpetual inner peace was swiftly smashed by a mass of voices competing for his attention. Like a stockbroker on the trading floor during a financial meltdown, Duncan struggled to comprehend one single stream of words.

"Hi Poppy, welcome to Westminster Mall! Poppy, you haven't bought any make-up from us for over fifty days now! Poppy, you have put on some weight since we saw you last – have you considered Diet Xtreme? Hi Poppy, we've analysed your skin and you could do with some dermatological treatment. Poppy, your testosterone levels are high for a young lady your age – have you tried the latest oestrogen tablets from Pharmara?" Duncan tilted his head, banging the opposite side and removing the ear receiver, giving it back to Poppy along with the handset.

"How can you wear this thing? It's driving me mad after a few seconds."

"You get used to it," Amy replied. "But I must admit, this place is extremely in-your-face. I've never seen or heard this many messages without my ear device. How can anyone comprehend all this junk?"

"You learn how to tune into the interesting ones; it takes a lot of shopping trips to learn how though."

Duncan pointed to something just to the right of him. "Look, I've got a bloody body builder guy just here flexing his muscles. Go away!"

Amy and Poppy tried to subdue their laughs. "Just ignore them, Duncan," said Amy as she started walking. "The trick is to stay on the move. If you stand still by a shop or billboard then that's when they really start hassling you."

Amy linked arms with Poppy, trying the big sister approach to extracting information. "So, where's this parliament shop we're going to?"

"It's just up here, across from the Westminster Abbey Sportland store, the golden building with the big clock at the far end."

"Oh yeah, lovely isn't it? Is it a jewellers or something?"

"No, it's where the country's politicians work and run the country."

"I've heard of them. They're corporate board members who get voted into a club by rich people, right?"

"Not quite," Poppy replied.

"That's exactly who they are," Duncan countered, before ducking beneath a terrifying holographic alien from the latest computer game blockbuster.

The Westminster Abbey Sportland store was preaching the virtues of a huge pre-Easter sale, a three-day extravaganza, resurrecting prices from five years ago – advertised with a large inflatable football slowly rolling back and forth in front of the main entrance (but no one knew why). Like every other church and cathedral in the land, Westminster Abbey had been resurrected as a sports store, confirming the nation's new religion, elevating sport into a higher realm than mere pastime and canonising its stars into saints. Westminster Abbey Sportland had a bigger congregation now than it had ever had in its entire history. The daily sermon was delivered through a hundred metre wide holographic display broadcasting the biggest sporting events to a packed Parliament Square of thousands.

There were no games or matches until later on in the evening, so the square was comparatively sparse, with a few kids chasing balls, wondering what teams Winston Churchill, Benjamin Disraeli, Nelson Mandela and the others had coached to get themselves imposing statues in the centre of spectator sport. They were too old and fat to be athletes.

Poppy led Duncan and Amy through a throng of tourists taking photographs of an entrance into the golden parliament building. A big wooden door loomed in front of them with a government security guard standing beside it.

"Good morning, sir," Poppy said with plenty of excitement and expectation. "I have a meeting with George Ray. He should be expecting me."

The guard looked over Poppy's shoulder to assess Duncan and Amy before speaking into his device. "Mr Ray, you have visitors. I'm sending their details over now." The guard scanned their DNA and waited for a response. It came back quickly so he opened the door, allowing the group into a reception area. "If you wait here, Mr Ray will be with you shortly."

Duncan took a seat in the gloomy room, looking around the hallowed walls to see if there was still any life in this old dog. "Are we safe in here from Pharmara Security?"

"Yes," replied Poppy in a hushed voice. "Government buildings are free from corporate tracking."

"So, what are we doing in here?" Duncan asked quietly, unsure why they were whispering.

"We need to access 'C.O.V.E.R.T.' so Amy can analyse the data and identify the best areas in the country for my father to take his carnival."

"What the hell's C.O.V.E.R.T.?" Duncan interrupted, looking at Amy to see if she mirrored his puzzlement.

She didn't. "'The Central Observatory for Viewing and Exchanging Reconnaissance Transmissions'."

"And what the hell is that?"

Amy explained, "Basically, it's the government central database collecting all the information being captured out there."

Duncan breathed out. "OK, central database, let's stick with that."

Amy continued, "It was originally called 'The Database of the Treasury' but they renamed it in 2036 ..."

Poppy continued, "The information we get from C.O.V.E.R.T., I mean, the central database, allows us to focus resources and target the promotional campaign to a far greater degree than if we use existing public and black market information."

"Aren't there any hackers out there who can break in?" Amy questioned.

"No, it's impossible. All corporate and government databases are protected with quantum cryptology and are impossible to break into. The only way to get this info is through an insider."

"George Ray is a mole?" Amy whispered her surprise.

"Actually, a government whip."

"I knew all these freemason freaks were kinky." Amy quickly hushed when approaching footsteps echoed round the wood panelled walls.

A thin middle-aged man of average height with thick white hair and large black shoes walked the shadowed hallway like an escaping floor lamp. George Ray brightly entered the room and waddled straight over to Amy.

"Miss Gold, so nice to meet you finally. Your father has told me so much about you."

"Er, no, I'm Amy – this is Poppy."

Poppy shyly stuck out a hand to be shaken.

"Oh, I'm so sorry, madam. Miss Gold, how lovely to meet you. I'm George Ray. I'm sure your father has told you a little about me?"

Poppy spoke quietly. "Yes, a little. He says you can help us garner some sensitive data."

"Yes, yes, come, follow me." George Ray quickly turned on his heels and led Duncan, Amy and Poppy through the dark hallways of parliament. "It's OK, you can speak freely, there are no cameras, microphones or any other such malarkey in the Houses of Parliament – about the only building on this island free of some contraptions."

Amy was a mixture of astonishment and outrage at such a notion. "Why ever not?"

"It doesn't bode well for a free exchange of ideas. That's the official line anyway. The real truth of the matter is that the members here like their privacy. Business and diplomacy is best done behind closed doors. Privacy is the buoyancy that keeps a viable government afloat."

Duncan increased his speed to catch up with George Ray. "It's such a pleasure to finally walk through these corridors of power."

George smiled at Duncan. "I never tire of bringing the older folk into parliament. They hold it in a much higher esteem than is currently deserved."

"What do you do here, George?" Amy asked.

"What do we do?" George repeated to himself. "Now that is a question. What do we do? I'll tell you what used to be achieved in this place to warrant Duncan's appreciation and then I'll tell you what we now do." George stopped at a door and opened it to let the others in.

The room was another wood panelled office with desks, media displays, drinks cabinet, a couple of oxblood Chesterfield leather sofas and a window into the Thames so the fish, seals and dolphins could watch the wildlife on the other side.

"Please, sit down." George sat on the edge of a desk facing his guests. "We administer the people. That's the proper terminology. In actual fact, we record the people. We record everything companies track. We used to run the country, create laws, regulate business, help other countries, help citizens – but that's all gone now. We're just a centralised department for businesses to collect information. The work is outsourced to us because we're the only organisation in the country officially independent of any corporation and big enough to handle the amount of data being recorded. Both government and businesses want to track and measure people for the benefit of global organisations and foreign governments – and they expect transparency and certain data protection policies being in place. UK businesses have reluctantly deemed the government as the central information database keeper of choice. We're the last piece of public ownership, but only because corporations allow it for their own benefit."

Poppy, having already heard this kind of talk from her father, stood up and asked George to let Amy into C.O.V.E.R.T. and download the necessary information.

"Yes, yes, I'm sorry, I get side tracked easily. Amy, please sit at this desk here. It has full access to the database." George opened the drawer of another desk and removed a small device from it. "You can download whatever you need onto this."

"Thanks." Amy took her place behind the display, cracked her knuckles and began tickling the old laser-beamed ivories. "What's the username?"

"*Admin.*"

"OK, and the password?"

"*Password.*"

Amy turned around to see if George was being serious. He had already turned around to continue his talk with Duncan and Poppy. The advancement in computer security was so great that basic human safe guards had eroded. Amy dived into C.O.V.E.R.T., refreshed and energised to be held within the familiar arms of binary and data once again. It had only been two days but she couldn't remember two days when she had been without her only love.

This experience was one she had secretly looked forward to. The C.O.V.E.R.T. database held the data of every citizen, every item and every business in the country containing CBID satellite tracking technology, which, by the natural economic laws of competition, had to be every company. Those companies who could not afford CBID integration (or delayed it) severely lacked the detailed information gleaned from consumer behaviour, and succumbed to faster, more equipped predators. This tagging revolution was swift and unforgiving of brand or balance sheet; both large and small businesses thrived and died depending on the speed of their CBID adoption and the application of its analysis.

For a tracking analyst like Amy, this was the Holy Grail. The Pharmara database held a massive amount of information from all its products, customers, sister companies, parent company, associated companies, suppliers and distributors but it was nothing compared to this. Like an individual plankton swimming against oceanic currents, Amy selected bits of data to download and analyse later, trying not to get swept away by the sheer volume and trying not to drown in what could be learned if she stopped for one second to look a little closer. This was a smash and grab exercise: head for roughly the right area, fill your boots and examine the spoils later.

"... and that's why there are no taxes anymore, because the citizenship sold their privacy for a tax free economy. Politicians were constantly making bad, partisan decisions to suit their own benefits, which magnified an already existing disconnect with the public who saw no real choice between parties and therefore no real chance of change. This led to business being increasingly seen as the main mechanism of bringing change and improvement, so it was business that stepped forward to fill this power vacuum. This culminated after The Great Recession in the twenty-teens when government effectively did nothing of any real effect while business lifted the country out of the doom and gloom. The fact that business didn't want the government to tighten regulations or change laws escapes everyone now, but history's written by the winners, and the winner this time wasn't a government. The main parties merged into one homogenous voice, relying on petty arguments and one-upmanship to differentiate themselves from each other, so the electorate thought not only would a new government built on pure, demonstrable facts bring real, measured results, but it would also give them the added benefit of living tax free." George picked up a mug of cold coffee and took a pained sip.

"How can the government afford not to tax people?" Amy asked whilst tapping away.

"The information collected from the citizenship and corporation tax is more than enough to pay for the smallest government in the UK's history. The switch to a tax free system was made financially viable by enabling the tracking system we now have. Business could maximise profits with the tracking people had allowed them to initiate and then government could tax those increased profits. The whole system became so much more massively efficient than forecasted that the originally promised lower taxation was further amended to be a completely tax free system. Of course, the problem is this financial disconnect from the state also leads onto a social and cultural disconnect, letting corporate interests in to take a more pro-active role in how the country is run."

Duncan, having listened with interest, repackaged Amy's original question. "So, what exactly do MPs do nowadays? How can the government run without public participation?"

George looked down as though he had been reminded of the death of a childhood dog. "MPs are the new royal family; tradition, ceremony and custom run their official lives. There is no real form or function for the modern MP. His real work is a form of regional corporate representative to satisfy the international convention that this is a fair and democratic land. MPs come in here a couple of times a year to make sure no revolutionaries are trying to restrict trade or commerce and then retire back to their boardrooms. The judiciary and law enforcement is run by legal and security departments across the land, and everything else may eventually find itself here, but only to rot in a lonely, forgotten inbox somewhere. It runs quite easily without public participation. Parties are virtually the same so no one in here really cares who wins, and the people out there don't care because they don't know."

"Surely the separation of all this information keeps the government in control over any third party organisations?" Duncan questioned.

"If I can let in three strangers fairly easily and access the C.O.V.E.R.T. database with the login details thought up by a retarded newt, then I think others are probably doing the same thing. Believe me: they have far less scruples than me."

"But this was the whole thing!" Duncan exclaimed. "The government allows corporations to track people if they then shared that information with the government. The government then got the complete picture with its own tracking information and tracking information from the corporations. If corporations have access to all that information too then what's to stop them—"

"Nothing," finished George with a wry smile and raised eyebrows. "They do not have complete access to one hundred per cent of the information as that would require a large amount of analysts to walk through the door and stay here for weeks, pouring over the data. But as I have already demonstrated with young Amy here" – George motioned towards Amy who was oblivious to the on-going lecture behind her – "it is possible to download nuggets of data to research later, off campus."

"My God," Duncan sighed to himself rather abruptly. "This information is basically out there for anyone to get their hands on."

Amy turned around. "Yeah, pretty sweet, isn't it?"

Poppy tried to help ease Duncan's emotions. "But the information is private, right? Unidentifiable, I mean. Non-governmental organisations are not allowed to store private information such as names and addresses, right?"

George slid off the edge of the desk and slowly paced the office floor. "Technically, that's true, but what's in a name? If you track a human male called 'Dave' then what else does knowing his name give you? You already know his DNA, so you can differentiate him from other males. Why would you want to know his name? Do all 'Daves' act differently from 'Georges'?"

As George paced towards the door, it suddenly opened and in walked a middle-aged lady stylishly attired and fashionably blunt. Her slicked back blonde hair and pale face with expensively minimal makeup made her look as though she had just come out of light speed.

"George, what are these people doing in my office?"

Amy shrunk in her chair with a conceding smile, conscious of being caught red-handed at her media display downloading masses of highly classified information.

"… and what is this woman doing here?"

George stepped up to the plate. "Mary, allow me to introduce you to some constituents: Duncan Hartley and Amy Jay. Duncan and Amy, allow me to introduce Mary Portofino, MP for Wigthorn."

"Well, well, well. I heard that constituents sometimes come to us but I've never experienced it." Mary took off her long red coat and hung it up. "May I ask what young Miss … I assume its 'Miss', with those nails … is doing at my consul, George?"

"You know that bug you've had when attempting to login into Googazonbay? I've put in request after request to IT and no one has come to fix it. Well, Amy and I got talking and it turns out she can fix it for you."

Amy, surreptitiously and with plenty of allegro, played a brief piece on the illuminated keyboard before turning around to cement George's quick thinking by adding some foundation. "There we go …" – Amy tried to think what the proper protocol might be for addressing an MP – "… Your Excellency. All done. It was just a simple conflict error."

Mary eyed Amy suspiciously and then checked the screen. It was clearly showing Googazonbay.co.uk, a site she had not seen for some weeks now – a welcome sight. Those long, boring, inconsequential parliamentary debates could now be filled with shopping once again. "How can I assist some of my constituents? I can't believe you came all this way to fix your representative's technological problems."

"Indeed not, Mary," George replied, still keeping an air of coolness about him. Amy removed herself from the display as quick as possible and, in doing so, tried to hide the fact that she was also removing a small device loaded with information. With a quick twirl out of the chair and some fast hands, the device was placed in a trouser pocket and she was seated beside Poppy on the sofa, glad to be out of the spotlight.

Mary stood next to George at the end of the desk facing her three guests. "I don't believe you have introduced me to this pretty young thing, George."

Amy felt Poppy trying to sink further into the sofa. Amy tried to sink with her. "My goodness, my apologies. This is Poppy Gold." George was glad of the change of subject.

"Another constituent?"

"No, Poppy is from Shaded Vale."

"Really? How very nice. I don't suppose you're any relation to an old friend down there are you? A certain William Gold?"

"He's my father," Poppy replied quietly, not wanting to attract further attention or interrogation but knowing her answer would do the exact opposite.

"His daughter!" If Mary Portofino's eyebrows raised themselves any higher, they would have made rather awkward additions to her expensively styled hair. Luckily, her eyelids noticed the escaping eye furniture and reached up as wide as possible to bring the adventurers back from the fringe. "Good heavens above, they say the world is getting smaller but this is quite claustrophobic." Mary focused her eyes on Poppy, looking for an answer to an unspecified question. "I can see a resemblance ... hmmm ..."

"Everyone says I have my father's eyes." Poppy reached a hand up to her cheek to scratch away a little self-consciousness.

"No, no, someone else." Mary remained lost in thought.

Sensing Mary Portofino had been suitably distracted enough to allow for a polite yet swift getaway, George motioned to Duncan, Amy and Poppy that the performance was drawing to a close and they could bow out gracefully.

"We'll leave you in peace Mary, let you get on with your business."

"Yes, thank you very much for your time, and lovely to meet you." Duncan stretched out a hand to seal his old school charm offensive. Mary Portofino willingly succumbed and shook Duncan's hand, not taking her eyes from Poppy. The two girls were already halfway out the door and merely nodded their goodbyes, so keen were they to leave.

The noise of the heavy wooden door slamming against the old wooden doorframe snapped Mary Portofino out of her daydream, bringing her back into the present to fully assess the face she had just seen.

It was a pretty young face and yet reminded her of an older woman: a friend, an acquaintance or a foe? She could not be sure. Westminster's power to rule may have faded but its power to blur and confuse personal boundaries still held true.

Mary slowly turned away from the door to sit at her desk, her brain rifling through fifty-five years of memories, trying to find the correct folder to file away this most recent experience. Images of people she had met, however brief or aesthetically challenged, flashed through her head like a huge security photofit program running through its entire database of eyes, noses, mouths, chins, foreheads, ears and haircuts. Mary minimised this to the back of her mind as she scoured the photos on the wall to the right of her desk.

From left to right, she analysed photos of friends, family, colleagues, famous guests and the occasional positive news article. As she briefly reminisced upon a photo of herself with a famous tennis player, famous for his beautiful backhand and also for his even more beautiful backside, her mental photofit was halted by the photo next to it. Mary had her arms around two other woman of similar age, they were grinning at the camera after a wine or three too many.

There was a match.

Mary sat back in her chair, pleased at having solved the mystery but even more pleased that her old friend had some dirty laundry that needed airing. Scrolling through her mobile device, she found the friend in question and called her.

"Estelle! Darling! Long time, no speak." Mary smiled as she sensed this was not a convenient time. "You'll never guess who I've just seen."

CHAPTER 9

"Amy, you really should get some sleep, you've been up all night," Poppy pleaded.

Amy had been up analysing the stolen data since they had rolled into their hotel room at 10pm the previous evening after heading south out of London. Under the cover of darkness, and their DNA under the camouflage of foreign tourists, Poppy was able to find a hotel independent of any of Pharmara's sister companies, located outside of London on the outskirts of the ex-commuter town of Serville. Amy insisted on buying a computer of their own rather than using the one in their hotel room so they could dispose of it later. Remaining undetected from any networks would require Amy to make some modifications.

Duncan rose with the sun after a much needed sleep, going next door to call in on the girls' room.

"Has she been to bed yet?"

"No. I've told her to rest but she won't listen."

Amy's tired face lit up with a smile as she turned to Duncan and Poppy. "Finished!"

"Great," Poppy answered like a relieved mother. "Now will you get some sleep?"

"Yeah, just got to send my analysis to your father and then I'm gone." Amy switched on Poppy's mobile device, ran the wireless thimble on the end of her finger over the desk and tapped it twice. "Done!" Amy lifted herself out of the chair as though she had put on fifty kilograms overnight, and fell heavily into bed.

Duncan sat in the warm office chair and by the time he swivelled around to face the two double beds, Amy was already in a deep sleep, curled up fully clothed with Poppy watching over her.

"I'm just going to have a look to see what Amy's found," Duncan said, swivelling back around to the desk.

"OK. Do you want me to order room service or anything?"

"Yeah, OK. I could do with a black coffee and a bacon sandwich."

Amy was still sleeping three hours later. Duncan and Poppy had eaten breakfast and Poppy was now watching reruns of *Only Dad's Office in Adder Towers*, a popular comedy mashup of golden oldies. The only original productions were news and advertisements – both of which only required CGI effects. The lost arts of acting and presenting were now only used in boardrooms or training centres. Creative writing was the domain of legal departments and accountants.

Duncan was deeply engrossed in the data Amy had been analysing overnight, only briefly looking despairingly up into space and tutting when something did not meet with his approval.

"This is unbelievable," Duncan said to no one in particular.

Poppy could sense the rhetoric and remained silent. Besides, the classic scene when Pike eats some of Manuel's finest 'green' and dances so idiotically that he falls behind the bar was just coming up and Poppy didn't want to miss it.

"How ...? This ... I don't understand ..." Duncan kept mumbling his way through the data, not revealing any articulate analysis or indeed any positive vibes.

Poppy stood and started to make her way to Duncan's side to see what was keeping his words from escaping in a coherent sentence when her mobile device alerted her to an incoming call.

"Hello, Father." Poppy stepped back away from Duncan, lowering her voice so not to disturb Amy. "Good. So is the show on the road? Excellent. Good luck." Poppy's voice then lowered even more, this time out of concern. "So is she on her way here? Why didn't you tell me that Mary Portofino knew my mother?" For the first time, Duncan saw Poppy's veil of serene calmness lower just a little as her world entertained uncertainty, trouble arriving at her doorstep for the very first time. "Yes, OK. We'll leave now."

Duncan got Poppy's attention, rubbing his thumb over the tips of his index and middle finger. Money. If Duncan was now a mercenary, he had to start acting like one.

"Father, do you have everything you need to make payment?" Poppy looked at Duncan as she received the reply. "Good, I'll pass them on." Poppy ended the call and spoke to Duncan, relaying The Colonel's orders. "My father is going to send me bank details soon for the both of you, but first we have to leave, and now. My mother knows we were in London with Mary Portofino and no doubt she'll be trying to track us down. We should wake Amy, apply some D 'n' Away and get out of here."

"And go where exactly?" Duncan asked without lifting his eyes from the screen.

"Wigthorn. My father says he has all the information he needs from Amy. Now he wants to keep us safe."

"Can't we stay near here rather than travelling. Won't it be safer?"

"No, he can't influence what goes on round here or keep my mother and Pharmara Security at bay. My father wants us close so he can protect us."

"That's what they say about enemies, isn't it?"

"Wigthorn is the nearest, safest place. We'll be closer to your granddaughter, and your seeds will be closer to the coast and en route out of here. We have to go now. We have to keep on moving."

"OK, OK. Let's wake Amy and get out of here."

Having calmed down after being prematurely awakened, an under-slept Amy plied herself with sweet doughnuts and coffee from the hotel to help wake herself up. Duncan led the girls down to a bus stop – not something that existed in Shaded Vale, or even Wigthorn, but a well-known key component of a poorer neighbourhood such as Serville.

"A bloody bus?" Amy replied with a mouthful of iced raspberry doughnut.

"Yes," Duncan calmly replied, not wanting to irritate Amy anymore. "Getting a hire car would leave us too exposed to tracking, so we need to use other means to get down to Wigthorn, such as shopper shuttle services, hitch hiking or walking."

"Walking?" Amy thought about it.

"Yes."

"The bus it is then." Amy scoffed the last bit of doughnut. "And why are we going back to Wigthorn? Home to our monolithic nemesis and its favourite daughter ... sorry Poppy, I'm sure your mum is great at baking cupcakes and stuff."

"We have to make sure Poppy gets back to The Colonel safely. Plus there's the crude issue of remuneration."

Amy's sugar rush fuelled her early morning ire. "We're following the instructions of a clearly insane, eccentric billionaire with delusions of grandeur ... sorry Poppy ... whilst babysitting his daughter and being pursued by her pit bull, ice queen mother ... sorry Poppy ... and all for what? Because your wife ate a bloody tomato!"

Poppy smiled. She had always thought her life (and family) to be impossibly boring, sheltered in an exceptionally wealthy gated community with a privileged yet sterile upbringing. Amy made it all seem so much more interesting.

"It's a crazy world."

"Yeah, I don't think that's quite going to cover it, Duncan."

"No, it won't. In fact, it's not crazy at all – it's completely measured and with purpose. How deeply did you analyse the data last night?" Duncan asked as they reached the bus stop. It was a huge sign lit up with various encouraging messages about the wonders of the destination. No one else was waiting to experience these wonders.

"As deeply as anyone could in only twelve hours, why?"

"Did you ever take a step back and try to gauge the bigger picture of all that information?"

"I can't say it was ever part of the brief," Amy said defensively.

"It wasn't, but I think all this tracking information is being used for something else other than consumer behaviour research and real-time census data."

Poppy voiced her own interest. "Like what?"

"Population control, product testing, foreign town planning, social network interference, experimental advertising techniques and a whole lot more."

"And how do you figure all that out?" Amy asked, intrigued how Duncan had seen all that by looking at the same data she had examined all night.

Poppy was also intrigued. "We haven't seen any of this control and experimentation in Shaded Vale. Have you seen it in Wigthorn?"

"No," Amy replied definitively.

"We haven't seen it because we're lucky enough not to live in an 'O.C.'."

"What's that?" Poppy asked.

"An 'Outsourced Council'. It's where a town's council has run out of money to effectively run their town, and the highest earning citizens of a particular town move away to better-off towns such as Wigthorn, leaving behind a town with decreasing tax revenue. Eventually they are left penniless, and this is when big business moves in, initially sponsoring flower displays on a roundabout, and eventually bankrolling the whole town, leaving the council toothless until they're just an ineffectual middleman. The town we're currently in, Serville, is one such town."

Amy and Poppy looked around with newfound knowledge of their location. Nothing really stood out immediately as being unusual about Serville.

"Why would a company want to buy a whole town?" Poppy said, trying to find a saleable asset amongst the broken buildings and cracked streets they were walking through on the outskirts of Serville.

"Control. They control how the town's money is spent, they control the advertising within the town, and they control what the citizens are exposed to within the town. They have a captive audience and all they have to do is keep those citizens alive and breathing, consuming and spending."

The 'Serville Shopper Shuttle' silently hovered around the corner before slowing down to let on new passengers. The modern-retro double-decker bus was a moving neon sign illuminating its desolate grey surroundings, displaying so many advertising messages in such quick succession that Duncan could have sworn that eight out of ten cats recommended the latest sports car to make your whites whiter. Modern advertising had no space for punctuation and no time for reflection.

Amy looked through the windows and saw beautiful, stylish people talking, sharing jokes and having fun. A handsome mechanic wearing overalls stained with manual labour was sitting alone reading; Amy earmarked the spare seat next to him for herself.

"Everyone looks all right, Duncan," Amy said, encouraging Poppy to get on the bus quickly to pay for the three of them before that spare seat disappeared.

The door slid open allowing a bright light to emit from the doorway, blinding Poppy as she walked on and scanned her mobile device. As Amy walked on through the curtain of light, she waited at the front to allow her eyes to adjust to the darkness inside and then scoured the bus to find her seat. The initial image of beautiful people sitting in clean, padded seats disappeared and was replaced by the reality: a seatless bus with a few miserable people sitting on the unkempt floor or standing against the sides holding onto a bar.

"Where is everyone?" Amy asked, gutted her eye candy had been deleted.

"Here," Duncan confirmed unhelpfully.

"Yeah, I mean the good-looking guy."

Duncan held on to a bar. "That's just to get you on the bus. Packaging has always been more important than the product inside."

The bus started moving and the little lighting there was soon lowered until it was almost pitch black. Gradually words, icons, logos, products and voice-overs increased their regularity and intensity with the speed of the bus.

"What the fuck is this?" Amy shouted towards Duncan above the din. Duncan couldn't hear a thing but could feel one of his arms being grabbed by Amy and then the other by Poppy. The three of them stood there in silence, eyes closed and holding onto each other to remain upright as the sensory overload was trumping their own remaining sense of balance.

Poppy tried activating the music player on her mobile device to help drown out the advertising. Looking down at the device, she hit play but no music was heard. Scrolling through the device's options, she soon found the wireless signal was being blocked by the bus. They were a captive audience unaware of a perfumed fog enveloping them within the darkness until the mist rested upon their lips and tasted like a popular beer. Amy saw a couple of kids spluttering in the background whilst a parent admonished them, "Well, keep your mouths shut then." Amy could hear the satisfaction in the mother's voice at such an ingenious advertising medium and an effective parental control device to keep her kids quiet.

The ten minute journey to Serville Central Mall took its toll on the bus's occupants; everyone stepped off convinced they could look better and had a shopping list of products to help them achieve this. Duncan had never thought about his personal grooming ritual in any depth before, but was now wondering if he had time to quickly get dermatological laser treatment – his forehead would be wrinkle free and he'd look younger.

Serville Central Mall was a huge building, unimaginative in design and bland in colour to encourage the customer inside quickly and not stand outside in architectural appreciation. This monstrosity was given life as the surrounding area contained neither outstanding natural beauty nor residents who placed aesthetics above superior choice and lower prices. They walked up to one of the entrances and joined the long queue behind families and groups of teenagers; no one entered alone.

"What's with the queue?" Amy asked, impatiently and unconsciously needing to look in a mirror to see if she really looked as bad as the bus advertising had now made her feel.

Duncan looked ahead to see what was going on but couldn't see anything. "Excuse me, sir."

The middle-aged man ahead of Duncan in the queue, wearing apparel that was neither guilty of subtlety or couture, turned around and eyed Duncan up and down, his face turning from disinterest to suspicion as he quickly began to realise that none of Duncan's sartorial choices were either in fashion or manufactured by any recognisable brand. A suspicious reply was tossed back. "Yeah?"

"Why is there a queue outside the mall? What's going on at the front?"

"Searching, in't they."

"For what?"

"I dunno, maybe a satellite is busted and they out catching foreigners. You ain't from foreignland, are you?" The man played with his mobile device, which was currently attached to his wrist, then looked up at Duncan again. "You don't seem to be hooked up."

Amy, realising the native's unrest and suspicion stepped in, dressed with her familiar logos and self-assured confidence. "How often do you see someone unhooked?"

"I ain't never known no one unhooked."

"Well then, don't you think you better turn around before you find out why?" Amy put her hand to her ear and looked up into the sky as though she was in close contact with a secret omnipotent agency. "One-seven-bravo, we might have a tango-delta down here. Please be on stand-by, over." By the time she looked back down, the man had turned back around.

The queue quickly diminished until Duncan, Amy and Poppy were due to be padded down by the armed security guards. Duncan hated queuing and always asked at the front for reasons why such a wait couldn't have been more swiftly dealt with; it drove Nicole mad that Duncan couldn't accept this British tradition as readily as he accepted a roast dinner every Sunday.

"I don't understand. There's heat, infra-red, x-ray, sonar and numerous other scanning technologies available and yet you choose to pad us down."

"Put your arms out, sir." The security guard kept eye contact with Duncan.

"Doesn't make sense, does it?"

"Sir, what brand is that jacket you're wearing?"

"It's a Millyla, I think."

"Never heard of them. You'll not be allowed entrance into Serville Central Mall today, sir."

"Why not?"

"Your clothes are not correctly branded, sir."

"OK, if you could just let me in then I'll purchase some new ones."

"I'm afraid that won't be possible, sir. Please, move aside – you're impeding everyone's patriotic right to shop."

Amy butted in, "Can he go in naked?"

Duncan looked at Amy and then back at the guard. "That won't be necessary."

Poppy, partly through embarrassment of not being let in and partly to engage with the natives, had begun speaking to a bunch of girls queuing behind them. They had informed her of the old High Street just down the road, which not only contained shops but also transport to Serville Southern Mall, another monstrosity Poppy imagined, but on their way south to Wigthorn, nonetheless.

Estelle and Gerard were travelling back to Wigthorn after an unsuccessful trip to London, having lost the whereabouts of Duncan, Amy and Poppy. Estelle remained motionless in her seat, seemingly powering the car by her icy stare alone. Gerard was sat at an acceptably professional distance at right angles to Estelle to avoid eye contact, and so his breathing would not affect her stewing.

The in-car communications broke the silence, allowing Gerard to take the deep breath he'd been desperately craving for the past hour.

"There is an incoming call for you, Estelle."

"Who is it?"

"Charles Sand."

Estelle raised her eyebrows and revealed for the first time to Gerard a turn of events she had not been expecting or was even prepared for. Gerard was intrigued enough to exploit this momentary lapse. "Why is he contacting you?"

Estelle's lapse was indeed only fleeting; the muted reply froze Gerard's wayward oratory functions, of which he was glad.

Estelle glanced at her reflection in the window to help neutralise her initial surprise before connecting the call. "Put him on."

The window opposite Estelle tinted over and was replaced by a communication screen focused on the face of Charles Sand, a face dominated by his genetically altered light blue eyes, made all the more prominent by his heavily tanned and hairless head.

"Charles, this is most unexpected. What have I done to deserve a call from my favourite Rooftech director?" Gerard could feel Estelle's jaw and cheekbones creaking under the pressure of a forced smile

"Estelle, always a pleasure. How long has it been?"

"Too long."

Both exaggerated their smiles even more, tossing their heads back whilst never relinquishing each other's gaze, not even to blink. Gerard could see Estelle's nose twitching through the strain as though it were trying to attract help.

Estelle continued the conversation and steered it down a more familiar, direct route of pure deed and no fluff. "So, Charles, unless you're organising dinner for next year's Domestic Energy Conference, I guess you have more immediate business plans on your mind."

"Indeed I do, Estelle."

Gerard sensed both combatants relax as the small talk was swiftly escorted out of the room to make way for the main event.

Charles continued, "Information has just landed on my desk that could prove, let's say, very timely."

"Such as?"

"I believe you're trying to apprehend three people in violation of Pharmara genetic copyright laws."

"You believe?" Estelle smelt a white lie.

"I know."

"You know the whereabouts of these people?"

"You don't?" Charles feigned a half convincing quizzical look.

Estelle's cheekbones creaked back into action. "Dearest Charley, you're a devil."

Charles smiled and slightly turned his head to one side as though shielding any onlookers from his eyes, which were now shining the brightest blue.

Estelle smelt blood, and was damned if she was going to loosen her grip on these outlaws now. She just needed Charles to give her their whereabouts. "You wouldn't just phone me with this information without a deal in mind. I obviously have something you want, so spill the beans. How can I help you?"

"We want the girl."

"Which one?"

"Poppy Gold."

Estelle feigned an unconvincing look of shock. "Poppy?"

The car suddenly slowed, nudging Estelle and Gerard forward in their seats as it turned onto the hard shoulder of the motorway and stopped. Estelle looked at Gerard. "What are you doing?"

"I haven't done anything."

Charles toned down his smile. "You're currently driving on one of the roads operated by a sister company of Rooftech: Roadtech. Please listen carefully as I don't want to see you having to hitchhike back to Wigthorn from here."

"Wow! You must really save money by just skipping the whole company name brainstorming sessions."

Charles ignored her. "The girl, Estelle. We want Poppy Gold. We'll give you their whereabouts in exchange for the girl."

"Why not just get her yourself if you know where they are?"

"They haven't violated any of our rules," Charles snapped back.

"That hasn't stopped you before. Anyway, Poppy Gold hasn't violated any of our rules either. We're only after the other two."

"Now who's getting bogged down in details?"

"Why do you want her?" Estelle asked.

"That's not really any of your concern."

"It is when it's my daughter you're talking about."

Charles turned to his side, silently addressing someone else off screen. A few seconds later, a smile spread across his face as he turned back to address Estelle. "Well, well, it is a small world we live in. Maybe I should be pulling you in for questioning, too, because we believe Poppy's father is planning to compete against Rooftech when the first home energy contracts are up for renewal in the next few months."

"And what would Poppy know? She's only a child."

"I don't know, but she obviously knows a fair bit if her father sent her into hiding with two fugitives. So, do we have a deal? You pull all three in and give Poppy an accomplice charge then transfer her over to us as we run the local jurisdiction so it's all above board. We don't want any technicalities to affect our bonuses this year."

Estelle paused and took a breath; she was stranded with no other choices. "Yes, Charles my dear, we have a deal. Now can you get us back on the bloody road so we can catch these reprobates?"

"Of course. I only pulled you over because you need to turn back. Plus, you'd nearly exited Roadtech space." Charles flashed his eyes one last time, like a lighthouse sweeping the horizon. "My apologies."

Estelle simply raised her eyebrows, willing the car forward. The trail had been found again and the scent was stronger than ever. Estelle pulled on the lead.

CHAPTER 10

"Duncan, I don't understand why we have to get on this chairlift to cross the main road," Amy asked through clenched teeth, gripping onto the bar lowering across her waist as her vertigo unhelpfully demanded she stare onto the street below.

"There's no other way to get across, look. There's no footbridge or crossing and the shuttle to Serville Southern Mall is on the other side of the road."

"But look over there." Amy quickly removed a hand, pointing in a vaguely southerly direction along the road, then grabbing the bar again without moving her head. "There're the remains of a perfectly good footbridge over there."

Duncan saw two adequate yet unconnected sets of steps leading upwards into thin air on either side of the road, the walkway connecting the two long gone.

Amy glanced at Duncan in a subdued panic as the chairlift began to rumble along the cable. "Why! Why would they remove a perfectly good footbridge and replace it with this rickety old thing!"

Duncan smiled, watching Amy out of her comfort zone, and looked back to see Poppy talking quite happily with a fellow passenger behind.

"Amy Jay, you need to live a little."

"What do you mean? I just don't like heights. What's living got to do with it?"

"This is the real world; it's not constructed of numbers, probability and patterns ..."

"Actually, I think you'll find—"

"No, no – I know what you're going to say, but you're missing out on the human element. Have you contacted any of your friends to let them know where you are? Family? They'll be worried about you. Is there a boyfriend or girlfriend waiting by the phone for your call?"

"No, there's no one, all right? Happy? I'm the statistical opposite of a node. What's that? A dead end? A loser? A sad case?"

"Unique."

"Ohh, give it a rest, Duncan. Now's not the time to start flattering me with faint praise." Amy screamed as the chairlift swung on its hinges; she gripped the bar so hard her knuckles turned white. "What the fuck was that!"

"Just a breeze, calm down." Duncan couldn't contain another escaping smile. "I bet I know what your problem is."

"Surprise me, great prophet."

"At the first sign of a love interest coming into your life, I bet you analyse the hell out of them until you find a pattern, giving you an excuse not to pursue them anymore so you can go on hiding away behind your numbers and graphs. No one's life would be able to stand up to that level of scrutiny."

Amy looked down to avoid looking at Duncan. It was an easier view to stomach.

"People aren't defined by the footprints, history and patterns they leave behind, Amy." Duncan lightly placed a hand on Amy's white knuckles. "Let go a little. Don't look back and don't look down. Look forward."

As they arrived on the other side, Duncan told Amy he'd have to lift the bar so they could jump off. Amy's reluctance to let go was soon quashed by the realisation that if she didn't allow the bar to move up so she could jump off then she'd simply turn around, remaining on this chairlift for all eternity. Amy's disembarkation was not graceful, but it was swift.

As they walked down the steps of the chairlift platform, Amy was still unsure why the town had deemed it necessary to replace a perfectly good bridge with a chairlift.

Duncan answered, "Serville is populated by the poorer citizens of this country and their council has had to sell control of various facilities and assets to private interests as the public purse cannot support them. Replacing a bridge with a chairlift is ridiculous. The toll money won't cover the costs, but the council don't pay for it, the shops in the mall do."

Poppy was just as confused as Amy. "So why do it?"

"The footbridge is unsafe, too expensive to repair and a law suit waiting to happen if anymore people cross it, so they sell control. I can only think that they maintain a loss-making venture because this is an experiment commissioned by a foreign government or company. Remember what your father said about the numbers not adding up? Well, I think this is where the missing figures come from." Duncan looks at Amy. "Remember what I was saying about the data we analysed? This could be evidence explaining anomalies there, too. Third party organisations are commissioning domestic corporations to conduct tests and experiments in the towns they effectively control, like this one."

"But a chairlift? I don't understand," said Amy exasperated, still in shock.

"Yeah, it's not too clear to me either. Maybe there's a region wanting to test whether it would be feasible to build a shopping mall on a mountain or a cliff, or they want to test how effective it is to change the way people enter a shopping mall or something to do with traffic flow. I'm not sure about the exact reason but, other than for experimental purposes, why would anyone swap a bridge for a chairlift in a town centre?"

"Was the security at the mall another experiment?" Poppy enquired.

"Maybe. I can't think of another reason why they'd refuse customers based on the brands they were wearing. A sale is a sale, right?"

As they arrived at street level pondering Duncan's comments, they were met by a throng of shoppers walking up and down the street. This old fashioned scene of shoppers scouring the streets for bargains under a blue sky instead of a mall reminded Duncan of his youth, except the street was completely barricaded, allowing only a few select exit points. The shops were renovated old-fashioned buildings knocked through five or six at a time to house the masses of stock. There were no small, independent shops – just a few mega retailers occupying the retail space of the whole street.

As they explored their new habitat, Amy walked over to one of the two metre high angled mirrors dotted along the pedestrian area to check her appearance, the bus ride still having an affect on her self-esteem.

"What are all these mirrors for?" Duncan asked Amy's reflection.

"These are 'street level viewers'. Satellites limit you to a bird's eye view. When you gain control of a satellite camera, you can view what's going on at street level by looking at these forty-five degree mirrors. They're cheaper than CCTV, though not as effective, but the locals don't complain about them." Amy realised she could be giving someone a prime view of herself, so she let her hair down and quickly walked out of view.

Another aspect that differed from Duncan's youth was the lack of small market or newspaper stands on the pavement. There were only market researchers – hundreds of them probing shoppers after giving them a quick scan to identify the best method of approach.

"Ma'am, I have a discount on a new shampoo for you!"

"Ladies! You looking for a great nightclub tonight?"

"Sir, you're looking for new clothes right?"

Just walking a few metres down the street meant getting shouted at, propositioned and almost accosted by multiples of people with electronic pads wanting a slice of information in exchange for a special offer. The information age meant everyone – no matter your education, personal assets or location – had something worth knowing. Whether you were a highflying executive wanting to hire a private jet, or were living on the breadline wanting a pint of milk, all information was profitable and therefore necessary for corporations to succeed.

"Sir, just want to know if you've ever considered moving to Serville permanently?"

"Madam, is it Spain or Italy this year?"

"Have you thought about kidnap insurance?"

People hurriedly walked down the street with researchers latching onto them, asking a few questions, and then leaving to pair up with another shopper. Like busy bees going from flower to flower extracting pollen, the researchers were methodically assessing the best flora to approach, and efficiently collecting the information necessary for the hive to survive.

This onslaught of researchers demanding information in exchange for offers made the unexciting experience of shopping into a truly unpleasant one, yet Amy was intrigued to know why this level of intrusion was not only tolerated, but also how it could contain value. Surely DNA tracking augmented with personal finances, product use and social interaction would give any corporation all the data it would ever need to get a full understanding of how its products and services were being used?

Amy looked for a researcher not only interested in her as a subject, but with a face suggesting willingness to exchange information for secrets rather than discounts. A girl soon caught Amy's eye and she made her way towards her. Amy, just as quick in her assessment, allowed the approach to result in conversation. Duncan and Poppy followed behind, keeping an eye on how to exit the mall and onto the shuttle service heading south.

"Excuse me, madam? Hi, I'm Sam, nice to meet you. I just wanted to ask you a few questions about your body."

"My body?"

"Yes, I see your breasts could do with some firming up."

Amy initially responded with a shocked look before glancing down at her chest in disbelief. "What are you talking about? There's hardly anything there!"

"Well, we can help out with that, too. Can I just ask you a few questions?"

"Sure, only if I can ask you a few first?"

Obviously desperate to achieve her quota for the day, Sam the researcher agreed.

"With all these satellites tracking people and products, why are you asking me questions?"

"Just plugging the gaps. Satellites and products can't tell us about emotions and desires. We're told to avoid the facts and collect feelings."

"And how do you quantify and measure feelings?"

"I don't know, ma'am, I'm just told to go out, ask these questions and tick boxes. The satellites measure people's physical state, whereas we assess their mental state. What are they looking forward to? Where do they want to be? What do they wish for?"

"OK, I think I understand now." Amy saw her previous job had lacked this information, and knew it was vital. Of course it was – all the facts and figures she had immersed herself in were only scratching the surface. You can't understand a human by their vital statistics alone; you must know their desires, too.

Amy fired off one more question. "Are you from Serville?"

"Oh, God, no. This helps to fund my studies at Rooftech Technical College in South London."

Sam sensed Amy's questions had ended and resumed her own line of questioning. "So, are you happy with having smaller than average breasts or have you ever wished for larger?"

Duncan and Poppy saw Amy's interest in genetic breast enhancement go a little deeper than was previously imagined after a few pointed questions from Sam the researcher, so they sauntered over to the fountain situated in the middle of a small square to give her some privacy. It was a matt metallic black and quite unimpressive, simply a giant bowl of water with a few large pipes sticking out the middle, spraying water. Its one saving grace was the seated rim around the edge, which provided respite for shoppers – a rare commodity when shoppers on the move are considered a more profitable proposal.

Duncan led Poppy to the fountain to sit down, weaving through the crowd of people either shadowed by researchers or researchers themselves attempting to shadow them. Duncan simply kept his eyes down, shook his head and opened both palms as though the little information he might possess would be completely useless to anyone whatsoever.

"How often do you wash your shirts, sir?" A researcher unskilled in the art of understanding body language, or skilled in ignoring it, intercepted Duncan's path.

"Hey, this is my guy!" Another researcher tried to claim Duncan for his own. "Sir, I have a far superior product offer for your clothes."

Duncan dispensed with manners and raised his eyes to look at one of the men. "I have a rare form of contagious leprosy. I suggest you ... huh ... huh ..." And with two sharp intakes of breath, Duncan sneezed in the researcher's face.

Poppy stifled a smile and sneezed in the other guy's face as she walked passed. "Father, I think my nose just fell off!"

Duncan sat on the edge of the fountain with Poppy at his side. They both stared out into the hectic maelstrom of consumer research for a second before Duncan broke the silence between them.

"How are you feeling Poppy? It's been a busy couple of days for you."

"I'm OK. It's been busy for all of us."

"It has, but you've been dragged away from your home after having done nothing wrong and had to stick around with a couple of strangers – one old man and a crazy girl."

Poppy looked at Duncan and gave him a smile to let him know this was the best time she'd had in a long time. "It's been fun. Well, more interesting than my usual days spent at home in Shaded Vale, my brain rotting along with everyone else's." Poppy looked around the square, soaking up the atmosphere. "This place has life – look at it. Look at the people. They may not have as much as people in Shaded Vale and they may get questioned about how they feel about not having as much, but there is life here. There's much more variety here – in the people, I mean."

Duncan was pleased to hear Poppy's positive outlook in this dilapidated backwater of God's green and pleasant land. She was right, too. The buildings and businesses dominated to the uneducated eye, but looking closer there was far more going on here than in Shaded Vale or even Wigthorn. The sterile, unadventurous summit of Shaded Vale housed the rich and contented – there could never be any struggle or art in a place like that. The very meaning of survival had been erased from the lexicon of Shaded Vale many seasons ago. Duncan now wondered if the lack of consumer research in Shaded Vale was a result of marketers not caring what the residents in such a privileged place thought, the people so predictable in their habitual ways that research was not deemed worthwhile. Residents in towns like Shaded Vale paid a premium to live outside the everyday challenges of constant, incessant advertising and marketing, but in reality this was probably another unnecessary product packaged up to look irresistible. The rich were so boring and entrenched in ritual they were not worth researching as the patterns gleaned were always so familiar and unsurprising.

Consumers at the bottom were so much more interesting: trying to find new ways to emulate the rich, using their wits to step up the ladder, foraging new paths up the greasy pole to find somewhere easier to live. The methods and ideas to lift oneself from a backwater such as Serville had to be fought for and risked. There was no way a mere satellite reading or a DNA signature could measure or predict how this group of people were going to think or act.

This was all relative, though. Duncan may have thought the people here were more interesting than in Shaded Vale, but that wasn't really hard. The most interesting people were from his generation – people from the past, people who had lived in the freedom of open competition with social institutions to protect that freedom. Slowly, over the years, the toxic waste of consolidation and monopoly seeped into the public supply almost unnoticed, almost without side effects.

That is, unless it was viewed by someone who had spanned a few generations unscathed by self-imposed virtual isolation – someone like Duncan. Sometimes being a hermit holed up in his lab at the bottom of his garden did have its advantages.

Duncan felt like one of the last leaves on a rotting evolutionary branch, enjoying one last look as the breeze tore him away to bury him in the shadow of a tree. But who would listen to an old man's mutterings about the good old days? The days that included poverty, hunger, huge waste, destruction of natural resources and overbearing governments strangling the life out of both enterprise and countryman alike.

"Do you like this place?" Poppy asked in an effort to snatch Duncan back into the present.

"No, it's a prison, but I like the way you're thinking. It's good to get out of the house once in a while, isn't it?"

Poppy shifted in her seat to face Duncan. "Can I ask you a question?"

Duncan, slightly taken aback by Poppy's directness, replied, "Yes, of course."

"Why did you leave Pharmara?"

"Your father didn't tell you?"

"No, the first I really heard of you was the day you arrived. Before that, you were occasionally referred to as the 'Veggie Man'."

Duncan left a little pause, hoping that Poppy would get distracted and change the subject, but she was not so easily thrown off course. Seconds later she was still staring at him expectantly.

"I used to work in the research department, testing drugs to fight various genetic diseases. It was important work and I loved it. We established cures for quite a few diseases but then the bottom fell out of it. All foetuses were getting screened and having genetic treatment before birth to treat problems. A generation later, a huge amount of diseases had been flushed out of the human genome, which meant there was virtually no need for these kinds of drugs anymore. This resulted in Pharmara's massive expansion into other businesses and the consolidation of the pharmaceutical industry into just two companies: Pharmara and Black Star."

"You got made redundant?"

"No, they kept me on. I was the team leader of the most effective research team in the country; many others got made redundant but not me." Duncan declared this curriculum vitae highlight with some shame and regret.

"You were good?"

"I was too good for my own good."

Showing the first signs of impatience, Poppy was determined to get to the bottom of Duncan's Pharmara exit. "So why did you leave?"

"We were under pressure to literally find problems to cure. Pharmara had the market share but with birth screenings and genetic therapies rapidly cleaning up the gene pool, the demand for advanced, life-saving drug treatments was drying up, so they went into more scientifically grey areas: restless leg syndrome, stutter vision, fast weight loss, hair growth, permanent tanning, etc. – crossing over into beauty-based treatments. They weren't interested in solving real problems, just selling product. So one day I came up with 'drugphobia'. It was a joke. I told them there was about ten per cent of the population who were fit and healthy, they ate well, they exercised and were well within their ideal weight limit, blood pressure, heart rate, etc. I told the Pharmara board that we could target these people as having a phobia to drug treatment. No one is perfect, everyone could do with something, and therefore if you weren't currently taking any kind of drugs then you had to be drugphobic. You probably also had an undiagnosed narcissistic streak, were ignorant in the ways drug therapy could help you, and so were a perfect subject for a course of antibiotics to treat your drugphobia."

Poppy's look changed from engaged interest to a horrified disappointment. "You invented PerFixx!"

Duncan's head dropped. "Yes."

"I was on that crap for three years before my father stepped in and questioned its actual use. I used to get headaches, my knees hurt, I had the worst dreams."

"Yeah, I heard the side effects for some people weren't very pleasant, but believe me, I didn't develop it any further than my initial joke. When I realised they were taking me seriously, I left. That was the artistic difference your father mentioned. The next day I walked into the lab where there was a huge meeting in progress involving every department to fast track development and get a product into market. PerFixx was the next big thing and Pharmara were betting on it big time. I stormed into the hastily arranged meeting uninvited and told everyone this was nuts and against everything we should be doing, but no one listened. The bonuses for this project were too significant to ignore. I walked out and never returned."

Poppy could see the remorse stamped across Duncan's face. He was talking to her as though she represented everyone that had taken PerFixx. Duncan was confessing everything to Poppy and she felt empowered with the gift of forgiveness on behalf of all PerFixx users, if she so wished.

Poppy shuffled closer to Duncan, touched his hand and kissed him on the cheek. "It's OK, you had nothing to do with its development, and if it wasn't you, some other smart alec would've come up with the idea sooner or later." As she stood up to check on Amy, she grinned. "Just don't tell anymore jokes."

"Yeah, I know. I kind of lost my sense of humour after that."

As Poppy stuck her head above the pulpit, the nearest researcher saw movement out of the corner of his eye and immediately turned to question her. "Ma'am, do you ever get period pains?"

Poppy, realising her faux pas, quickly dismissed him before another, more restrained researcher ghosted in and very quietly asked an inappropriate question any basic satellite data could have answered. "Miss Gold, do you spend much time with your mother?"

Poppy took a step back, which was lucky as Duncan stepped forward and, aided with the element of surprise, grabbed the man by the arm and threw him into the fountain. Duncan linked arms with Poppy, forcefully leading her away into the crowd.

"He knew my name, Duncan."

"He must be working for Pharmara."

The splash and commotion caused everyone to look. Researchers, not missing the opportunity of people letting their guards down, started questioning every distracted head, including Duncan and Poppy.

"Sir, madam!" It was one of the researchers from before.

Duncan answered before the question came, "You got laundry products, right? That guy in the fountain, he really needs your product – quick, ask him." Duncan turned to other researchers. "He'll need your product, too – quick!"

Poppy turned to the girl who had questioned her not a minute before. "He said his girlfriend has really bad period pains, go!"

Duncan looked back and saw the fake researcher stand up in the fountain before getting swamped by questions and handheld media devices.

"We need to find Amy and get out of here."

Duncan and Poppy quickly found Amy still chatting to Sam the researcher amid the chaos and, in tandem, linked both of Amy's arms with one of their own and led her away down a side street and out of the crowds.

"Why are we leaving in such a hurry? I was well on my way to getting twenty-five per cent off a natural breast firming treatment," Amy demanded as she agitated herself free from her rescuers.

"They've found us. We need to get out of here." Duncan's eyes were fixed firmly ahead as he concentrated on furthering their escape. They continued down the side street.

"Was it Estelle?"

"No, it was someone else," Poppy answered.

Amy looked at Poppy. "Who?"

Duncan spoke up. "I don't know, but I don't think it was a Pharmara employee. He was more interested in Poppy than you or I."

Amy looked back to Poppy. "What does he want with you?"

"I don't know, but I don't think my mother is far away." Poppy lost herself in thought, trying to determine how the questioner knew her name, what he wanted with her, and why she suddenly felt the presence of her mother.

"Stop!" Poppy immediately halted and turned to face Duncan and Amy. "Don't ask me why, but I think my mother is nearby. I feel it."

Amy looked unimpressed with any metaphysical revelations at this moment in time. "And?"

"Look, we need to know who sent that guy and who we're running from, right? You still got that DNA scanner Leroy gave you, Amy?"

"Yeah, it's in my rucksack."

"Get it out." Poppy stood purposefully, hands on hips.

"What are we doing? We've got to keep moving," Duncan insisted, nudging himself forward to back up his words with action.

"No," Poppy replied, out of character. "Scan me."

Amy, not wanting to get in the way of Poppy's ambition, activated the scanner and took a reading. "Now what?"

"Use my reading as a base and then scan within a one or two mile radius for the closest match you can find."

A grin spread over Duncan's face whilst Amy looked up at Poppy with some admiration. "Nice one."

They waited for what seemed like ages for some kind of life from either the scanner or Amy.

"Got it!" Amy looked down the side street the way they had come. "She's going to be walking around that corner in about twenty seconds – we better move!"

Amy swung her rucksack over her shoulder and the three of them started running down the street and round the first corner to get out of sight.

Amy put the ball firmly in Duncan's court. "How are we getting out of this? We can't run forever."

Duncan, not the fittest of runners, struggled to keep up with the girls whilst organising some semblance of an escape plan. They continued running down another side street that led onto another square filled with people and researchers. In the centre was another water feature, but not a fountain. Water simply shot out of the ground like tall pillars stretching into the sky before collapsing under their own weight, crashing back down. It was a sunny day and kids were stripped to their pants playing in the water, chasing each other around.

Duncan stopped in front of the country's number one hardware chain and posed a question. "How do you think they found us? We've altered our DNA signatures."

"Facial recognition software via the town's CCTV." Amy's answer was prompt and definite.

"Is that the best way to track us?"

"No, DNA is always the preferred method. Faces can be changed or hidden."

"OK, we need to get back on their DNA radar because that is the only way we have to lose them. Follow me." With that, Duncan ran into the fountain and got himself utterly drenched, scrubbing his arms, his head and his hair. The girls looked on in bemusement.

"Quick, we need them to start tracking our DNA so we can lose them again later. We have to get rid of this fake DNA."

The girls understood and jumped straight in.

The men walking through the square couldn't believe their luck as two young and attractive ladies dressed in summer wear showered themselves in the middle of a busy shopping centre.

"Go on, darling!"

"Got room for one more?"

"I'll scrub your back if you want, love!"

Amy took a second to enjoy the attention before Duncan came over to her. "Amy, get those D 'n' Away sequencers ready. We need to make up a solution with each of our own DNA."

"Our own? Why would we want to do that?"

Duncan pulled out a hair from his head. "Look after that; I'll be back in a minute. Just get those solutions ready."

"Wahey! Get in there, granddad!" Another reveller shouted, enjoying the spontaneous wet t-shirt show along with a growing crowd.

Duncan ignored the caterwauling and ran into the nearby hardware shop to gather the necessary tools to execute his plan of escape.

Amy and Poppy stepped away from the water as Amy organised the D 'n' Away sequencers to take readings of Duncan's, Poppy's and her own DNA. As she did this, Poppy took the DNA scanner and tracked the whereabouts of her nearest genetic relative.

"Where is she?" Amy asked on her knees, preparing the equipment.

"She's down the side street we came from. We haven't got long. What's Duncan got planned?"

"I'm not sure."

Another audience member voiced his disappointment in the show's lack of progression. "Come on, girls, leave your mobiles alone and start dancing again!"

Duncan returned, still soaking wet but with three empty garden weed spray bottles. "Quick, fill one of these with the D 'n' Away liquid solution, we'll be able to spray everyone around here a lot quicker. Amy, you take the left, Poppy the middle and I'll spray people on our right. Let's see Estelle try and track a whole shopping square full of Duncans, Amys and Poppys."

Stepping up the level of entertainment for the crowd from showering themselves to showering everyone else was received with much cheering and encouragement. Both Amy and Poppy stepped into the role of sultry eye candy with relish, though neither would have admitted it. Duncan merely stood behind them, spraying his side of the crowd and keeping an eye on the scanner to see when they needed to put down the weed sprays and run. None of the audience noticed Duncan's lack of enthusiastic participation, although a few more mature female members had made their way around to Duncan's side and were egging him into performing more flirtatious manoeuvres.

Estelle had utilised the heel reduction facility in her shoes and was running down the side street. Behind Estelle were three security personnel, and behind them was Gerard, puffing and panting.

They stopped at the end of the street and surveyed the square before them. The square had retail shops all around the edge with a fountain in the middle containing a large crowd of people cheering and shouting.

"They stopped here, ma'am." The lead tracker kept his eyes on his device to avoid any eye contact with Estelle, confirming his perpetual submission.

"And where are they now? I don't wish to simply chase them."

The tracker played with his device, somewhat confused at first, quickly descending into blind panic.

"Well?" Estelle inconveniently piled on the pressure.

"They ... err ... there are loads of them." He looked up at the crowd around the fountain. "There are about twenty Poppys over there."

Estelle grabbed the device and looked at the screen. There were indeed twenty red dots in the square signifying twenty

DNA matches. Estelle threw the device to the floor, angry she'd let modern technology blind her.

"OK, we need some good old fashion scare tactics and CCTV." Estelle engaged her mobile device and contacted the town's security department. "Re-activate facial recognition on all cameras in this square and the surrounding shops. Let me know when you get a match. Do you have a speaker system here you can plug me into?" Estelle waited for the reply. "OK, connect me into it."

Estelle instructed her security personnel to cover the main exits out of the square. "Gerard, you stay here with me."

Connected to the surrounding PA system, Estelle announced her presence. "Attention shoppers, this is a customer announcement."

Estelle then spoke covertly to the lead security guy. "Fire two shots into the air."

BANG! BANG!

Shoppers ran everywhere. Estelle watched the commotion spread as people criss-crossed each other, not knowing where they were running to or what they were running from. This was a rare moment of job satisfaction for Estelle; causing mass panic was such a bigger buzz than scaring people individually, one-on-one. Estelle made a note of the time so when she was back in the office she could download the satellite video footage and watch this again.

The wet t-shirt show abruptly came to an end. Duncan lost Poppy in the panic but saw Amy and ran over to her.

Amy had her hands over her face, squinting through her fingers to find Duncan and Poppy. She saw Duncan approach. "Quick, cover your face! This is a 'crowd flush'. They're using facial recognition software to track us. Find someone!"

With that last command, Amy led by example and latched onto one of the young male revellers and hid her head in his chest and arms, the noble gallant's automatic reaction was to cover her up and lead her into one of the shops.

Duncan quickly followed suit and saw an older woman with a small sun umbrella. He played the gallant hero and put his arm around her, leading her into the same shop whilst keeping his head hidden. But he also couldn't see very well and led the woman into a door. She looked at Duncan in disgust before abandoning him in the doorway.

Amy took his arm, pulling him inside. They made their way into a shop window display behind a couple of mannequins, looking out into the square to find Poppy.

With the square effectively cleared, Estelle contacted the security centre. "Any matches?"

The answer returned was obviously in the negative due to Estelle's jaw clenching rippling through the side of her face. Gerard took a step back.

Estelle contacted the security staff stationed on the exits. "Tell me one of you saw someone."

Another negative was returned, precipitating Estelle rotating slowly towards Gerard in search of answers. Gerard tried to fade into the near distance.

Just as Estelle's glare caught up with her body in facing Gerard, a late call came through. Estelle put a finger to her ear. "Where? In the middle of the fountain?"

Estelle walked into the deserted square to see who was standing in the fountain. There was one figure standing motionless within the towering water columns, hidden by the falling cascades.

Amy looked in the shops across the square whilst Duncan looked around inside the shop they were in. Neither could see Poppy, until Amy caught a glimpse of her. "Duncan, look there, in the fountain."

There she was, hiding amongst the water jets spurting upwards, viewable from only a few certain angles. They could see Poppy looking around, presumably looking for Amy and Duncan. Amy waved her hand a little to catch her attention; Poppy saw her and stared at them.

"She's saying something. What's she saying, Amy? I can't see."

Amy stared intently, trying to make out the words she was mouthing. "I'm not sure. Hang on …" Amy looked more closely. "She's only saying one word, I think."

"What is it?"

Amy looked round at Duncan. "*Run.*"

"Turn off the fountain," Estelle commanded in a monotone, reconciled voice.

The square's water feature quickly died, leaving behind one soaked girl standing in the draining water.

"Hello, my darling."

"Hello, Mother."

CHAPTER 11

Poppy walked over to her mother, cold and wet, but warming the closer she approached. In the years since she last saw her mother, Poppy tried to assess how much she had changed herself. Not much, still sheltered under her father's wing. Her mother was the complete opposite and probably harboured an intense disappointment of her daughter. Why else had she not visited? At her age, Estelle had already burnt bridges and stepped on toes; Poppy had only just completed her first bus ride.

Keeping her head down, Poppy allowed her hair to fall over her face to hide the unworthiness beneath. She walked over to her mother, willing her to open her arms.

Estelle zipped up her jacket and opened her arms to invite her daughter in. She'd seen this reaction in many movies, and it seemed appropriate. "Darling, come here. I'm so glad you're OK. Did those fugitives harm you?"

Poppy ignored the question and buried her face in her mother's neck, releasing a repressed smile that had been imprisoned for so long. Estelle was slim but she stood strong and firm. Her grip was not tender, but Poppy tentatively imagined this was the overwhelming emotions of a mother reunited with a long lost daughter.

Estelle didn't want to let go because Poppy might know where Duncan and Amy had gone.

Looking over Poppy's shoulder, Estelle silently motioned to Gerard to keep searching the surrounding area.

"Darling, you're cold and wet. Let's get you out of these clothes and somewhere warm." Estelle put her arm around Poppy, leading her back to a waiting car with instructions to get in, tint the window, turn up the heating and remove all her clothes. Estelle walked into a nearby clothes shop, whizzed round like a fashion conscious cyclone, expertly mixing and matching before flashing her mobile device at the till and walking back to the car, leaving behind an audience of shoppers pushed further into shock by the sight of such a commanding and controlled performance in the aisles. Estelle opened the car door slightly and threw the clothes inside.

Whilst she waited for Poppy to dress herself, Estelle took one last look around the square and the surrounding retail outlets, then down at the front of her jacket, which had become damp from holding her daughter. Her look changed from one of attention to one of aggravation.

"Damn kids." Estelle removed her jacket, and took one last forlorn look at its Italian leather before chucking it onto an empty seat and sitting down adjacent to Poppy. Estelle took a quick look at Poppy then addressed the car's computer. "Mossyface Wood, and don't hang around."

A period of awkward silence accompanied the pair out of Serville and onto the motorway. Poppy finished getting dressed, examining her new shoes whilst she frantically tried to think of an apt conversation starter, one that was neither too heavy going nor too trivial. Never had a simple pair of slip-ons taken someone so long to put on.

Estelle was deep in thought, trying to establish how she could extract the location of Duncan and Amy from Poppy before they got to Mossyface Wood. The added complication of this being a family matter, which clearly meant more to Poppy than herself, required a little more tact and diplomacy than usual – skills Estelle was fully aware she lacked, which was one of the many reasons why she steered clear of family. Estelle watched Poppy making a meal of putting on a simple pair of slip-on shoes. Any maternal feelings that may have been floating around quickly drowned under a wave of disappointment.

Finally, Poppy thought of something to say, a question she genuinely wanted to know the answer to. "What's in Mossyface Wood and why are we going?"

Estelle raised an eyebrow. "You really don't know?"

"I don't know why my own mother would take me there."

Estelle relaxed with a smile. "You're not a child anymore, my darling. Your father has taken you down a route I would not have taken you down personally, but since he was the one who wanted to raise you, I suppose you had no choice."

"You didn't want me?"

"No, I just didn't want to fight for you. Why should I take you away from someone who wanted you more? I'm not a spiteful person, despite what you may think."

"So why even have me in the first place?"

"The benefits for a wealthy young woman, like I was, to have a child is immense. Once that second, faint heartbeat is detected by a satellite, databases go mad and before you know it you're being sent free this, free that, special offer on X, discounts on Y and the whole world is flung onto your doorstep. Add that to the incentives these same corporations pay to doctors not to abort any foetuses and you'll see the desperation of business to attract new consumers far out weighs any woman's individual choice."

Estelle slid across the back seat to be within arms reach of Poppy. To further her bargaining power, she reached for Poppy's hand.

Poppy took it, convinced the warmth emanated from her mother's heart, not the car's climate control.

"Darling, you think I'm heartless and selfish, but who else is going to look out for number one? No one, that's who."

"That's because you have no one."

"Don't I have you?"

Poppy was slightly taken aback by such a weak attempt to engineer some emotional guilt, realising that without the ability to glean any information from the hand she was holding or the eyes she was looking into, Estelle had to rely on responses learnt from the wide screen. Poppy removed her hand from the emotionless grip. "Why are you taking me to Mossyface Wood?"

"You know why I'm taking you there."

"You just can't help giving me away, can you?"

Poppy was sat in a solitary chair in the middle of a circular room walled from top to bottom with uninterrupted glass. The roof and the floor were tiled in white, whilst the view out of the window in every direction looked over the tops of the trees of Mossyface Wood. This was the headquarters of Rooftech.

Mossyface Wood had been a sleepy village located in the north of the Sussex countryside. In 2024 it was chosen for a party political experiment. A safe constituency for the opposition party of the time, it was deemed expendable by the administration so they completely ignored it, hoping to save resources when no votes could ever hoped to have been won there. The borough of Mossyface Wood declined, leading to it becoming the first completely corporately owned and managed conurbation in the UK. Rooftech's parent company bought eighty per cent of the land in 2032 to locate the headquarters of its rapidly growing solar technology subsidiary, Rooftech, so it could give birth to a huge economic shift in energy production within the protective arms of Mother Nature.

Poppy sat there somewhat aware of the company's history and economic might within the country's balance sheet, but was far more interested in the view out of the window. Wherever she looked, there were just the tops of trees with the occasional hill jostling for attention in the distance. The birds flying from branch to branch made her feel like a goldfish stuck in a bowl. Within the middle of this expansive and panoramic view, she felt pangs of claustrophobia.

The peaceful silence broke when part of the floor slid open, lifting Charles and Estelle into the room, like a magician and his assistant making a dramatic entrance onto a stage.

"Desk." Charles said to no one in particular as he walked to the centre of the room. A rectangle slice of the ceiling began to lower itself until it reached waist height and remained hovering in the same position, precisely poised between magnetic polar forces. As it froze in mid-air, three small squares lifted themselves from the floor slightly to provide adequate seating for the desk's occupants. Charles sat down and then Estelle, her ankle bracelet reaching into the air as the magnetic forces lifting the desk and seats gave it life.

"Sit," Charles demanded with no hint of playing the graceful host.

Poppy sat. "Who are you and what do you want with me?"

"I'm Charles Sand, CEO of Rooftech Industries. What do I want with you?" Charles pressed a button on the side of the seat and a back rose up so he could lean back in his chair. "I want to know what you know."

"And what do you think I know, Mr Charles Sand?"

"I know that you know what your father is planning."

"My father couldn't plan a teddy bears' picnic."

Estelle enjoyed her daughter's spirit and at the unarguable truth that Billy Gold indeed could not plan himself out of a proverbial paper bag.

"That maybe so, but his money can buy planners, organisers, schedulers, administrators, the works. So please, if you think this is some fun little game you're playing, you'd be very much mistaken. My sources tell me your father is planning to setup competition against Rooftech to coincide with the domestic energy contract renewals."

"Scared of a little competition?" Poppy felt empowered next to her mother.

Charles looked at Estelle in mock surprise. "Man! Who would've thought you two were related?"

Estelle suppressed a growing sense of pride and kept a stony face. "What is your father up to, Poppy?"

Poppy stood up suddenly. "Oh! Since my wonderful mother is asking me, I'll let you know!" She walked over to the window and looked out. "If this is the HQ for the biggest energy supplier in the country, why is it so small?"

"It's all underground." Charles stood up and walked over to the opposite side of the room. "All those trees, they're not real. The leaves are all solar panels feeding energy down the trunks and into the grid. The trees are growing on the roof of the building, the biggest building in the country. As far as the eye can see is the tree topped roof of Rooftech."

"There's no wood in Mossyface Wood?"

"Not anymore, no."

"That's progress?"

"With the increase of desert communities throughout the world, it is. In the growing flood plains and coastal areas where the higher sea levels have devastated local foliage, it's a giant slice of progress."

Poppy looked closer at the tainted view of nature painted by an android apprentice of Constable and saw solar panels hiding in the brushstrokes of the lush facade. Now it was clear why there were so many birds flying around – none of them actually wanted to land.

Charles stared intensely at the back of Poppy's head, his face tensing up as he waited for her to turn back around. This young lady was not showing any signs of revealing her face or any pertinent information, so Charles ended his charade of playing nice and began a new offensive.

"Stats!" Charles said firmly to the room's computer, and with that the windows quickly faded to black, shrouding the room in complete darkness. Poppy looked back around into the centre of the room and saw Charles march to his desk before disappearing into the blackness, only his sky blue eyes indicating his presence and state of mind.

After two seconds of complete darkness, the room burst into life with bright, multicoloured lights. Words and numbers slowly scrolled down and rolled around the blacked out windows, which were now acting as vast screens. Poppy looked around, trying to take in the wealth of information flashing before her:

0.6% of East Wigan are taking a warm shower.

1 male is having a cold shower.

3,556 men in Newcastle are sitting on the toilet.

23 megawatts of energy is being generated by homes in Glasgow per hour.

Washing machines are using a combined total of 34 megawatts in North Yorkshire.

Plymouth is currently the UK's least energy-consuming city.

Statistical facts were scrolling up and down, from left to right with the actual numbers changing every second ... Now 0.7% of East Wigan were in the shower. Poppy turned on her heels to view the whole circumference of real-time data being presented, from the seemingly inane to the obviously significant. Within the space of just the few seconds it took to circle the room, 4 people had died, 6 were born and 18 new heartbeats had been found. If a heavenly stock exchange dealing in the shares of human souls was in existence, this might be what the trading floor looked like, minus the angels and demons in their multicoloured jackets trading life and death.

Poppy saw Estelle taking all this information in, too, her face reflecting the many colours of constantly changing statistics, bar graphs and pie charts dancing before her. Charles was motionless, staring straight at Poppy.

"This is what it's all about!" Charles sauntered towards Poppy. "Facts! Certainties! Indisputable evidence! Call it what you will, without it modern industry would collapse." Charles rested a hand on Estelle's shoulder, which refocused her attentions on Poppy. Charles lowered his voice. "We track, we measure, we record, we trend and we forecast."

Charles continued his slow, purposeful walk towards Poppy, his body only made visible through the reflection of the multicoloured light show racing round the room, yet his eyes never got lost amongst the distractions. "All this data is gained from the products and services offered by Rooftech, its holding company and its sister companies. It allows us to listen to our customers. Our customers can talk directly to us simply by using our products in the way they want to use them. If they change, we change."

"If you change, they change." Poppy countered, stepping forward.

Charles' impatience was wearing thin. "I don't think you're taking this situation as seriously as I had hoped."

"I don't know what you want from me," Poppy pleaded as Charles continued advancing towards her.

Charles could sense betrayal within her voice. He leaned in close to her and whispered, "Stop fucking me around."

Charles turned to face Estelle. "What do we need to do to make this girl talk?"

"Squeeze her where it hurts," Estelle responded with her natural reflexes, only to realise that what might hurt Poppy might also hurt her. That first feeling of being connected to someone via the intangible vagaries of lineage both surprised and strangely comforted her – before the fear set in.

"Exactly." With that, Charles grabbed Estelle by her jacket collar and dragged her towards the desk.

"What the fuck are you doing!" Estelle was in hysterics as Charles, who remained calm throughout, threw her onto the desk. Clamps firmly fixed her to the desk, clasping her ankles, legs, waist, wrists and neck.

Poppy ran over to her mother but was blocked by Charles. "Leave her alone! Let her go!"

"Shut it!" Charles screamed at her, knocking her back with pure sound waves alone. Charles turned to face Estelle who was still struggling to escape. "You can shut up, too! Stop moving – there's no way you're getting out of there until I let you go, so you may as well rest."

"Get me out of here immediately! Your superiors are going to hear about this!" Estelle's proclamations fell on deaf ears.

"They already know!" Charles pointed a small remote control at a screen. A boardroom of faces looked back.

"*Carry on, Charles.*"

Charles stepped towards the head of the table and gave Estelle a short, sharp slap across her face. "Can I get some bloody silence now?"

Poppy looked on in disgust. "You've gone mad."

"Have I finally got your bloody attention now? Life at the top ain't all champagne breakfasts and international conferences, you know. Sometimes you have to get your hands dirty." Charles stepped away from the desk and pressed another button on his remote control so the desk rotated one hundred and eighty degrees. Now, facing Poppy, it tilted Estelle's head up so she could see forward.

"Now where were we?" Charles theatrically said to no one in particular. "Oh yeah, you were going to tell me your father's plans."

"I'm not telling you anything."

Charles pressed another button and the roof spiralled open like a camera's aperture, letting in more light. The evening's glow lightened the room slightly and filled it with occasional, distant bird song. Charles pressed another button and a small single ray of light appeared on Estelle's forehead.

"How about telling me something now?"

Estelle couldn't see the light, but the reaction on Poppy's face told her she was now the focus of something unfavourable. "What is it, darling?"

"There's a beam of light on your forehead."

Estelle moved her head as much as she could to try and see the beam. It was only when she tilted her head back so much the clamp hurt her neck did a slight glint of light register. Estelle was immediately sure of this textbook negotiating tool. She'd attended the same training course as Charles. "Fuck you, Charles!"

Charles glided towards Poppy, completely ignoring Estelle's protestations. "Let me tell you what's going to happen before you leave."

Poppy looked into her mother's eyes until the view was blocked by the advancing Charles, who wanted Poppy's complete and undivided attention. He looked slightly embarrassed by the uncommonly savage tactics he had just employed and continued in a calm and professional manner.

"I know what your father is planning. I know what he has done and why he has done it. I know that he sent you up to London with the old man and the girl to cause a distraction. I also know he is a foolish man to take on Rooftech."

"If you know so much, why do you need me?"

"I also know he is stubborn. He is not going to stop marketing his new energy company simply because I tell him to. He isn't going to do anything I tell him to do."

"Looks like you're out of luck then."

"Not quite. *You're* going to tell him."

"Tell him what?"

"You're going to tell him to stop this whole stupid game."

Poppy smiled a genuine smile of incredulity. "He won't listen to me."

"No? Not his only girl? You better hope he does because if you don't, you'll never see your mother again."

Poppy laughed; a false, forced laugh. "My mother? Ha! You're seriously using my mother as a bargaining chip? I think your research is lacking in that department. I hate my mother!"

"Do you?" Charles lifted his remote device to the sky. Poppy moved past Charles and saw the light on Estelle's forehead had become slightly wider and brighter. Poppy ran to her mother and placed her hand on her forehead to shield her from the beam. Poppy gritted her teeth as she looked into her mother's eyes, her hand shaking, the intense heat burning into her skin.

Charles looked on admiringly, yet undeterred. "I started an account with a new power company this morning, 'AlbionSol'. You may have heard of it. This new company appears to provide a good, well-priced service. I thought I'd give them a test run and have them power this room. Good job, I think. Everything seems to be working."

Estelle looked pleadingly towards Charles. A tiny breath of smoke was rising from Poppy's hand, the hair and skin starting to burn.

"Enough!" Charles pressed another button, returning the beam to its original, harmless state. Poppy snatched her hand away, putting it to her mouth and using her tongue to help cool it down.

"Are you OK?" Estelle asked, still struggling to remove her wrists and ankles from the clamps.

"Yeah, I'm fine," Poppy answered whilst blowing on the back of her hand.

"Rooftech currently powers about twenty-eight million homes in the UK. That's about eighty-four per cent." Charles' words were echoed by graphs and charts on the screens behind him. "We're expecting a small one per cent growth this year as the new contracts are rolled out. However, your father is throwing a spanner in the works with his new enterprise, meaning I may not achieve this year's targets. This, as I'm sure you are now aware, is not acceptable. To help your motivation in convincing your father to stop what he is doing, I have programmed the satellite that is currently beaming a harmless glow upon your mother's head, to do so in direct proportion to AlbionSol's market share."

On the screen flashed up what looked like a very one-sided score line, but was in fact the total amount of customers Rooftech had versus AlbionSol. Currently the score stood at Rooftech 28,034,344 against AlbionSol's customer base of 1,355.

Poppy looked at the score and then back to Charles. "These numbers worry you?"

Charles looked back at the screen; AlbionSol had just gained 4 customers. "They should worry all of us. Once those 1,359 customers increase to 20,000, the beam changes from simply emitting light to becoming a tiny source of heat. When I start to lose one per cent of market share then ... well, let's just say that Estelle's anti-aging treatment won't be at the forefront of her mind anymore." Charles smiled at his own word play rather than the thought of Estelle's forehead implants melting.

"How am I meant to stop my father from launching AlbionSol? He's been working on this for years!" Poppy's eyes flittered from Charles to the score board and back again as she spoke.

"He's your father; you're his daughter. Surely you have ways to wrap Daddy around your little finger? If you don't, then you'd better get your thinking cap on because Mummy is going to be fried bread before the day's out if you don't succeed."

A short, subtle, electronic crescendo sounded, indicating newly updated sales figures. Poppy and Charles looked at the scoreboard. AlbionSol had gained one new customer. The swing 'o' meter graphic displayed centrally under the two competing scores wasn't detailed enough to register this slight fluctuation but Poppy could still picture in her mind one person walking from the large, safe arms of Rooftech and venturing over to the new, more financially rewarding side of AlbionSol.

The thought of more people defecting from Rooftech to The Colonel's new company, AlbionSol, which was offering a far better deal, buying energy generated at home and fed back into the national grid at a much better rate than Rooftech, had always seemed so exciting and romantic to Poppy. Now this dream was a nightmare. As her eyes moved from the scoreboard to her mother, there was nothing she wanted more than to keep the status quo.

"I better go." Poppy held her mother's hand.

"Wait! Charles, we can make a deal."

Charles looked at Poppy, then examined his nails. "What kind of deal?"

"Let me talk to The Colonel. Poppy's too soft. I know how to bring him round. Let me go and AlbionSol will be dead by the morning."

"And my collateral?"

Estelle said nothing. Her eyes didn't even move but Charles knew the answer.

"Come on Estelle, not even you ..."

Poppy joined the dots. "Mother?"

"Poppy, my darling. I can do so much more than you. I can finish this thing before dinner time and you'll be in your own bed by midnight. No harm would come to you at all, I promise. I'll speak to your father, tell him the danger you're in ..."

"No, please don't say these things ..." Poppy valiantly reached out a hand in hope as she stepped backwards for survival. "Mum, please."

Charles guided Poppy out. "Poppy, go. Find your father, tell him to stop AlbionSol and show your mother something about love."

A panel on the floor lit up to reveal an exit. Poppy walked over and stood on the panel, waiting to be lowered out of the room.

"Run along now, you don't want to leave your mother in the spotlight for too long." Charles walked over to stand next to Estelle.

As Poppy was lowered down, she looked at her mother.

Estelle just about managed to see Poppy sink below the floor line, a tear falling from her cheek as she turned her head sideward.

When her mother had disappeared from sight, Poppy took a last look at the scoreboard. AlbionSol had just gained another twenty-three customers. The Colonel's years of preparation were now being put into action – years of planning, recruiting, secret meetings – and now she had to convince her father it had to stop. It had to stop to save her mother, a woman who had abandoned her willingly and had never shown any sign she ever wanted her back. Poppy was going to have to think of something more effective than bursting into tears and storming off to her room to enforce a change of heart from her father.

With Poppy gone, Charles ran his fingers through Estelle's hair. She squirmed as he did so. "Just me and you, Estelle."

"'*You and I*', you fucking idiot!"

Charles grabbed her hair and pulled her head back. "I'm going to enjoy watching you burn."

"Already resigned to the fact you're going to lose business this week?" Estelle replied, spitting out the words.

"I'd gladly lose one per cent to see the last of you."

"You'll never get away with this. You've fucking lost it."

Charles let go of Estelle's hair and laughed. "Oh my God! You think they actually care about you? Holy shit! Estelle Hawthorne, the coldest fucking bitch on the planet actually thinks her employers care about her." Charles' laughter grew louder. "Is that laser frying your brain already?"

Charles walked over to the returned lift. "There are a hundred people willing to throw you to the lions to get your job. Gerard for example ..." With that, Charles exited the room.

Estelle stewed on her mistrust of Gerard as she watched the scoreboard show a spirited fight by AlbionSol. It had just gained customer No. 1,446.

CHAPTER 12

Duncan and Amy pushed their bikes up the remainder of an old footpath and headed into Wigthorn from the east, parallel with the coast, in the shadow of the Pharmara offices snaking across the top of the South Downs like a modern Hadrian's Wall. Their strength had taken them this far but the remaining few metres were too steep for them to cycle their old pedal-powered bikes up, especially since the bikes were in such bad condition, having been found behind a barn some fifteen kilometres previously. Duncan had often reminisced over his own pedal-powered bike he'd owned as a kid, but now all nostalgia withered along with his energy reserves as he fully appreciated the modern solar-powered bicycle, the sun powering electromagnets that repelled an adjustable ducted fan within the wheels, like a river turns a mill.

"Nearly there," Duncan announced breathlessly, trying to encourage Amy who was noticeably lagging behind.

As they both reached the top of the hill and walked into the all encompassing view of Wigthorn down below, the sun raised itself from its own slumber and peaked over the horizon behind them.

"What a view! Home sweet home," Duncan said, energised by the sight of his hometown in the warm morning light.

"Yeah, yeah beautiful." Amy threw down her bike, collapsing on the grass without a second glance towards Wigthorn.

Duncan saw Amy virtually passed out on the wet grass and let her take a moment's rest before they made their descent into Wigthorn itself. Looking out over Wigthorn and along its coastline, Duncan could clearly see the raised sea defences keeping out the English Channel. The rising sea levels had forced many parts of the UK coastline underwater, and indeed many parts of the world, but Wigthorn had rapidly built a solid wall of concrete along the old promenade to protect itself from the encroaching waters of Wigthorn Bay, bullied by the English Channel, itself overwhelmed by the might of the Atlantic Ocean. This wall proved to not only save the town from drowning, but to also save it from bankruptcy as it housed a huge shopping mall within its entire length, meaning a new sandy beach could be situated on top of it, replacing the old shingle beach. The new pier formed the centrepiece whilst the old pier became one of the most popular diving sites in the South East, a wreckage from the past containing ancient treasures such as a theatre, a wooden walkway, facilities for disabled people and arcade machines.

Seeing Wigthorn again helped renew Duncan's motivation. He had only been away for a few days but so much had happened to change his outlook on life, it felt as though years had passed since he'd been here last. His thoughts immediately turned to his granddaughter. He was desperate to see her, to let her know he was all right.

"Amy? Come on, we have to go."

"What's the hurry? We can rest here for a bit. The Colonel's crazy road show extravaganza stuff isn't happening for a few hours yet."

"No, we have to go now. I want to see my granddaughter before she goes to school."

"You're joking right? We can't go around visiting family members in Wigthorn right now, I don't know if you remember, but we need to lie low at the moment, plus we're carrying illegal equipment, illegal seeds and a ton of data stolen from the government. The last thing we ought to be doing right now is delivering Abby chocolate and teddy bears." Amy remained seated on the grass to emphasis her point. "We'll rest here for a bit, hide out in Wigthorn with The Colonel's help, then fly off into the Swiss sunset to collect our money. You can then get your seeds to the Doomsday Vault and I can go find somewhere with comfortable sun loungers and cute pool boys."

"You can stay here if you want, but I'm going into Wigthorn now to see my granddaughter. I may not get another chance."

"Later, you'll have all the time in the world to play grand-dad. Let's stick with the plan and get this thing done."

Duncan got on his bike. "Look, I'm going now. I'll catch up with you later."

"How are we going to meet up with each other?" Amy called to Duncan, who was already starting to freewheel down the hill.

"I don't know," Duncan shouted back.

"Bloody kids." Amy spat out dismissively to herself as she achingly got up and on her bike to chase after Duncan. Duncan had left everything with Amy, including the D 'n' Away sequencer; she knew Duncan would never survive without it.

Duncan knew it too.

Huddled under a large oak tree surrounded by hedges and weeds, part of a forgotten, overgrown end of someone's garden in the west of Wigthorn, Duncan and Amy were putting on a fresh coat of D 'n' Away after their sweat from cycling left them vulnerable to detection.

"I'm running out of juice here, Duncan."

"Here, you can have the rest of this." Duncan handed Amy his device.

Amy took the device and checked the display. "Hang on, you're applying the foal mixture. I've just put on a teenage boy's concoction!"

"Don't worry about it, as long as you don't raise any flags with your own DNA then you'll just be a glitch in the system."

"Being a glitch is still going to make me stand out though."

"Just put it on, who's really going to notice?" Duncan replied, impatient to visit his granddaughter.

Amy thought back to her own experience of seeing anomalies on the screen and somewhat agreed it would be all right. She just hoped the operative viewing this anomaly wasn't bored enough to want to investigate it further.

Having previously dispensed with their bikes in a boating lake, Duncan made it clear to Amy she needed to stay out of sight for just ten minutes. "I won't be long, OK? I'm just going to knock on her window and say hello."

"Your family don't do front doors or something?"

"I can't let my son and his wife know I'm here."

"Why not?"

"They'll tell Pharmara Security – they'll have to. They'd be breaking their employment contract if they didn't and I don't blame them – they wouldn't be good parents if they suddenly allowed themselves to become unemployed and lose their Wigthorn citizenship privileges."

"OK, don't be long. I'll stay here and wait for you to get back."

"See you in a minute." Duncan ran through one of the hedges and made a stumbling effort to scale a fence into his son's garden.

Crouching down on the other side of the fence hiding behind some bushes, the ones he planted for his son two years ago, Duncan picked up some tiny stones and gently threw them at a window just in front of him whilst whispering his granddaughter's name. "Abby!"

The time was about 7.30am, fifteen minutes before Abby was due to be woken by her parents for school. Duncan wasn't sure if she was a light sleeper or not. When Abby had stayed at his house, Nicole had always been the one to wake her and put her to bed. Duncan was always down in his underground greenhouse preserving the purity of Mother Nature's offerings. Sitting out here, not totally confident this was actually Abby's room he was chucking stones at, Duncan questioned whether he had organised his priorities as meticulously as he had organised his crop rotation. Today felt like the first time he had ever placed family above his work.

"Abby!" Duncan whispered again after another stone had rattled the window, a little too loudly for his liking.

Fortunately for Duncan, his limited climbing skills were no longer needed as Abby's bedroom lay on the ground floor. A light came on through the curtains, illuminating cartoon dancing characters and bringing a sigh of relief to Duncan. Then, a few seconds later, the curtain itself started twitching. Duncan stuck his head out from the shadows so Abby could easily see him.

Through the gap in the curtain an entangled mess of light brown hair protruded, then came a hand to wipe away some of the hair, revealing two tired eyes and a yawning mouth. Duncan stepped out of the shadows with a broad grin.

"Abby!"

The yawn widened into a grin and the tired eyes brightened as both hands framed the front of her face to tie back her hair. Through the glass, Duncan could see her mouth the word 'Granddad' excitedly. She had a smile like Nicole's, a genetic echo Duncan never tired of appreciating.

Abby told the house computer to open the window and as it slid up she stuck her head and arms out and they hugged, Duncan looking into her bedroom to make sure her door was shut, Abby looking out towards the garden wondering what her granddad was doing here so early on a school day.

"Abby, Abby, it's so good to see you."

"Granddad, where have you been? Mummy says people are looking for you to make sure you're all right. Is it because you miss Grandma?"

Duncan looked into Abby's eyes. "I'm OK. I miss Grandma but I'm OK. What about you?"

"I'm OK, too, Granddad. I miss Grandma as well. Do you want me to make you breakfast?"

Duncan smiled at her. "No, I can't." Her selflessness was not a character trait from his side of the genetic coin. "I've only passed by to say hello to you as some people are still looking for me, but it's important they don't find me, do you understand?"

"Why are they looking for you? Are you in trouble?"

"They think I've done something bad, but I haven't, I promise you. I need to go and make things right and then I'll be straight back here for you. I'm going to be a better grand-dad from now on. We're going to do a lot more things together."

"Good." Abby reached out and hugged Duncan again. An eight year old didn't need explanations. Their instincts are still finely tuned and uncomplicated by adult life. As they stood in the morning sun hugging each other, Abby trying to keep her family together and Duncan clinging onto the past, they heard a door closing on the floor above.

"Abby, someone's awake. Don't tell Mummy or Daddy I was here, OK?"

"OK." Abby's face suddenly lit up as she remembered something. "Granddad, wait a minute, let me just get some-thing." Abby left the window and ran to her bedroom door, opened it and disappeared. Duncan moved to the side of the window in case a parent walked past.

A few seconds later, Duncan heard the bedroom door close and carefully peered through the window to see if it was Abby returning. It was. "Granddad, look its Grandma's 'mobbie'!" Abby handed Duncan one of the mobile devices his wife had used. "I heard Daddy say you better come home soon to tie up Grandma's loose ends before they start tying you up. What does he mean, Granddad?"

"Your father means that Grandma did everything for Granddad and now she's gone I need to dig my head out of the sand and start organising my own life like an adult."

Abby chuckled. "You *are* an adult, Granddad. You're old!"

Duncan smiled. "Thanks!" Time wasn't on his side. Now he had to pass on his inheritance. "Abby, can you keep secrets?"

"Of course, Miranda told me once that—"

"OK, OK," Duncan quickly moved on. "I've written a letter to you. It's in this envelope but ..." Duncan passed it to Abby, not letting go until he'd finished his sentence. "... I don't want you to open it until your eighteenth birthday."

"That's millions of years though, Granddad!"

Duncan put his fingers to his closed lips and twisted an invisible key. Abby copied her granddad with a cheeky smile.

"I know. It seems like it now but, believe me, it'll come round soon enough. Look, I've written on it *Don't open until you're 18*, so if you're ever tempted, remember that Grandma will be keeping an eye on you."

Abby's face dropped. It broke Duncan's heart to be so cruel, but the letter, containing a small amount of words and a large amount of money in a Swiss bank account, just had to be kept secret for a little while longer.

"Come here, my princess." Duncan reached up and gave her a hug. To hell with anyone who might come in. He wasn't going to leave his granddaughter on a cruel lie. "I love you, Abs."

"I love you, too, Sugarpops."

Amy was crouched down against a tree, hidden on all sides by bushes, drinking water from a bottle and enjoying getting some rest from the night's journey to the south coast. A mixture of public transport, hitch hiking, walking and cycling had finally brought them to Wigthorn.

Occasionally Amy would take a look over the hedge to make sure no one was about. Someone walked their dog past a few minutes ago and an early commuter had left the house over the road but apart from that, everyone else was still tucked up in bed, somewhere she'd like to be.

Whilst looking over the hedge one more time, something small landed on the ground just in front of her. Amy turned round to see what it was, but she couldn't be sure as the ground under the oak tree was covered in twigs, leaves, stones and other remnants of suburban foliage. Amy then looked upwards to see where the unidentified object had come from; she wasn't expecting to look into the green eyes of a strange man sitting on a branch looking back down at her.

He raised a finger to his mouth to preserve the peace, nudged himself off his perch and glided gracefully to the ground, a thin cord slowing him down at the last minute. Amy scrambled backwards away from the tree trunk, further into a hedge. He greeted Amy with a smile. "Don't be scared, I'm with The Colonel. He wanted us to bring you in."

"Who's 'us'?"

"I'm James. I'm an Unrecorded." James stepped forward towards her and stuck out an open hand, inviting her to stand closer to him.

"What are you doing?" she said, stepping forward at the same time.

"We need to go. Duncan's whereabouts have been discovered by Pharmara and they'll be here any minute."

No sooner had James finished speaking, the surrounding area lit up with flashing blue lights from two Pharmara Security vans silently hovering around the corner at top speed. James grabbed Amy, pulling her down behind a hedge.

"We have to go, now."

"I can't leave without Duncan."

"He's just about to jump over the fence."

Just as predicted, Duncan landed on the ground beside Amy. "We've got to go ... Who's this?"

James introduced himself quickly and succinctly, eager to get this rescue mission off successfully. "I'm James. We have to disappear immediately. Amy's D 'n' Away solution is deteriorating and we're sticking out like a sore thumb. They'll soon notice a half horse, half human anomaly and realise we're no longer living in ancient Greek times with centaurs." James gently squeezed Amy's arm and winked to let her know he was joking. Amy smiled at his wink, not having the faintest idea what 'ancient Greece' or 'centaurs' were but enjoying the intimacy nonetheless.

Another guy descended from the tree like a panda falling from a bamboo feast; well built with short cropped black hair and a black eye. "Jimbo, we having a picnic or something? Let's get a shift on, old son! Come here, Granddad!" Duncan was unceremoniously grabbed by two tattooed arms and just as he turned towards Amy in shock they sped upwards into the oak's canopy.

James wrapped both his arms around Amy's waist. "Hold on tight, Amy Jay."

Amy reached up and put her arms around James' neck. "Don't let go of me." Amy reeled herself in, embarrassed at how easily she fell into the damsel in distress role at the drop of a pair of kind eyes and strong arms.

"I won't."

"Mummy, Mummy! There's someone at the door." Abby came running up the stairs to alert her mother who had only just got up and was in the bathroom. "Daddy! Wake up!"

"OK, OK, darling. I heard Sissy the first time." Ryan, Duncan's only child and Abby's father, got out of bed and put on a t-shirt and tracksuit bottoms to answer the door. Abby followed close behind, wanting to hear every word but trying not to let on that anything out of the ordinary had happened today.

"Who is it?" Ryan asked the house computer.

"Gerard Abbot, Pharmara employee, position classified."

"OK, open the door."

As the large faux mahogany door slid to the left, two men stood in suits, one looking intently into a small device, the other awaiting the house owner.

"Good morning, sir. I'm Gerard Abbot of Pharmara. I believe colleagues of mine have been here before with regards to your father, Duncan Hartley."

"Yes, they have. Have you found him?" Abby stood behind her father with her arms around his waist, peering up at Gerard who returned a discomfited smile.

"We are still looking, sir. I'm afraid he has been eluding us up to now. The reason I am calling though is we recently picked up a reading of one of Nicole Hartley's personal devices and were wondering if you had switched one of them back on?"

"No, we haven't touched any of them. I think we have three in the kitchen, all of which have been switched off for a few days now."

"Would you mind checking to see if those three devices are still in the house, sir? We picked up one of them being activated not far from here."

"Yes, of course." Ryan walked into the kitchen and opened a drawer where he found two of the devices. Pulling the drawer out further and rummaging around did not reveal the third device. Ryan hastily searched a couple more drawers but found nothing.

Meanwhile, Gerard was exposed to a child, a non-entity in his world of consumer rights and copyright protection. Abby was exposed to potentially revealing a truth, still a student of the nurtured art of lying.

Gerard took the adult step of papering over any awkward silences. "So, do you enjoy school?"

Abby noticed his eyes drift over her shoulder towards her father looking for the missing device in the kitchen. "I want to be a farmer like my granddad!" she said emphatically to regain his fullest attention.

It worked. "Really? And what exactly does a 'farmer' do?"

"She grows things." Abby slipped in an oft-repeated phrase from Duncan.

Gerard shirked at the sheer blasphemy. "You'll get all dirty though. You don't want to mess up that beautiful hair of yours, do you?"

"I'd wear a hat." Abby turned to see her father returning down the hallway.

Ryan put an arm around Abby. "I'm sorry but we seem to have lost one. It's not in the house. You mentioned picking up a transmission outside our house – can't you still track it?"

"No, it was only switched on briefly about ten minutes ago. Has anyone been here this morning?"

"No one's been here. We've only just woken up."

Gerard looked over Ryan's shoulder into the house. "OK, I'll take those two remaining devices with me and leave you in peace."

"Huh? You can't take these – they're my mother's."

"They're evidence in a criminal investigation and still the property of Pharmara. Your employment contract stipulates full co-operation in internal contract breaches ... Unless, of course, you wanted to end your contract with Pharmara?"

Not only was this man hunting down her granddad, but now he was being mean to her father on their very doorstep. A genetic mutation inherited from Duncan skipped past her father and landed at Abby's feet. She pulled at her daddy's arm, paraphrasing a line from her homework in a whisper. "Not good idea to remove the bait from the trap, Daddy."

Ryan looked at Abby in horror. His job, their house – everything was on the line with this level of insubordination. Ryan looked at Gerard, hoping he hadn't heard, or at least, understood.

Gerard smiled. He'd been interrogating the wrong Hartley. "Oh, don't think I swallow bait offered by the enemy so easily, my little general. I know the bait is you, not the phones."

Gerard snatched the devices from Ryan's hand and left without ceremony, secretly pleased his latest assignment pitted him against worthy adversaries. It was in their DNA.

Ryan remained entranced by his daughter. "Where the hell did you learn that?"

Abby looked back, exasperated and unimpressed. "Daddy, don't you know anything? We've started Sun Tzu in Business Management class this year. Come on, I'll be late for school again."

Ryan shouted up to his wife as Abby ran to her room. "Darling, do you know our eight year old daughter is learning warfare strategy at school?"

An indifferent reply from the master bedroom surfed down the stairs on the hairdryer's breeze. "Yes, love."

CHAPTER 13

"Are we ever going to move out of this bloody tree?" Amy exclaimed.

The two guys had lifted Amy and Duncan up towards the tree where, unexpectedly, a car hung motionless. Hidden amongst the leaves and branches, directly above the metallic road, the car used a specially enhanced magnetised system to elevate it further.

"Surely we'll get spotted up here?" Amy tried to restrain her panic, the vertigo taking control once again, yet she couldn't tear herself away from looking out the window.

James turned around from a display at the front of the box shaped vehicle. "Don't worry, kids, we've got a holographic display on the base disguising us from wondering eyes below, and there are enough leaves and branches on top to confuse spying eyes from above, making them think we're actually ten centimetres off the ground and not ten metres."

James turned back to the display and addressed the big guy who was sitting next to him. "Al, looks like they're going. Get us down from here and we'll head into town."

As the two Pharmara vans drove off down the road, Al de-activated the holo-projection and started their descent onto the road. As soon as they were on the ground and moving along, Duncan sat back in his chair at the rear of the car, pulled out Nicole's old device from his pocket and started to scroll through various emails.

Al set a course for Wigthorn's town centre and remained at the head of the car working on some other matters. James left Al to it and moved back to see how Amy was. Amy greeted him with a smile, moving to one side to give him some space.

"Who are 'The Unrecorded'?" Amy asked, interested to see how his explanation might differ with Julius'.

"It's more of a way of life than an organised group. There are no central tenets, meetings or funny handshakes. It's simply a bunch of people that do business the old fashioned way: bartering face to face. We aren't on any databases, we stay out of sight from the satellites, we buy everything from independent sources, and all our communications are done on a closed network. That's how we stay unrecorded."

"Why stay unrecorded, though?"

"Basically, so we don't get hassled and given the hard sell. We're like an 'anti-target audience'. The satellites, the DNA recognition, product tracking, the huge network of domestic computers and appliances, this is not simply for control. As you know, this is research to better product offering. If everyone stopped eating cornflakes tomorrow, they'd stop making cornflakes – they're not forcing anyone to eat cornflakes. The thing is, they know that people like cornflakes, there's no chance everyone in the country would stop eating them, and so they want to know more about how, where, why and when do people eat cornflakes. Over the years, competition has forced every company to up the ante, improve or die. Now cornflake manufacturers know everything about every packet of cornflakes they've ever produced."

"And the problem with maximising profit is …?"

James leaned in closer. "There are limits. Business has come as close as it legally can to gaining information and maximising profit. There is no more third world to exploit, no more information that can be squeezed out of consumers, and materials cannot be manufactured or purchased any more cheaply. Now, companies have to push at the one limit that can still be pushed against."

"Which is …?"

"The law. What they legally can and cannot do is the only barrier stopping them from maximising profits even further. You've seen for yourself how government information can be accessed and shared without too much difficulty. Legally, that should be highly private and sensitive data."

"That's not all. Duncan and I found some disturbing trends in the data we retrieved." Amy looked towards Duncan, but his head was buried in Nicole's device, so Amy continued. "We think domestic businesses and government are not only selling data to foreign businesses and governments, but are also conducting tests and experiments in the so-called 'corporately owned' towns on behalf of themselves and these foreign interests."

James sat back pensively. "Yes, we've thought this for a while, but haven't had any tangible evidence to support it. Of course, this evidence is all well and good, but it means nothing without the public institutions around to enforce any kind of change."

"You could use it as leverage."

"Against what? To gain what? It's not as if we can use the media to expose this –all lines of communication are controlled. You think the people who are being used want to take action? Being a guinea pig is their job! Without it, they'd be living on the street eating out of bins."

Al turned around from his display. "Jimbo, we just got confirmation from London. The internet is shutting down in one hour. We've got a window of three hours, until midday, or until we get shutdown beforehand."

"Great stuff. Tell The Colonel."

Amy looked at James in disbelief. "You can *shutdown the internet*?"

James laughed. "Well, only in this country, for a few hours. Plus, it's not really us doing it. We aim to stay off the record but we like to remain in the loop, if you know what I mean. We're small and flexible, we can move around easily, cover our tracks – but they can't. We like to keep our ear to the ground and see which way the wind is blowing."

Amy raised an eyebrow at the volley of sayings. "Which means what in English?"

"We've infiltrated the communications systems of the two main media outlets in the UK. They think Al here is a sales director in both their holding companies. Over the past two years we have been setting things up for today."

"Shutting down the internet will cause chaos!"

"No, that's not what we want. We want to shut down the internet to get people outside. We want them to stop watching TV programmes, visiting websites, emailing friends, chatting to family, liking cat videos – we want them to leave their houses. We've convinced the two media companies to experiment in controlled media output, enhancing the symbiosis between media consumption and retail consumption. The current cannibalism between the two is costing money; greater controls can produce savings. This will result in their retail outlets increasing profits whilst all the entertainment is switched off."

"They bought that?"

"It took two years of hard work and co-operation by a few likeminded people, but yes, they'll taste anything that smells like profit."

"So they're going to pull the plug on all internet access to boost retail profits ... That's not bad going, Jimbo. So, what do you plan on people doing with all this free time?"

"That's when The Colonel starts selling AlbionSol."

Amy's smile started to recede as the positive aura emanating from James faded into the ether. "So, you're going to use all this free time to continue selling to people? Isn't that hypocritical?"

"What do you mean?"

"You're getting people out of their homes because you're not able to buy airtime?"

"Yeah, exactly."

"So all this, 'The Unrecorded', is just a creative sales technique, a hacker's version of direct marketing? All this talent and potential and you're using it to *promote a product*? You're just a fucking salesman!"

"Hey! Easy, sweetheart, don't get your knickers in a twist," replied James. Al looked round in surprise. "Not so long ago a little bird told me you would be getting a financial reward in direct proportion to the success of the information you stole."

It was true. Amy was working on commission, too. What kind of businessman such as The Colonel would give away most of his wealth for the good of the common man? He was simply creating a new business and recruiting the necessary help to make it happen. What made AlbionSol so special? Amy had been seduced by The Colonel's ranting, about wanting to change the balance of power; the trouble was, he wanted to move it in his direction.

"You know, James, you're absolutely right – I'm no better than you. Thinking we're Good Samaritans, helping those less fortunate than us, people with fewer choices to better their lives before they're stuck in a corporate town, going to a sponsored school that only aspires to give them the skills for a menial position with minimum wage and loyalty points ... We're fucking idiots!" Amy got up, moved to the back of the car and sat next to Duncan, whose head was still buried in the device, not listening to a word that was going on. "We should be doing more to corrupt this monopoly of power. You have the tools and yet you choose to serve a different master, but a master all the same."

James and Al were getting restless at this surge of aggressive questioning. "A master who pays for us quite handsomely to live the rest of our lives in sunnier climes and with, may I be so bold, hotter, more palatable chicks than you get here! We help you and this is the thanks we get?"

Amy sat back and toned down her accusatory approach. "You're a fake. Just because you don't do the nine-to-five, doesn't make you a rebel. Just because you're unrecorded, doesn't mean the footprints you leave behind have any less of an impression."

Al had heard enough. "Jimbo, shut this fucking bitch up. We don't need her going loco at The Colonel and halting our tasty little transaction once the data's handed over."

Amy smiled. "This is a game, isn't it? A rich kid's game. You get everything as a kid living in an iPatch town, not wanting for anything, and then when it comes to breaking free from Daddy's purse strings, you put all that education and opportunity to good use, finding the quickest way to live the easiest life – which is to find a surrogate Daddy."

Al turned around in his seat to get a better view. "Man! She's got a fucking mouth."

James remained simmering just below boiling point. "You got any more?"

"Just one thing," Amy remarked, as she gestured for Duncan to give her the mobile device. Duncan gave it up without a word, unaware of the tensions within the car, focused on the streets passing by and the wife who'd left him behind.

"I need to inform The Colonel I've analysed the data in more depth." Amy's fingers danced over the screen.

"He's already been informed that we've rescued you and you're on your way."

Amy held up the mobile device. "But what if this new analysis is destroyed? It might affect your payment, right?"

James looked at Al incredulously, making a move to grab the mobile device. As soon as he did, Amy shouted, "Sky roof. Omega, gamma, gamma, bravo!"

This outburst of Greek resulted in three events happening almost simultaneously. Firstly, the whole of the roof slid back to reveal the open sky above. Secondly, two beams of light appeared from the heavens and locked on to both Al and James. Lastly, Al and James looked up into the sky, tracking the beams onto their own persons before recoiling in excruciating pain and falling unconscious on the floor.

Duncan immediately snapped out of his daydreaming. "What the hell was that?"

Amy remained seated. "That, my friend, was justice from beyond the grave. Nicole subscribed to a crime protection service helping people in need by zapping any potential intruders or attackers. You may have heard of them: 'Thor Security'."

Duncan felt like he had just stepped into another dimension. "No, never heard of them."

"We got a discount as they're a sister company of Pharmara … but anyway, whilst I was talking, I messaged them via Nicole's phone, told them my husband and I were getting car-jacked inside our hire car and our attackers had threatened us with violence. They told me to open the sky roof so they could disable them."

"What was all the 'gamma, gamma' stuff?"

"Well, I don't own this car but Thor Security sent me the override code, and there you have it." Amy got up from her seat, straightened herself out, grabbed her rucksack and got out the car. "Duncan, we better leave before either of those two wake up and Thor's security staff arrive."

Duncan grabbed his own bag, following Amy. "So those guys were going to attack us?"

"I don't think they would've seriously hurt us." Amy stopped. Duncan seemed to be elsewhere. "Duncan, what's up? You have no idea what just went on and you look like you've seen a ghost?"

"It's Nicole. I think she was having an affair."

CHAPTER 14

A courtesy car had driven Poppy from the Rooftech headquarters in Mossyface Wood south to a public car park in the centre of Wigthorn. It was now parking itself in a hive-like structure consisting of five hexagonal towers with a central atrium so cars could be magnetically lifted then rotated into an available space.

Before the car even rose from the ground to its new home, Poppy was already running out of the parking structure on the hunt for her father to stop the nationwide AlbionSol sales drive. Driving into Wigthorn, Poppy had seen an impressive laser show in the sky, alternating between the two stages of the hills to the north and the sea to the south. Going into town Poppy could see unmanned advertising vehicles driving a pre-programmed patrol to rally the home owners of suburbia. These travelling salesmen preaching the good word of an end to energy monopolisation were cubes dressed in display screens on each side, showing five second snapshots of AlbionSol's selfless mission statements …

A father leaning against the wind turbine erected at the back of his house, smiling as he watches his young children play in the garden :: AlbionSol – Paying YOU and your family a fair price!

A young couple walk through a shopping mall arm-in-arm, clearly pleased with their day's haul :: AlbionSol – Keeping the three day working week a reality!

A man in his fifties sits in the latest luxury sports car with his peers in the background, all very impressed :: AlbionSol – Earn more than Rooftech!

Patriotic images of flag and country :: AlbionSol – The Soul of Albion!

The messages were simple and unsophisticated; they didn't need to be anything else. Anything involving any subtlety or thought processes on the part of the consumer would have been lost.

Poppy ran down the quiet street from the car park into the main town centre. All around her were tributes to her father's energy company: lasers and zeppelins in the sky, leaflets on the ground, advertising vans on her left, homeless people wearing sponsored clothing on her right, and all around were bubbles and balloons in the AlbionSol corporate colours of orange, blue and white.

She continued running through the busy town centre like a slalom skier, avoiding all the shoppers who seemed happy with the distraction. Kids loved the balloons, the zeppelins and the lasers; an unexpected party had appeared for no reason and everyone was invited. The adults were admiring the rarity of actual leaflets in their hands, immune to the electronic messages hitting them from all angles on their mobile devices, home and in-car computers, at work, on the motorway, in town, everywhere. How nice, they thought, to have a piece of paper in your hand. It seemed so classy and old fashioned.

Poppy stopped in the middle of the main square to see if there was any sort of command centre for this supposed chaos. She couldn't see anything obvious. During the planning stages, all command centres were going to be mobile. Poppy pulled her mobile device out, trying to see if she could get through to her father; his device had been switched off for the past few days. It still was. She tried to call Julius, but his device was inactive, too. In fact, all external functions of Poppy's device had been rendered inactive. Poppy looked up and noticed others were also struggling to use their devices.

Suddenly a voice started speaking in her ear. It was an advertisement for AlbionSol. All mobile devices were now receiving this message. People in the square were getting out their devices with obvious disgust and switching them off. Others were intrigued and excited by this electronic kidnapping. Poppy recognised the voice even though hearing it was strange: it was her own.

Gerard had told Poppy her father was in Wigthorn, but now she was here there was no way to contact him.

In the commotion of a town under siege by the forces of marketing, both traditional and modern, a countdown was heard from above in a non-threatening voice so as not to scare everyone. Pedestrians, shoppers and residents all looked up and saw the bottoms of the four zeppelins were now displaying a countdown of twenty seconds. As the countdown continued to be announced from the four zeppelins of the apocalypse, kids joined in from below, excited at whatever would happen when the zero came.

Poppy had come up with this idea herself one day after reading about a zeppelin that had travelled across the Atlantic to New York many years ago. Pandemonium was sure to follow, that was the plan, so Poppy made a rapid exit out of the town square and into a street leading away. As she heard people count down to one, she looked up with the rest of them and saw all four zeppelins explode and the sky fill with multicoloured smoke and fireworks. The surrounding crowds made approving sighing noises when the clouds started to rain down glittery ticker tape and streamers shimmering in the morning sunshine, captivating the audience with sparkling messages of improved energy compensation.

Poppy allowed herself a proud smile; the scene was more beautiful than she ever imagined, like getting front row seats to see the last breath of a supernova and being showered in its stardust.

She noticed her imagination was being appreciated by others, too, but she had no time to enjoy it. Any more time wasted meant the increased likelihood of her mother meeting a similar but less flamboyant end.

Poppy ran down the street with no handle on her destination or direction. No matter where she was going, she would get there quicker by running, so she ran faster.

Halfway down the street, people started coming out of their houses, one by one. Pale faces, unblemished by vigorous activity or sunlight, appeared at their front doors, curious as to what was going on outside but wary of what may lie in wait. Neighbours turned to face each other for the first time in years, some started conversations and others smiled at each other, all awoken by the complete lack of distractions being pumped into their brains. The satellite transmissions had gone dead and in its wake, eyes stuck in the skulls of people who could only relax when consuming a million bits of information a second, were suddenly left to stare at a blank display and their own reflection in the screen of a lifeless mobile device. Out they crept, smelling the un-air-conditioned outdoors, feeling the non-carpeted garden path and seeing perfectly rendered three-dimensional people. This was almost too much information for them to handle.

Poppy sprinted past these slow motion pedestrians, dodging in and out of them as they shuffled onto the pavement. Running was becoming increasingly hazardous as more people emerged from their houses, turning their heads upwards so virtually everyone on the street was keeping their eyes on anything but the street.

Poppy could hear people as she slowed her sprint to a brisk walk:

"Well, hello Daisy. How're the grandchildren?"

"Dad, look at the fireworks!"

"Dave, are you ever going to mow this lawn? Look at it!"

"What's this leaflet doing here, Dad?"

"Mum, look at the monkey riding the dog!"

Poppy had to turn around for that one. There it was, a monkey riding a Labrador. The monkey had a bag over its shoulder and was chucking leaflets all over the place as the Labrador jumped over walls, hedges, through gardens and across roads. The monkey was no more a skilled rider than strapped on for dear life, but his commitment to delivering the leaflets was admirable. As this unusual postal service sped past Poppy, a leaflet was thrown in her direction so she picked it up: 'We pay YOU more than Rooftech for YOUR energy – Visit www.AlbionSol.com to find out more!'

Once again, the message may not have been as expertly honed or uniquely delivered as the leaflet itself, but its simplicity was as equally attention grabbing.

Poppy screwed the leaflet up and chucked it back on the pavement. She looked around erratically, not knowing what her next step should be, panicking that wasted seconds were contributing to her mother's melt down. Poppy's heart beat faster, the adrenaline kicking up a notch, her breathing increasing, the sweat seeping through her skin and her face straining to keep the oncoming flood of tears at bay. Frustration was boiling up within her as she sensed a countdown to her own dramatic explosion.

A small vibration in her jeans pocket halted the mounting pressure as Poppy's mobile device alerted her to a text message from an anonymous number.

"Follow me."

Poppy looked at her device for more information such as a link to a map application, co-ordinates or something more hidden within the message, but she couldn't find anything. Disappointed, she placed it back into her pocket, returning her dejected gaze to the floor where a small light shone on the pavement just ahead of her. She stepped forward and saw there were words within the light:

Follow me.

She looked up to follow a beam of light, but there was nothing. Looking down again, the light danced on the paving slabs, urging her to follow. She obliged, relinquishing to a stronger sense of purpose and direction.

Poppy tracked the illuminated words down the road, constantly looking over her shoulder, keeping an eye out for anyone following her, but everyone seemed much more interested in the various street and air shows going on all around them. If this light were a trap by Pharmara Security, why wouldn't they just send a few goons along to apprehend her rather than conducting this charade? No, Poppy was fairly confident this was her father reaching out to her, keeping his location a secret until he was sure she wasn't being followed and couldn't be tracked. Poppy put an extra spring in her step knowing she was closer to saving her mother. She kept walking ahead of the light, urging it to speed up and quicken their journey.

The voice of a young Wigthorn resident interrupted her thoughts, bellowing out of a bedroom window on the other side of the road and directed at a man standing in the front garden below holding a mobile device in one hand and an AlbionSol leaflet in the other.

"Dad, we're back online!"

The father looked around to his neighbour. "Here, Dave! I just signed up with this AlbionSol company and they've got me back on the internet, increased my energy payments and credited my account a month in advance, all in about two minutes. You should give it a bash – might keep the wife quiet!"

"Good call," Dave agreed. His wife was a nightmare.

Dave retrieved the mobile device from his pocket and began to switch his account. Poppy watched, realising this must be happening all over Wigthorn and in every other town and city identified by Amy, giving AlbionSol the greatest chance of taking a sizeable share of UK domestic energy production.

The light continued forward without Poppy as she watched this sideshow of the main event. Poppy sprinted after it, a new sense of urgency turning the heat up and reigniting her panicked state. Good news for AlbionSol meant bad news for her mother. She soon reached the light, shouting as she ran past, "Come on!"

The light reached a crossroads. It headed down the smaller road leading into the old part of Wigthorn. Poppy waited for a moment at the crossroad to see if the light had made a mistake – there was nothing much in the old part of town – but the light waited for her, encouraging Poppy to follow with a ritual-istic dance.

Poppy followed, less enthusiastically, as she was leaving the crowd behind. She supposed it made sense for her father to hide out somewhere the ubiquitous camera was less focused and the omnipresent satellite less overbearing.

The light stopped outside the old library. Unused for dec-ades, it sat in a derelict state of repair due to the long arm of redevelopment not stretching this far east. Windows smashed and doors on their hinges, yet the entire collection of books still sitting on the shelves, damp, dusty, deemed useless by the web, and now slowly being deleted by spiderwebs. Not worth stealing and not worth protecting.

The light disappeared. This must be her destination. The old library was deserted but satellites could track undisguised human activity here and access would be easy for any security forces.

Poppy heard a door open at the side of the library, but no one came out. She went round to investigate what had caused the door to open. The more she approached, the more the doorway revealed its occupant: an arm, a head, a body, legs, a man standing. Then she saw who it was: Julius.

"I can't come out." Julius pointed upwards.

Poppy, relieved she had trusted her instincts, walked through the doorway and gave Julius a big hug to anchor her scattered emotions. After a few seconds of relaxing in Julius' arms and allowing his calmness to permeate, she caught her-self in the act of hugging an employee of her fathers and retired, apologetically.

Julius smiled at her. "Come on, your father has been wait-ing for you."

"It has to stop, Julius," Poppy told Julius as she followed him down a dark stairwell. "It all has to stop now!"

They went down the stairs, along a few corridors and down some more stairs, until Julius stood in front of a door before opening it for Poppy. "The Colonel is in here."

Poppy strode in, knowing she had to stop the AlbionSol promotional drive to save her mother's life. A simple concept to convey, and yet she knew her father's suspicions of simplicity.

"Father!" She ran to The Colonel and fell into his arms. He held her tight, relieved to see his daughter had survived her excursions intact.

"Where are the others?"

"We got split up. They should be down here in Wigthorn." Poppy lifted her head to address him face to face and distract his attention from the quilt of media displays blanketing the far side of the room. "Father, this must stop. All this has to stop. Mother is being held by Rooftech. Charles Sand is going crazy trying to protect their market share. He's going to kill her unless you stop gaining customers!"

The Colonel looked into Poppy's eyes. "Mother? You call her Mother?"

"She's my mother, yes. You have to stop it now, Father!"

"She has been no mother to you, my darling."

"Please! Just stop this game!" Poppy rushed to the nearest display and tried to press buttons on the touch screen display but nothing happened. "This has to stop, Father!" Poppy saw footage of a street promotion happening in an old town square. Looking at the text below, she saw it read 'Chester'.

A promotional co-ordinator was sitting by the next display, running the scheduling of marketing attacks on Bristol. Poppy pleaded with him in a whisper, "You must stop this now, just tell them all to stop what they're doing and go home."

The Colonel walked over to her, gently leading her away. "This can't be stopped. It's too late. Too much planning has gone into this. You know that – you helped with it." The Colonel pulled up a chair and sat Poppy down, turning it away from the rows of displays that showed the vast scale of the AlbionSol promotional blitz.

The Colonel got down on one knee in front of the chair and spoke softly. "We're making progress, Poppy. Look over there; we've got a million customers already."

Poppy's head shot up from her hands, tears silently streaming down her face as she tried to read the display for herself. If ten thousand customers meant the laser started to generate heat, then how hot would it be with a million customers? Was Estelle dead already, or was there still time?

Poppy leaned forward and held both of her father's hands. "Please, just stop this. Estelle is dying. You can save her."

The Colonel stood up sharply, throwing Poppy's hands away. "Enough! Save one life and stop a revolution that will free millions? Would that one life do the same if the tables were turned? You think your precious, part-time mother would help save others?" The Colonel crouched down quickly and filled Poppy's view to emphasis his point and block the screens. "No."

Poppy held out her phone, pleading with her father. "Just call Rooftech, tell them it was all a mistake, just a demonstration and not real. Tell Charles he can have all his customers back so he can release Estelle straight away." Poppy played with a few buttons. "Here, it's ringing; you can speak with Charles directly. Please father ..."

The Colonel took the phone and held it to his ear, waiting for someone to answer. When they did, The Colonel replied, "No, it's her father."

The Colonel laughed at the response. "This is no game, Charles. This is for real. How does it feel to see market share slipping through your fingers by the second? Seems you've forgotten the art of competition. Too many victories have made you slow and lazy; you better put this year's bonus on ice, old boy!"

The Colonel smiled to himself as he paced around in front of Poppy.

Poppy's frustration grew at not being able to hear both sides of the conversation until she could no longer contain it. "It's just a demo, Charles! You can let Estelle go! Please, it's not real!"

The Colonel turned his back on Poppy. "Oh, it's for real, Charles, don't worry about that."

The Colonel hung up the phone then walked over to a nearby desk, picked up a legal electronic device and handed it to Poppy.

"This is our weapon of choice: the competitive contract. The fight against corporate monopolies will be signed, sealed and delivered via contracts. We can't rely on government to break it up. Genuine competition has to evolve from the outside and infiltrate the ..." Poppy had read the contract, hearing her father's diatribe many times before. She glanced through it whilst attempting to think of one last way to free her mother.

The Colonel could see his daughter's thoughts were drifting elsewhere and tried to change tack. "It's not us bearing arms, Poppy. We're fighting a fair fight. It's up to us to not only win, but hold those who do wrong accountable. All this isn't going to stop for one single person and especially not for your mother. This is too important. Can't you see we're turning the tide here?"

Poppy remained buried in the contract, her eyes glazing over as she searched for watertight reasoning to convince her father but only found ramshackled long shots. "You could just pause the promotional drive, get Mother and then resume it once she's safe!"

"No!" The Colonel reigned in his outburst. "It's too late. Momentum is on our side and we have the advantage of surprise."

Poppy also tried changing tack. "Since when have you wanted to be the boss of an energy company? Why do you want to throw your money and free time away? It's not Monopoly money."

"It's anti-monopoly money! I've created the only weapon up to the challenge: a completely independent company with no board, no shareholders, and all the bean counters shut in a darkened room, their sole responsibility to file taxes and financial documents. Unemployment greets any of them brave enough to comment on product or marketing budgets – the part-time office cleaners outrank them." The Colonel looked around to check no one was in immediate earshot. Julius was talking to a promotional co-ordinator and the other operators were deeply engrossed in their tactical stewardship, so he continued, "This is part of a wider plan."

Poppy looked up at her father for the first time, her intrigue trumping her dejection. "What wider plan?"

The Colonel bent down again with both hands on Poppy's knees and spoke softly. "Election victory and premiership of the country. That's the only place from which to directly affect the country."

Poppy had to clear all thoughts of her mother with this bombshell so she could fully engage with what her father was saying. "Hang on, you want to be elected to parliament? But you have no party, you have no supporters. Plus, you always said government was impotent."

The Colonel chuckled at this last point as he stood up. "It's true, they're spineless idiots. I'm going to put some backbone into it, resurrect it. This new party and its manifesto will grow from AlbionSol's customers. I don't want to run another company again; I'm building a means to an end. Once AlbionSol serves its purpose of establishing an organic, grass roots political party and recruiting voters then I'll cast it upon the waves and leave it to steer its own course."

"You've planned an organic, grass roots organisation before the company has even launched? Can you foresee who will lead this great democratic voice of the people?" Poppy snapped back sarcastically.

"Me. It'll need a well-known face, a natural leader to help it get started …"

"Oh my God." Poppy bowed her head, shutting her eyes in disappointment. "My father has delusions of grandeur. Can't you just live the rest of your life on the golf course and find a trophy wife like everyone else in Shaded Vale?"

"I don't want power." The Colonel spat out his contempt emphatically. "I want to hand power back to ordinary people.

Remove it from boardrooms and put it back in the street where it belongs." The Colonel bent down again to be at the same level as Poppy. "What's the matter, Poppy? Are you scared of people having dreams? Are you scared of people having ambition? If I hadn't had any dreams or ambition I'd never have developed PMP Resurfacing, we would have been stuck on the poor side of Wigthorn, and you'd be at a corporate college right now learning how to flip a burger or make a cappuccino."

He put his hand on hers. "I know it sounds like rambling, but look out there. People are listening, things are happening. I just want to throw a few spanners around and mix things up a bit."

Poppy shook her hands free. "Why did you keep the part about going into politics quiet?"

"Getting you to believe and work with me on AlbionSol was hard enough; imagine if I laid all this out in front of you? You'd have reacted like this. I needed you with me."

"The people out there are only interested in their bank accounts. They don't care about anything else you have to say unless it gives them more free time or money. How are you going to turn them into voters?"

"That's the easy bit. Our policies will benefit the pockets of voters and not the profits of energy companies."

"Bribery, that's the best policy you can come up with?" Poppy lifted the legal device, placing it on her lap to give her hands something to do. Looking at it, she noticed the version number had changed since she'd last read it a few weeks ago. Examining the change log of the document, she traced the exact changes.

The Colonel, still bent down in front of Poppy, pointed at the legal device. "This is just the beginning. Once AlbionSol has recruited enough customers to give a realistic chance of gaining a majority in the House of Commons, then we'll start communicating the political messages to our customers, educating them on how to vote and what it means to vote. We'll be handing an otherwise hidden and forgotten form of responsibility back, not taking it away or replacing it with something equally ineffective. Like Rooftech, the political parties will be unprepared and inexperienced in fighting such an unorthodox opponent." The Colonel stood up, satisfied with his arguments, convinced Poppy had been subdued by his reasoning and passion.

"This can't be right." Poppy was rapidly trying to make sense of the contract in front of her. "These extra clauses you've added to the contract ..."

The Colonel said nothing.

"You can't do these things, surely?" Poppy looked up at her father. "You're asking people to give away their personal information, allowing their DNA to be tagged and identified." She ran her finger down the contract. "Here, this clause allows privately held information gained by AlbionSol to be sold to any third party without prior approval – you can't do that!"

"The government is already doing that."

"Yeah, but corporations aren't. Anyway, just because the government is doing it behind everyone's back doesn't mean you can."

"I'm not, it's in the contract!"

"You're no better than any of the others ..."

"You think people care?" The Colonel mixed up a cocktail of a smile and surprise, delivering it awkwardly to Poppy.

"You really think people are concerned about what happens to their personal data? People don't give a shit! You know why they don't give a shit? Because there's nothing to give a shit about! Since DNA satellite tracking has been introduced, society, business, homes and government have been revolutionised in terms of efficiency. The amount of money we used to waste in miscalculated utilitarianism or poorly selective sampling, it would make your head spin! We've got accuracy like you wouldn't believe, and this?" – The Colonel grabbed the electronic contract from Poppy's hands – "This gives us more power, more information and more opportunity to better people's lives."

"But these improvements have only happened because of the people's trust in the mechanisms behind it. This contract pushes that trust to the limit." Poppy got up and pointed at a specific clause in the contract. "Just here, you can't sell private, identifiable information to foreign governments or corporations."

"Why not? Who's going to care if their daily activities are sold? Whose life is so interesting they want it hidden from view? The mundane routine of the lives people have been lulled into is about the only value they have anymore. Why not exploit this need for information and make it more valuable by improving the quality of it?"

"By removing all forms of privacy?"

"I think you overestimate the people out there. No one's causing dissent, no one's putting up a fight and no one's putting on a red beret and making speeches. The old adage protecting privacy was 'If you've nothing to hide then you've nothing to fear' but this doesn't apply anymore, not when the individual has been surpassed by the herd. In herds, companies

don't need identification; groups of people are defined by location, activity, age, gender, habits, etc., information measured
by satellites. People don't realise they will only ever be seen
as products, meaning they need to reposition themselves as
such. It's not a step backwards, it doesn't change who each
individual is, it's an acceptance of how they've always been
seen. The consumer has finally achieved self-consciousness.
Add identifiable information to this new improved, premium
product and the population can demand more in recompense.
Sell this improved product abroad and the sky's the limit."

"Obviously not. This blanket of satellites watching our every move keeps us grounded and now you want to put names to
faces? Dissenting voices will be silenced, undesirables relo-
cated, genetic traits refused entry, personal histories collated
and disseminated, receipts and journeys cross-referenced. The
patterns helping to keep everyone on a fairly equal footing are
removed, exposing the frugal and highlighting the spendthrift;
a consumeocracy is created."

"Nice word, did you just think of that?"

Poppy's natural calmness gave way to a manmade anger.
"Don't be facetious with me! By removing the patterns people
hide in, you suddenly expose every single person to identifiable scrutiny, and when they find out they're being railroaded,
the herd are going to cause a stampede to your door."

"They already know! Look here, it's written down in plain
English. I'm not hiding anything!"

"Who reads the small print? You tell people what they
want to hear about continuing to earn high energy payments
enabling them to remain in their comfortable lifestyles and
they'd sign anything. You're not advertising the fact every
blank face recorded by a satellite will soon be accompanied

with a photo and vital statistics." Poppy turned her back on her father and surveyed the displays. Scenes from all over the country were beamed back, crowds of potential customers being sold and attended to. Poppy thought of her mother. Her late mother. Her father had seen to that.

Poppy turned around to face her father. "Caveat emptor?"

"Change is a necessary step, part of a bigger picture."

"This picture is getting pretty big – are you sure you can still see it all?" Poppy walked out.

Julius looked over his shoulder, making eye contact with Poppy as she walked past. The Colonel clutched his legal document device as he watched Poppy leave the room, then took one last look at it. If this weapon was to sever the relationship with his daughter, then so be it. He was sure he could still see the whole picture.

Charles Sand heard a small chime from the display on the wall. He stepped back from the window with the view of the treetops to see AlbionSol had reached the two million mark.

He addressed the computer, "Inform the board I wish to convene a meeting."

Charles walked over to the elevator in the floor, turning around to absorb the pristine view of immaculate trees as he descended, all the while ignoring Estelle's lifeless body slumped across his desk, smoke billowing out of a large hole where her face used to be, her grey hair extinguished.

CHAPTER 15

Duncan strode briskly down the street, Amy in tow struggling to keep up, skipping every few steps to close the gap.

"Where are we going? What's the hurry?"

"The Passion Fruit Café. It's just along here I think."

"Yeah, we're nearly there, I know it well. It does the best toasted sandwiches in town – you hungry?"

"There are payments to the café from our joint account."

"And?"

"I've never been there."

"And?"

Duncan stopped, scowling at Amy. Amy took the opportunity to get her breath back. "The payments amount to more than just a sandwich and then, on more than one occasion, about an hour later a couple of tickets are bought at the old Holo Theatre further down the road."

Amy smiled at the old fashioned use of 'Holo Theatre'; nowadays it was a 'Holoma'. "That doesn't mean an affair, don't be silly."

Duncan glared into Amy's eyes. "Do you know something?"

"No, no! I swear. In fact, I'm just as intrigued as you. I didn't think she had it in her."

"You want her to have cheated?"

"No, no!" Amy continued walking. "It's just down here. I'll keep my mouth shut."

Duncan followed. "Yeah, if it's not too much bother for you, that'd be just dandy."

The Passion Fruit Café was filling up with brunch customers, more than usual due to the AlbionSol promotions and the downtime of the internet. People were treating themselves to an extra bagel or pastry on top of their tea or coffee as a reward for switching to AlbionSol and increasing the earning potential of their home's energy. The café was alive with talk about plans for these extra funds and the spectacular nature of the whole event.

Duncan pushed to the front of the queue, searching out the owner, a middle aged man overseeing his staff of three. Duncan gestured to the owner that he wanted a word.

The owner, not overly keen on direct customer interaction, shuffled his way to the end of the counter where Duncan and Amy were waiting.

"Yes?"

"Hi, I was wondering if you could help me."

The owner remained motionless and emotionless.

Duncan held his hand out for Amy to hand him the mobile device. "Yes, I was hoping you could tell me if this woman has been in here?" Duncan showed the café owner a picture of Nicole stored on the device, zooming in on her face.

The owner, once again, remained unmoved.

Amy, seeing the owner would only answer to pressure rather than goodwill, took over proceedings. Flashing her Pharmara ID badge long enough for the owner to see the logo and recognise it's authority but quick enough he couldn't determine the department or the fact that it was now void, Amy continued, "I don't think you fully understood my colleague's question, sir. Has this woman, Nicole Hartley, been in this café and who was she with at the time?"

"I don't have to tell you shit." The owner's soft pastry exterior contained a tough, bitter centre.

"It's true, you don't have to tell us shit." Amy looked at Duncan, then looked back at the owner. "It's also true that I don't have to talk to Pharmara's property department, maybe spread a rumour or two when certain leases come up for renewal."

The owner crossed his arms.

Amy took that as a sign to increase the pressure. "There's the supply chain, too. If it ever became toasted or fried, that really would be a shame. We just want the name of the person she came into the café with, that's all. None of this will be recorded and no one will know who said what and we can all get on with our miserable little lives like nothing ever happened."

The owner glanced at his staff, who were busy serving, then nodded his head for Duncan and Amy to come closer. "I'll tell you, but you ever come back and I'll inform one of the Pharmara directors when he gets his lunch that I'm getting hassled and it's affecting my sandwich making abilities. He gets very tetchy when he doesn't get his favourite sandwich in exactly the right way."

"No problem, this is the last you'll see of us. We need a name?"

"Louis Klein—"

Duncan interrupted, "I know that name. He's ..." Duncan closed his eyes as his brain scrolled through a multitude of faces to fit the name.

The café owner helped him out. "I think he's a teacher or something."

"Yeah," Duncan replied as he looked at Amy. "Mr Klein, he's Abby's teacher."

Duncan stopped outside Abby's school, feeling conspicuous by his arrival during teaching hours. Every Tuesday Nicole would pick Abby up after school, taking her home for dinner until her parents picked her up around 7pm. Duncan always looked forward to Tuesdays because he got to see Abby, but now he realised he'd only ever been to the school to pick her up a handful of times. He'd always left it to Nicole. A project in the underground lab always seemed more important than walking to Abby's school.

Amy broke the pensive silence. "You're not going in, are you? It's not even lunchtime yet – classes are still going on."

"I can't wait around, Amy. We haven't got any more D 'n' Away juice left so we're going to be popping up on someone's radar soon."

"You'll never get in. Schools are tighter than maximum security prisons, and about as much fun."

"In corporate schools, true, but here at Wigthorn Independent they utilise the old fashioned method of security guards – a disadvantage for electronic fraudsters but not familiar family members."

Duncan approached the entrance of the school, tall gates standing next to a security booth where a guard was watching something on his device. Amy immediately noticed the lack of logos, electronic billboards and the plainness of the school's unfettered exterior. The school looked empty and felt hollow to her.

Duncan approached the guard confidently. "Hi, Arthur."

The security guard examined Duncan for longer than was comfortable before eventually recognising him. "Hello, Mr Hartley, how are you? We haven't seen you around these parts for a while." The guard then put on a solemn face. "I'm sorry to hear about Nicole, my condolences."

"Thanks, Arthur. I'm just here to take Abby to the dentist. Her father forgot and asked if I could do it as he's busy."

"OK, no problem, sir." Arthur put down his device and pressed a button to open the gates. "Abby's been a strong girl. I know how close she was to Nicole."

"I've had to bring a colleague along, too, as we were having a meeting when my son called."

"No problem." Arthur got back to watching his daytime soap, 'East Neighbourdale Street and Away'.

Amy gave Arthur a smile as they both walked through, confirming she was indeed with Duncan and not a silent assassin.

Amy walked through the school behind Duncan, engrossed in the strange displays stuck on the walls. Examples of the children's work were unfamiliar to Amy's own corporate education at Pharmara High only a mile away. She stopped at some drawings of kings and queens. "Are they learning about fairy tales here?"

Duncan stopped and turned back to see what Amy was referring to. "No, they're some of the old kings and queens of England. Look, this one is Elizabeth I."

"Is she the one who said 'Mirror, mirror, on the wall'?"

Duncan looked at Amy, somewhat confused. "Huh? They are real people from history, not characters in a story."

Amy walked past Duncan. "I suppose you believe in Santa, too."

Now was not the time to highlight obvious holes in the Pharmara High curriculum, so Duncan carried on walking down the corridor to Abby's classroom.

They looked through the window in the classroom door, seeing a man about Duncan's age perched on the edge of his desk reading a story to the children. Amy pressed her ear to the door ...

" ... so the nanny was given the duty of measuring the two brothers so they could wear suits to their auntie's wedding in a month's time. The elder brother didn't want the nanny interfering with him; he could measure his brother and himself without the nanny's help ..."

"It's 'The Baggy Trouser Brothers' story." Amy smiled as she looked up at Duncan, her own fond memories of hearing this story at school coming back to her.

"Bloody hell, more corporate bullshit making its way into the school," Duncan commented to himself, markedly less enthusiastic.

Duncan knocked on the door as a matter of courtesy and walked straight in. All the kids and the teacher looked round.

"Granddad!" an excited call came from the back. Abby got up and ran towards Duncan as he bent down and embraced her.

"Hello, darling."

Abby then leaned back to look Duncan in the face. "What are you doing here?"

"I'm actually here to see Mr Klein." Duncan looked at the teacher. "Hi, I'm Abby's granddad and I was hoping to have a quick word with you."

Louis Klein approached Duncan and replied calmly but firmly, "I normally ask parents and relatives to organise an appointment. As you can clearly see, we are in the middle of a lesson."

Duncan upped the civility with a whisper. "I absolutely insist I see you now."

Louis looked around at the kids and saw they were being exceptionally quiet, aware of the tension. "OK."

Louis, not wanting to cause a scene with only twenty minutes until lunch, picked up the device he was reading from and handed it to Abby. "Abby, why don't you finish off this story and read it to the rest of the class whilst I go and speak with your granddad."

Abby, keen to impress her granddad, immediately accepted. As she hopped up on the desk to play teacher, Duncan and Louis joined Amy outside the classroom.

"I've been wondering when you would come, Duncan," Louis said as he gently shut the door.

"What do you mean?"

"There was no chance of 'if' – Nicole never made any effort to hide anything. You being here proves that. She just wanted you to notice."

"So you're not denying anything?"

Louis took a breath. "We saw each other, but it was platonic, and that was how she wanted it to be, Duncan, because of you."

"But it's not how *you* wanted it to be?" Duncan said sharply. "You wanted more from my wife?"

Louis held his hands up. "Hey, I don't think you understand. We were just friends. You need to realise why she wanted to go to the Holo Theatre, play tennis or go out for a meal with someone other than you."

"Because you pursued and pressured her?"

"Duncan! Listen to yourself. You think Nicole was a pushover? You know why, deep down, you know why."

Duncan remained silent, trying to plot another approach to pin down Louis Klein rather than looking for other possible reasons.

Louis continued, "When was the last time you took Nicole out? Surprised her? Even just spent some quality time with her? I'll tell you, shall I? Apparently it was over ten years ago when you spent a weekend in London."

Duncan remembered it well. It was her fiftieth birthday. He'd organised a whole weekend away: five star hotel, a show, an advertisement gallery, a top restaurant, a surprise night out with her sister. Everything had gone relatively smoothly especially with Nicole's sister giving him a helping hand.

"We're not teenagers anymore, Louis. I'm not sure if you realise, but marriage isn't just a series of first dates and unbridled joy stretching into eternity." In the absence of reasoned arguments, Duncan adopted the lowest form of battle: patronising sarcasm.

"I was married for thirty-five years, up until five years ago, Duncan, so I have an inkling of what marriage is about, and what you're going through now. My wife died, too." Louis, checked on his class. "Look, I miss Nicole. She was a special woman, but like anyone, she needed attention, not stress. The stress you caused ... it ..." Louis stopped himself and glanced at his class. "She wanted more than to sit at home and wait for you to come out of your underground greenhouse, or wherever you barricade yourself in all day. Your obsessions should have been split evenly. Nicole needed just as much tending and looking after as your damn tomatoes."

"Mr Hartley!" A shout from the end of the locker-lined corridor.

Duncan looked around and saw Gerard advancing with a security guard flanking him on each wing.

"... and Miss Jay! A bit old for school, aren't we?" Gerard was revelling in his newfound freedom as the newly instated Head of Statistical Acquirement and Analysis.

The heels of Gerard's shoes echoed their way up to the classroom door. "And who might you be, sir?"

"A teacher. I should be getting back to my class."

"But of course. We'll be out of here very shortly."

Louis could feel the aggressive undertones of Gerard's demands, and was glad to go back to his day job. He gave Duncan and Amy a silent recognition of goodbye and walked back into the class, asking Abby to continue reading another story.

"Duncan Hartley, at last! You've led us on a merry dance these past few days." Gerard held up a sandwich and took a bite out of it. "The best sandwiches in town, apparently, with a nice side order of 'information'."

Duncan took a nervous step forward to draw a line. "You let Amy go. I dragged her into this and she has nothing to do with any of the growing I've been doing."

Amy stepped forward drawing another line. "Duncan, shut up! This shitbag can go fuck himself."

Gerard enjoyed being argued over. "This pleasant female creature has broken the rules, Mr Hartley. Surely you understand that?"

Duncan understood, but the absence of constitutional law in the real world meant corporate rules could be negotiated.

Duncan suddenly moved behind Amy, wound his right arm around her neck, drew a pen out of his pocket and held the point to her jugular.

"What the hell are you doing!" she shouted, consciously refusing to look at Gerard for help.

"Shut up," Duncan said firmly, yet revealing a slight reticence in the background of his voice. "You and those guards just walk back down the corridor, otherwise you'll have the paperwork of a dead girl at an independent school looming over you for the next few months."

Without a pause to counter, Gerard responded, "And then what are you going to do?"

"I'm leaving."

"Before or after you slit Miss Jay's throat?"

"If you come any closer, I'll do it!" The reticence in Duncan's voice barged its way to the front.

"Let me get this straight. You're either going to escape with a hostage under your arm, which is going to massively slow you down, especially a man of your advanced years, or you're going to slit her throat and we're just going to let you run?"

Amidst Duncan's crumbling, ill-thought-out plan, he decided to stand his ground and say nothing.

Gerard glanced over at the guard on his right, who then withdrew a gun from inside his jacket and point it straight at Duncan's head. Duncan had never seen a gun, let alone had one pointed at him before.

Gerard enjoyed the look in Duncan's eyes. "Oh, would you look at that."

Duncan remained resolute. All he could do was project supreme self-confidence. He frowned and held Amy closer.

"First things first, Duncan," continued Gerard, "step back a few paces so your granddaughter can't see you through the window. We don't want her opinion of you to sink anymore after she comes to visit you in prison."

Duncan stole a glance of Abby reading her class a story before retreating out of view.

Gerard continued to be centre of attention. "Secondly, you got me on one point. You're right: I don't want a messy first day on the job. So I'm going to give you some leeway. I'm afraid your own fate is already sealed, but young Miss Jay here can reap the benefits of your rash bravery. You let her go without harm and we'll overlook her minor misdemeanours. There is no profit in Pharmara apprehending and imprisoning her. Luckily for her, the profit in your capture easily allows us to write her off as damaged stock. A loss leader, if you will."

Duncan immediately relaxed the arm around Amy's neck, gently placing it on her shoulder apologetically before finally removing it altogether. "I'm so sorry, Amy. It was the only thing I could think of."

Amy's initial glare was soon tamed by Duncan's genuine sorrow, and she gave him a hug. "Nicole loved you, Duncan. Even with your imperfections, she still loved you."

Gerard was numb to the moment. "Miss Jay, this very cosy deal is subject to you getting out of my sight in an extremely short amount of time."

Amy whispered ever so quietly. "Seeds, Duncan." She then turned her head, keeping her arms wrapped around Duncan, and looked down the barrel of a second gun trained on her by the second security guard. "I'll see you soon, Duncan. I'll get you out."

"No, just go." Duncan looked down at Amy with a resigned smile, gently pushing her away – a push disguising a handoff. "I'd appreciate it if you could look in on Abby every now and again. No doubt her parents will disown me now."

"Sure," Amy whispered, tapping her nose. "Doomsday Vault."

"Errr, Miss Jay? Run along now," Gerard stated impatiently.

Amy straightened herself out, surreptitiously sliding the bag of seeds into a pocket, before facing Gerard with an accusingly pointed finger. She spat out "Twat!" before walking back past Duncan to exit the corridor at the opposite end.

Gerard shook his head disapprovingly at the ill-mannered parting gesture. "Now, Mr Hartley, if you would be so kind as to conduct yourself in a more esteemed manner than your young friend, we can get out of here quickly and quietly."

Duncan heard a door close behind him as Amy made her way out of the school. He walked into the view of the classroom door, seeing Abby reading to the class. She turned and smiled at her granddad; he smiled back, giving a little wave.

Once on the other side of the classroom's view, a guard brought out a 'pacifier collar', a thin metallic device clipped around the neck that was said to reduce your IQ to one of a small lapdog. The guard then led Duncan away by the lead as he dumbly walked to heel, tongue hanging out and head bowed.

Gerard followed, informing his superiors of his first day's success.

CHAPTER 16

Poppy ambled along Wigthorn's Pharmara Promenade, against the flow of people rushing from East Wigthorn heading to the New Pier to catch the AlbionSol spectacular finale at 2pm.

After leaving her father, Poppy attempted to digest the full meaning and reasoning behind his grand plans. Why hadn't he told her everything from the beginning? Maybe he didn't trust her or didn't think she would fully understand. In the space of just a few days, her mother had shown her true colours by selfishly wanting to swap her position beneath the laser for Poppy, and now her father was slipping through her fingers, too. A life lived in a bubble didn't push people to the limit, so Poppy had no reason to question anyone's loyalty or worthiness, but now it seemed that even those closest to her put conditions on the depths they would go.

Poppy ambled alone and felt it, for the first time in her life.

Duncan and Amy were off-grid and Poppy had no idea where they were, so she reached out to someone who might give her a sympathetic ear.

"Hello, you have reached the office of Miss Portofino MP. How may I direct your call?"

"It's Poppy Gold. I need to speak with Miss Portofino immediately, please."

"Please hold and I'll see if she's available."

Opposite the Pharmara New Aquarena swimming pool, an old couple vacated a bench after their Jack Russell escaped their clutches to chase an Alsatian-sized robotic anglerfish that appeared to be swimming along the road with an AlbionSol logo rather than its own luminescent bait. Poppy sat on the bench.

"Poppy?"

"Yes, hi, this is Poppy Gold."

"Poppy, darling! Are you OK? I heard about your mother, I'm so sorry. Are you safe?"

Poppy was grateful for the concern and gravitated towards it. "Yes, I'm fine." As soon as the words left her mouth, she could feel the onset of tears. The strain of keeping them at bay showed in her voice. "I didn't know where else to turn. I know you knew my mother and I thought ..."

"I'm coming to get you now. Wait where you are." Mary nearly forgot herself and the access she and her fellow parlia-mentarians professed to abhor; she qualified her previous statement with a charade. "Where are you?"

Poppy looked around. "I'm outside the Pharmara New Aquarena swimming pool."

"Wait there, I'm coming to get you, you poor thing."

"Charles, darling, have you been up to your old tricks again?" Mary settled down into her car, doing her makeup as it drove itself from her constituency office in Wigthorn towards the swimming pool to pick up Poppy. Conversations involving multi-tasking with personal grooming were strictly audio-only.

"That bloody ex of hers is trying to ruin this year's bonus."

"Come now, Charles, there are more important things we're working towards. Was it really necessary to give old Estelle the heave-ho? She was proving to be quite useful."

"We've plenty of useful people already – one less won't make a difference. I hear the C.O.V.E.R.T. database has been compromised."

Mary pouted in the mirror. "Oh?"

"Yes, to be more specific, the data was downloaded to an external device from a terminal in your office."

Mary's eyebrow pen slipped to make her surprise even more pronounced. "My terminal? Are you sure about that, Charles?"

"The head of data security is positive. He's checked the visitor log and discovered a Poppy Gold, Duncan Hartley and an Amy Jay were there on the same day. Coincidence, Mary?"

Mary sat bolt upright, correcting her errand makeup. "No Charles, I don't believe in coincidence."

"Me neither. I've done some research and this Miss Jay could prove a problem to us and our goals. She's a statistical analyst at Pharmara – well, she used to be up until a couple of days ago. If she has the chance to study the data, and if she's as clever as her personnel reports claim she is, this could provide us a few hurdles. The board may want me to clean these problems up for them if they are not cleaned up sooner."

"I understand, Charles. I'm on my way to meet Poppy now, she'll lead me to Amy Jay and I'll find out what she knows and eliminate her. The board need not worry about a thing."

"I'm seeing them this afternoon, so I'd like to give them good news." Charles ended the call.

Mary snapped her compact shut, a puff of powder hanging in the air. Mary blew it away.

Mary's car silently approached the swimming pool, driving down a side road, past the car park and down the dead-end street where people could admire the view of the sea from the safety and warmth of their own car. Poppy was sat on a bench with her back to the road. Mary recognised the slouched out-line of despondency.

"Just here, pull over." Mary straightened her jacket as she shifted forward in her seat ready to leave. "Open."

Mary got out, putting on the attentively concerned mask, the one she saved for visiting down-trodden constituent voters when accompanied by the press. "Poppy! Come here, my dar-ling." Mary stamped on an AlbionSol balloon as she approached the bench.

Poppy wiped away a few tears before turning around and then hiding herself in Mary's outstretched arms. Poppy wel-comed the comfort. Mary looked around to see if anyone was watching as they walked back towards the car.

Inside, Mary tinted the windows, turned up the heating and kept Poppy close.

"I'm so sorry to hear about your mother. She was a special woman and a good friend of mine. I've already contacted Rooftech demanding an immediate investigation."

"He tortured her, Mary." Poppy let the tears roll within the cocoon of the car.

"They'll pay, Poppy." Charles' methods had always been a bit crass for Mary's more diplomatic tastes, but that was the price she was willing to pay to work with 'doers' and not 'talkers'.

"I see your father is rocking the boat, too."

"He won't stop, either. I begged him to stop to save Mother's life, but he wouldn't." Poppy blew her nose and sat up so she could look at Mary properly for the first time. "He wants your job, too."

"My job? Whatever do you mean, sweetheart?"

"He's gone mad, I think. He's gaining customers now but plans on converting them to voters later to gain a majority in parliament."

Mary let out a short laugh. "Oh my! Billy was always an ambitious man." Mary handed Poppy another tissue. "He doesn't stand a chance."

"Father has got over two million customers signed up to AlbionSol already, Mary – he's serious!"

Mary gave Poppy another tissue and a reassuring smile. "Darling, customers are one thing; getting them out to vote is quite another. Our democracy has evolved to accommodate this fact. To change it would be a step backwards into the past."

"Don't underestimate him, Miss Portofino."

"Oh, I won't, Poppy. I know your father very well and I would never underestimate him. How he produced a daughter as beautiful as you shows anyone the man has hidden qualities and Lady Luck on his side." Mary's smile glistened in the artificial light of the car. "Now you're safe. Are your friends safe, too?"

"I don't know. I haven't heard from them since yesterday afternoon when we got split up in Serville. They said they were going to be heading down here to Wigthorn, but apart from that, I have no idea."

"They could be in danger, Poppy. Estelle has been killed and I recently discovered the government's C.O.V.E.R.T. database had been hacked into and sensitive information stolen. You wouldn't know anything about that, would you?"

Poppy sunk in her seat. "Yes."

"Darling, you must tell me. Your friends could find themselves in serious trouble."

"Amy reckons she found something in the data, evidence about the way tracking data is being used and maybe sold." Poppy's sudden realisation of Mary's own obvious connections to government stopped her from explaining more.

Mary's political brain was quick to snuff out any suspicions. "She was right, Poppy. There are rogue elements in government and in business, hell bent on twisting this great country to satisfy their own selfish ends. They will stop at nothing, which is why we need to find Amy and Duncan quickly, with the minimum of fuss, to keep them safe from harm."

The saleswoman sensed she had closed the deal, so moved on to the paperwork. "Let's see if we can track them down." Mary turned to face the display on the opposite side of the car. "Computer, contact Gerard Abbot at Pharmara Security." Mary glanced at Poppy. "He might be able to help us."

Poppy kept quiet about her previous introduction to Gerard in Serville.

Gerard's voice darkened the atmosphere of the car. "Miss Portofino, a pleasure to ..."

"I'm looking for two people, Mr Abbot. A Miss Amy Jay and a Mr Duncan Hartley. I understand you are also looking for these people."

"I have already found them. Mr Duncan Hartley is currently detained in a Pharmara Detention cell."

"And what of Miss Amy Jay?"

"She was released."

"On what grounds?"

"There was no profit to be gained in holding her."

"Her safety is of paramount importance to me, Mr Abbot.
Profit is not a factor in this matter. Are you in a position to tell
me where she is now?"

"No. Since she was released without charge, we have not
kept track of her."

"Can you track her down now?"

Gerard answered after a couple of seconds. "No, there's no
trace of her DNA within a fifty mile radius. She couldn't have
got any further in such a short space of time."

"So where is she?"

"She could be disguised, underground, within a lead-lined
room – there are a few explanations."

"This girl is in danger, Mr Abbot, and you had her in relative safety. If anything happens, I'm holding you and
Pharmara responsible. Is there anything else you can tell us?"

The faint noise of security staff franticly working in the
background could be heard. "We did a weapons scan before
approaching the two suspects. Miss Jay had a mobile device in
her pocket, but not hers – it belonged to Mr Hartley's late
wife, Mrs Nicole Hartley. We've just tried contacting it but the
user is not responding."

"OK." Mary breathed a silent sigh of relief. "Mr Abbot,
may I suggest you join us in the hunt for Miss Jay as your personal well-being is irrevocably linked to hers."

"Yes, ma'am."

Mary may have lost all interest in the captured Duncan Hartley, but Poppy hadn't. "What are you going to do with Duncan?"

The line went dead.

"What are they going to do with Duncan, Miss Portofino?"

Mary was busy seeking out information on her device. "He's not your concern now, Poppy. He's safe. We need to focus on finding your friend Amy."

"But how?"

"She's obviously screening her calls, so send her a photo of yourself with a piece of information only you and she would know. That should be enough for her to answer."

Poppy got out her mobile device.

Mary looked up and put a hand on Poppy's. "No, no, not here. You're going to have to do it outside and alone." Mary stroked Poppy's soft cheek. "You have to be alone. You're so sweet that you wouldn't be able to lie with me being in front of you and Miss Jay doesn't trust anyone at the moment – no-one except you, hopefully."

Mary instructed the door to open. "Here's Nicole's number so you can try and contact Miss Jay." Mary stepped out of the car, followed by Poppy. She hugged her tightly to install some much-needed encouragement. "Amy needs you now. You can help her."

CHAPTER 17

Amy cleared her head with some fresh sea air, walking through a busy shopping street in Wigthorn, trying to lose herself in the crowds of people under the onslaught of street entertainment, air shows and AlbionSol slogans. She was mentally exhausted after spending the past few hours sitting on the seafront analysing more of the data she had downloaded from C.O.V.E.R.T., trying to recognise people in the numbers and find reasons for the patterns they formed. Her earlier conclusion of people and towns being sold off to the highest bidder to perform various social and urban experiments was proving to be correct, but not only that – there seemed to be more.

Gaps in the data suggested Amy's download was not as complete as she first thought and had either been corrupted or interrupted, but further analysis showed this was not the case. There may have been gaps in the numbers, but there were no gaps in the timelines. These gaps were fully intentioned, suggesting only one thing: control samples were being gathered. But why?

In the shadows of backstreets and alleyways, Amy occasionally caught glimpses of homeless people being bundled into the backs of vans, conspicuous by their foreign number plates and the unfamiliar uniforms of their occupants.

Amy looked through a small crowd of laughing children chasing AlbionSol balloons released by a giant AlbionSol teddy bear and saw another vagrant forcibly extracted from his makeshift hut beside some bins and unceremoniously chucked into the back of a white van. Amy weaved her way through the children and ran down the alley to discover more about the fleeing van, but only just saw it head for the seafront in an easterly direction.

As Amy got her breath back from this short sprint, her mobile device vibrated in her pocket. It had been doing this all day from unrecognisable and blocked numbers, all of which she'd ignored, but this one came from a number she knew: Poppy's. She let it ring a few times, deliberating whether it was safe to answer or not. If not, she would have to dump the device immediately and leave the area.

The curiosity was too great, even if she did wonder how Poppy had got the number to this device. She looked around to see if anyone was watching her, stood under the shade of a nearby tree and answered the call with silence.

"Amy? Hi, it's Poppy. It's OK to speak, it's just me. You're not safe. Have you given my father anything?"

No answer.

"No? Good. Don't."

Amy's reply crept out of the shadows. "You remember what you told me when we first met? Meet me there in ten minutes."

Having recovered consciousness before Thor Security personnel came to investigate their latest bolt from the blue, James and Al used the crowds as cover to escape back into anonymity. Once they'd found relative safety in an abandoned building, James contacted The Colonel.

"Colonel, the girl and the old man escaped."

The Colonel quickly reassigned them so he could focus on customer sales. "The old man is out of play from all accounts, but you have another target: Julius Talent. He's gone missing and is incommunicado. I think he may have reassessed his priorities. Your fee doubles if you get Amy Jay and Julius Talent."

"We're on it."

"Poppy has also left. Julius may have gone after her. You can track her through her phone. Don't trust her DNA signature. I repeat, do not trust her DNA signature as she's probably using an alias. You bring her back to me alive and I add a zero onto the end of your fee."

"Understood."

"Understand this: if any harm comes to her, the satellites and drones at my disposal will light you up like a Christmas tree and you'll have more followers than Elvis."

The Whale Café on the seafront, to the west of the New Pier, had about twenty tables outside it on the elevated promenade that kept the emerald sea to the south from flooding Wigthorn. Poppy approached and saw a few tables occupied but no sign of Amy, so she went inside to look. Still, Amy was nowhere to be found. Poppy sat at a table outside under the main canopy, thinking this would be the best place to minimise detection from cameras and satellites.

A waitress came to her table and Poppy ordered two soft drinks as she kept an eye out for Amy. An unusual vertigo unsettled her due to the water being visibly higher on one side of the high promenade than the town on the other. Not only did this huge structure keep a rising sea level at bay, but it also served as a windbreaker, and sitting on top exposed her to a refreshing salty sea breeze. Poppy waited for Amy, watching the seagulls bobbing up and down on the waves.

A few minutes later a woman in a headscarf and sunglasses approached the café, glanced at Poppy and the other customers, then went inside. After a few seconds, she came out and stood behind Poppy. Amy spoke. "You promise you're alone?"

Poppy had to turn around to confirm who it was. "Absolutely. It's so good to see you. Are you OK? I heard about Duncan. Is he going to be all right?"

Amy quickly sat down next to Poppy. "In a word, no. He's been caught and Pharmara are going to make an example of him. I'm more interested in you. Where have you been and why do you think I'm not safe?"

"I've just come from a meeting with Mary Portofino. She says the data you downloaded is highly sought after and you could be in danger if anyone else catches up with you."

Amy checked the café and the promenade in a panic. "Is she here?"

"No, it's just me."

"She must be following you somehow. There's no way she'd let you disappear. Do you still have any D 'n' Away juice left?"

"No, I'm out."

"Mine's wearing off; I can almost feel myself become more exposed by the minute." Amy got closer to Poppy and grabbed her arm. "Listen, Mary Portofino and all that lot up there in London are the ones I'm running from. They are the dangerous ones. I've done more research into the data and the government is definitely selling contracts to foreign organisations so they can perform experiments. Not only that, they are also selling them to domestic corporations via local government. Mary Portofino is one of the main players in this game. I've got evidence right here." She tapped her pocket. "She is an integral part of the success and expansion of this secret policy."

Poppy felt another pang of disappointment pierce her stomach as another member of her support network collapsed. Poppy questioned the last remaining pillar. "Why should I trust you? Seems like I can't rely on my father, my mother didn't care, and Mary Portofino is just using me – how do I know I'm not just another tool to you, too?"

Amy relaxed her grip on Poppy's arm from restraining to reassuring. "Why would I lie to you? What do I gain from meeting you here out in the open? I just wanted to see if you were safe."

Poppy looked up at Amy. "You're on the run, still. You could use me for escape."

"What am I going to do, jump on your back and force you to piggyback me out of here?" Amy waited for a reciprocal smile. It came with some coaxing.

Out of nowhere a voice broke the reunion. "Drinks, ladies?"

In unison, both Amy and Poppy forced their chairs back with a screech, turning the heads of the other patrons. This waiter was out of uniform, wearing a sombrero-sized hat. Though they couldn't see the top it was designed like an aerial view of a bin. In fact it was a dustbin lid stuck onto a sombrero, nothing more advanced. Any satellite looking down would dismiss it as a litterbin … that moved.

"Relax!" The waiter tipped his hat.

"Julius." Poppy moved closer to greet him.

Amy kept her distance. "What are you doing here?"

"You're not safe."

"Yeah, you're not the first one to tell me this. What about it?"

"We have to leave now. We're getting out of here."

Poppy was pleased her collapsing network had stopped imploding and had actually grown by one person. Amy was not so confident of Julius' loyalties.

"Do either of you have a mobile device?" Julius asked.

The two girls showed their devices to Julius who took them, ran towards a passing pair of AlbionSol dwarves on a tandem bike and chucked them onto the float they were towing.

"You won't need them where we're going. Let's move."

They walked swiftly down the promenade towards the New Pier, surfing the edges of the crowds to help conceal themselves but also allow for a quick escape if necessary. As they walked, they passed the hospital on the other side of the main seafront road, its entrance lining up with Italian registered vans, and the main entrance filling up with homeless people who were brusquely dumped, then carted off inside. Was Wigthorn giving its homeless free health care?

Julius looked down at the hospital and saw Amy's bemusement. "You're right about foreign experimentation." Amy looked at Julius as he continued, "Naples city council has a large homeless problem and a big tourist trade to look after. They want to know if giving all their homeless a check up, new clothes, a shower, a haircut and some money will help clean up their streets and improve tourist revenues."

"But why not actually test it on their homeless?"

"They've tried for twenty years to get forced health check up and personal hygiene for their homeless but EU human rights bureaucracy and Italian corruption won't pass any of this legislation. They need empirical evidence that it'll actually work before legislating for it."

"So they use the convenience of a tracked and apathetic society." In the afterglow of her own detective work, Amy realised her part in this exploitation; not the eyes or the ears, but the brain. Her job involved joining the dots, putting reasons behind the graphs and extrapolating patterns. A corporate clairvoyant and psychologist, giving meaning to the past and describing the future, every moment and every person accounted for. Only now, Amy was lost.

"Exactly." Julius looked at Poppy and saw the sparkle in her eyes had dimmed since he had seen her last. He put his arm around her as they walked.

"I've found gaps in the data, Julius," Amy pointed out, hoping he may have clues as to why they were there.

"Are there gaps because your download was incomplete?"

"No, these gaps are purposeful. The timelines are uninterrupted, yet gaps appear. You only see these kinds of gaps when iPatch towns are tracked, but this data is for regular towns."

"Like someone has turned the tracking on and off during certain periods?"

"Yeah, it's like control samples are being monitored."

"What if the government switched off all their tracking, what then?" Julius asked.

"They wouldn't have any data to help run the country or to sell on to corporations."

"But what is the government actively running at the moment? The decades of increased tracking are directly proportional to the decline in public services. What if these gaps in the data are control samples to see how corporations can cope without C.O.V.E.R.T.? What if they're stability tests in preparation for a big switch off?"

"Turn C.O.V.E.R.T. off?" Amy bumped into an old couple enjoying the elevated view from their deck chairs, as all her brain faculties were routed from navigation to incredulity.

"Why not? Downsize C.O.V.E.R.T. and outsource it until the database becomes incompatible and redundant. The corporations then have total control and government can be consigned to the recycle bin of history."

They arrived at the entrance to the New Pier, busy with crowds of families, couples old and young, as the AlbionSol events came to their climax at the end of the pier with a holographic light and sound show with fireworks.

"Do you know why the New Pier is called 'New Pier'?" Julius asked Poppy in a tourist guide fashion.

"Because there was an old one?" Poppy felt uneasy stating the obvious.

"Exactly. It lies underneath the new one. Halfway along, directly underneath, is the end of the old pier. It's used for smuggling by small submarines. There are people who wish to buy anti-surveillance equipment like D 'n' Away sequencers" – Julius tapped his jacket pocket – "by unrecorded individuals and groups across the world, all wanting to hide from the all-seeing eye. We have to escape with this data to save ourselves and aid other like-minded people."

Poppy and Amy looked at each other in solidarity. What had they to stay for? Julius wrapped an arm around Poppy again, leading her up the pier as Amy took one last look back at Wigthorn. The northbound view into Wigthorn from the entrance to the pier brought back memories: the fishing rod over her shoulder, a drunken boyfriend hanging off an arm leaving the nightclub, a face full of candy floss after taking visitors on the ubiquitous seafront tour and, more recently, walking back alone with only thoughts of an uncertain future from an afternoon spent at one of the cafés. At every stage of her life in Wigthorn, the pier had played a central role. It was a destination for all ages at all times, but now it was a departure. When a Wigthornian left Wigthorn, they never thought they'd ever leave via the pier.

As Amy savoured one last view for nostalgia, two sides began to wither under the increasing weight of reality: from the east came the flashing lights of a Pharmara Security convoy; from the west came two mercenaries, unknown to any database and unseen by any satellite, although Amy could see them quite clearly now.

She turned and ran, warning the others they should do the same.

CHAPTER 18

"Turn C.O.V.E.R.T. off?" Amy's voice recording was played back.

"They know everything, Charles, and they have proof." Mary Portofino was now back in her constituency office in Wigthorn town centre, leaning forward on her desk and watching a tracking icon blink upon a holographic bird's-eye view map of Wigthorn. The blinking red light was currently making its way along the pier. "I've used a good old fashioned bugging device on Poppy's jacket as their DNA signatures cannot be trusted, and Julius must be part of this group of 'Unrecorded's because we can't find his records anywhere."

Charles Sand was watching on remotely. "Mr Talent and Miss Jay must be eliminated immediately. Miss Gold will be used to barter with AlbionSol to guarantee us an electoral victory in a few months."

"Very good. I shall instruct the Pharmara Security detail currently closing in on them to carry out our wishes."

"I want this dealt with quickly, efficiently and with no public involvement. We can't afford any more leaks, Mary."

"Consider the matter closed, Charles."

Charles silenced his mobile device, slipped it into a trouser pocket hiding in his sleekly cut suit, and stepped out of the private, express elevator, one of the many 'beads' surrounding the glass structure in the centre of Docklands, London. Known as 'The Abacus', the bead shaped and multicoloured exterior elevators surrounding the building shot up and down like an uncertain stock market; dropping off winners at the top, downsizing the losers and dumping them off at the bottom near the Thames. The glass building in the centre was a literal zero – a numerical oval symbolising the break-even point of commerce, the bridge between profit and loss. The higher up the office building an employee occupied, the closer they were to the satellites that helped put them there. Employees were only allowed access to their own floor and below. Anyone hoping to stand on the shoulder of a giant and steal a glimpse of the great beyond were denied access by a primitive computerised voice from the ceiling, 'Access denied'. To do this in an elevator with those higher up the career ladder would only cause embarrassment for all until you had stepped out to allow the elevator to carry onwards and upwards.

With his guest access assigned, Charles walked over to one of the full-length windows at the top of The Abacus to survey the expanse of the London skyline. Sitting on a bed of magnetism, the top floor was physically removed from the rest of the building and slowly spun around at the top of the capital's financial district, relishing its elevated status amongst the mortals one mile below.

Adjusting his tie, straightening his jacket and checking the time, Charles made his way to the east of the building where, further to the east, lay the executive conference suite. Pressing his finger on the identification pad, the door opened showing the plus-sign-shaped transportation to take him across.

The executive conference suite was shaped like the number one, a much smaller building next to The Abacus consisting of just one floor with one room, but elevated a mile up to the same height as the top floor of The Abacus. The cross-shaped transport shuttle and the number one conference suite were suspended on the most powerful magnets ever produced, more powerful than the ones launching satellites everyday.

Charles closed his eyes, breathing out all anxiety in a short, sharp sigh and walked into the transparent cross, obtaining a view of the city on all sides. It promised to take its cargo from nothing to something, no strings attached. Charles kept his eyes firmly on the conference suite as he floated out into thin air, sweeping all of Docklands underneath it. He always hated this part.

A small wiry man stood up from the circular table, introducing Charles to the room as soon as he entered.

"May I introduce Mr Charles Sand, CEO of Rooftech Industries, the biggest provider of domestic and corporate solar roofing in the world today. He was a key figure in lobbying government to introduce subsidised solar roofing for UK homes to help combat carbon emissions, energy production and … to make sure we stay on top of things." The wiry man constructed a wiry smile from wiry parts. The rest of the room laughed along with the peer pressure.

Charles was shown a seat but he insisted on standing. Assessing his audience, Charles recognised the fourteen members of the Zenit Corp board dressed in their usual blandness, assimilating into the vacuous atmosphere of the conference suite. A leaderless organisation judged and guided by numbers alone, a CEO or chairman was an unnecessary conductor with so many mechanisms of measurement directing the symphony of moving parts.

If they had each swapped homes, their partners would have struggled to notice even with the differences in racial attributes and gender accessories because they merged into the background so effectively and effortlessly. Charles found it hard to find any variety or recognise any personality. These kings of brand were the masters of bland, the shoemaker's children.

There were two new faces seated at the far end, oriental men dressed identically to each other and to the rest of the room, sartorial chameleons, camouflaging themselves, eyes independently looking out for both threats and opportunity. They were in holographic form, each head and torso beamed from a device onto a real chair. The technology being used to do this was cutting edge, as Charles didn't notice they were built from light at first, until noticing the absence of shadow.

The wiry man continued his introductions. Charles heard nervousness in his voice, an uncertainty that revealed cracks in his limited confidence.

"Charles, you know everyone currently on the board. Let me introduce you to our two guests this afternoon, Mr Xiè and Mr Féng from the government of the People's Republic of China."

The two holographic figures nodded in acknowledgement, too polite to speak. Charles nodded back, convinced of their arrogance.

The wiry man quickly brought Charles into the spotlight. "Charles, if you could update the board and our guests, please."

"Of course." Charles acknowledged each of the board in turn before addressing the Chinese delegates. "Our preliminary tests shutting down C.O.V.E.R.T. have proved to be a success. As our hypothesis suggested, the data we're getting from C.O.V.E.R.T. is diminishing year on year, and the benefits we gain from it now are not worth the tax we're paying. As in the past with the justice system, roads, transport, military, media, health, education and local government, removing control from the state-run regulatory bodies opens up an industry to greater freedoms and opportunities. The central statistical ministry is no different. No longer will we have to use stealth and subterfuge to share data – we can do so openly. No longer will the state have an unfair advantage by having a hand in all data exchanges. 'The Whitehall Firewall' will shortly be pulled down, bringing with it greater freedoms and profits without having to support a cumbersome government."

The Chinese delegates listened with statue-like intensity. The board remained on tenterhooks, waiting for positive vibes from the Chinese.

The stony exterior was broken by Mr Xiè. "May I ask a question, please, sir?"

Charles was taken aback, expecting a stern challenge to his authority. He suddenly felt like the strictest teacher in school. He readjusted how the rest of the room saw him and straightened up even more than usual. "Of course."

"'Shortly'? When exactly?"

"There is to be a general election in three months. Once the status quo has been confirmed then we have a five year window to implement, imbed and develop this new industry."

The other delegate, Mr Féng, chimed in, "We see the status quo could be challenged if this newly launched company, AlbionSol, has any success."

The board muttered its contempt for such an action. One of the braver members voiced her concerns directly to Charles before cowering behind her blushes. "Why would this new energy business provide any kind of threat to the re-election?"

Mr Féng stuck his holographic neck on the line. "According to our data, AlbionSol are only fighting hard for customers in certain constituencies with small populations, a large percentage of home owners, educated residents and in relatively low corporately affiliated areas. They are also not trying to gain customers nationwide, only about forty per cent of the country. These strategies coupled with favourable policies would give them a good shot of electoral victory, especially if the opposition is ill prepared."

Charles reaffirmed his alpha male status with the reassurance of good preparation. "We have already identified this scenario and appropriate measures have been put into action."

"Such as?" said Mr Féng.

"This impressive debut performance by AlbionSol is actually a positive development as it helps subdue the common international view that the UK openly supports the current 'quintopoly' of the Big Five corporations. We have got assurances from the other four of a temporary partnership until the election has been confirmed in our favour in three months, our imminent takeover and freedom from government necessitating this momentary marriage of convenience. AlbionSol maybe a thorn in the side of one of us, but together it would be impossible to shift the balance of power."

The two Chinese representatives remained stony-faced at this response – a good sign. The board returned to grazing on reports, graphs and balance sheets.

Charles continued his presentation. "In another example of unprecedented co-operation between the Big Five corporations, we have nailed down a standard format for all statistical information. This means all our clients will be able to choose from a multiple of informational packages from each corporation and then very easily merge multiple data sets, making your job of extrapolation and conclusion infinitely easier and broader in scope than it has been up to now. The software to access and report this data will of course be free to all our customers."

Mr Xiè spoke. "Will the information be personalised?"

"Yes. Legislation will be pushed through as soon as the re-election is confirmed, and within days all DNA information will be assigned a name and the ease of cross-referencing will cascade from that. This personalised data will provide the key to unlocking specific data such as: consumer history, financial history, geographical movements, physical characteristics, medical records, education and employment history, family history and more. I don't need to explain to you the many applications this level of detailed information could have."

"Would there be opposition to such a change in personalised data?"

"There would no doubt be small pockets, but not enough to generate any interest from our customer base. Any opposition will soon be drowned out by the flood of special offers and deals we'll promote as a result of gaining extra revenue from the newly opened data market. We aim to pass on any improved profit margins to our customers ... enough to keep them acquiescent, anyway."

"As well as having access to data, we can also contract trials?"

"This will be the area of main interest to clients such as yourselves. With greater freedoms come greater responsibilities, and we plan on being responsible for more and more of your trials in the future, giving you better information to use in your own markets. One example I can give you is that right now the Indian state of Delhi has contracted a transport trial in the town of Leicester. With their increased middle class demanding a magnetic road system, they needed to see how feasible it would be to have an improved road system whilst still allowing the sacred cow to roam free. They wanted to see the effect it would have on traffic flow and human mortality rates because they plan on building a magnetic road system without the expensive automated safety features we enjoy over here. So we launched 'Operation Beef Ransack' by switching off the safety features in Leicester and releasing over two thousand cows into the city centre."

"And the results?"

"There is a client privilege here, but let me give you a brief overview. Cows have the most positive effect in decreasing human road fatalities – it's quite remarkable. Unfortunately, traffic flow suffers as a result. I think Vishnu and his fellow deities will have a job on their many hands keeping them under control. The secular entities our two countries choose to guide us are a lot more efficient and a lot less demanding." Charles sealed this with a knowing smile.

The holographic representatives grimaced nervously, not sure whether their diplomatic lessons in foreign political correctness allowed them to smile or not. So they settled for doing both. The board soon followed suit.

Charles continued to fill the dead air. "The Indian federal government are also interested in using certain sections of data, most notably medical, educational and family history to help re-enforce what they regard as a broken caste system. Arranged marriages involving British citizens moving to India have resulted in many brides and bridegrooms not living up to their billing." Charles eventually sat down on the chair he'd been hovering over. "We are not interested in your motives for this data or how you intend to use it, but we will assess each trial request to make sure our own population are not too adversely affected. It's in both our interests to keep British citizens functional."

"To a point!" A board member barked, the others laughed exponentially.

Charles shot back a raised eyebrow and then offered reassurance to the Chinese guests that those buried in numbers will stay buried and not interfere with important matters on the shop floor. "One of the key things I want to stress to you and all of our customers is that the businesses in the UK offering data and trialling solutions strive to maintain the utmost quality of service. We work together and have set up guidelines and best practises to protect our citizens, and of course, our customers at home and abroad."

Charles broke the pregnant pause. "Any questions?"

A lone sheep took a step forward. "Yes, I'd like …"

"For our distinguished guests," Charles said incredulously.

Mr Xiè, thinking there was a finely balanced culture gap to navigate, tentatively asked, "Mr Sand, will you be our main contact going forward?"

Charles nodded to keep his eyes from looking around. "Yes. You and I will be working very closely going forward as my new role after the election will be totally dedicated to working with our partners overseas in the Far East."

Mr Xiè's face visibly relaxed to the point of almost melting. "Excellent. We shall carry on with the contractual negotiations at a later date but we are very happy with the way things are preceding so far. We look forward to a productive relationship."

"As I do, too, Mr Xiè." Charles dug into his jacket pocket, fishing out a small device and ran it over the console on the desk in front of him. "As a sign of goodwill and a small sample of what we can offer, I'm sending you data on all flights from the UK to China over the next week. On it you'll find sixteen British citizens that will be of interest to you: some own books banned by the Chinese government, two of them have been arrested outside the Chinese Embassy here in London, one of them is a relative of a fugitive wanted by your government, and another practises Falun Gong. I hope this will prove useful and give you an appetite for more."

Mr Xiè looked down at his own console back in Beijing. "Yes, very pertinent information indeed. Thank you Mr Sand. We shall talk again soon."

"Indeed."

The two holographic figures disappeared from view and Charles leaned back in his seat, pleased with how the meeting went with one of his biggest potential clients.

The wiry man stood back up. "Splendid work, Charles, you handled our Chinese friends very well. I trust this AlbionSol business isn't going to cause us any problems."

"No, it's being dealt with."

"Good. Once this unprecedented process of working with the other big corporations is over, we can get down to the real business of crushing them." The wiry man produced a clenched a fist that even the weediest children wouldn't have flinched at. The board felt empowered with this fighting spirit and a wave of passion washed over them.

Charles watched his superiors, the meek relishing their inheritance. The one saving grace of working with foreigners to sell this perfect, detailed, real-time vision of England's green and pleasant land was the time he'd spend away from his fellow compatriots. They repulsed him. He would look forward to selling their freedoms and liberties to the highest bidders. Their apologetic disquiet, their emotionally retarded reserve, their joy at others' misfortune, their fortitude in dire straits and their incapacity to cause a fuss would be their undoing ... and the highlights of his sales pitch.

CHAPTER 19

Julius and the two girls sprinted down the pier, dodging day-trippers and regulars alike. Arriving at the halfway point, which consisted of a large restaurant complex, Julius ducked into a sheltered alcove, looking around to see if the coast was clear before shoulder barging a door open. Julius stepped into the darkness, and Amy and Poppy wasted no time in following him in. Julius shut the door behind them, telling them to wait whilst he activated a light from an old, chunky handheld device.

"What's that thing?" Amy asked.

"It's an old fashioned battery powered torch – no tracking devices on this old thing. Come on, we need to head down to the old pier."

Amy and Poppy followed Julius down, through doors and down stairs, into old, forgotten rooms swamped by a rising sea level and kept at bay by an old pumping machine siphoning energy from the distant sea turbines spinning on the Wigthorn horizon.

Amy shivered in the cold dampness, unprepared for such dwellings. Poppy took off her coat and gave it to Amy, who accepted it with thanks only after seeing Poppy was wearing a jumper underneath. In order to put the coat on, Amy looked for a dry spot on the floor to place her bag, not wanting to risk getting the seeds or data wet.

"We're nearly out of here, Poppy. Time to get this little lot to people who can actually do something with it." Amy tapped her bag before swinging it back over her shoulder.

"Where are you taking it?" Poppy asked.

"Julius can have the data, that's not important." Amy replied. "The important thing is to get these seeds as far away from here as possible."

Relieving herself of her coat didn't lighten the troubles occupying Poppy's thoughts. Julius and Amy were the ones who needed saving. They were important, they were useful, they knew what they were doing. She was just an extra weight, slowing everyone down. She had nothing to contribute. As soon as she questioned her purpose, she found it.

James and Al, chasing the biggest payday, ran after the red beacon on their tracking device. They went past the whale shaped café, down the promenade, past the pier and were virtually on top of their targets, but there was no sign of them. They kept jogging onwards, the red beacon under their feet.

"Where the fuck are they?" exclaimed Al, frustrated at having to exert precious energy.

"They should be here." James hit the side of the device. "They're moving at the same speed as us, just here!"

Al looked around as two dwarves cycled past on a tandem, dragging behind them an AlbionSol holographic display.

"Stop!" said Al. "Where are they now?"

"They're still moving east."

Al ran after the dwarves. "Oi! Yeah, you! Grumpy and Sneezy! Wait there!"

The dwarves stopped pedalling, not because they wanted to but because they had to – Al had run in front of them and stuck his hand up.

"Where are they now?" Al shouted at James.

"They've stopped." They both looked at each other, then at the two slightly worried dwarves.

Just at that point, a sizeable congregation of Pharmara Security vehicles whizzed past them along the seafront road, screeching to a halt outside the pier. Out streamed twenty security officers led by a man running onto the pier. A tide of tourists parted as they rushed through the entrance.

James saw the commotion and recognised the wild goose chase they'd been led down. "Al, forget these guys, we gotta follow that lot."

Gerard led his men with long, heavy strides so as to make as much noise as possible to emphasise their urgency and importance. Beside him strode a navigator, one eye following a red dot on a device, the other watching where he was going.

They got to the building located half way along the pier and the navigator stopped. "They've gone in here and are heading downwards. I'm not sure how, though, as there's only the sea underneath here."

Gerard weighed up his options. "Johnson, you take ten men and search inside the restaurants and bars. I'll take the others and we'll search the perimeter."

James and Al stopped running up the pier as soon as they saw the Pharmara Security personnel guarding the perimeter of the central restaurant building, scanning everyone walking past.

"Why have they stopped, Jimbo?" Al said as they both slid behind a couple of people looking over the edge of the pier into the sea below.

"I guess Poppy has gone into the restaurant to hide."

"She ain't going to get very far in there."

"No, which doesn't make sense. Why would she hide in there? Plus why is security searching people outside? Why not just keep guard on the exits?"

"Maybe they've lost them?" Al said, trying hard not to get distracted by the smell of salt and vinegar chips wafting over from the couple next to them.

James looked at Al, surprised. "You know what? You may have hit on something. I heard from some local Unrecordeds a while back there's an old smuggling route under the pier." James closed his eyes to think better, mouthing an old rhyme. "'*Facing the dawn, on the edge of Wigthorn, is a door in the floor, under the eye of the storm.*'"

"Huh?"

"A rhyme this old Unrecorded guy said to me when he was drunk. I always thought the edge was somewhere on the hills, but look at the pier – it's on the edge, too." James started to walk up to the central building. Al pinched a chip. "Facing the dawn – that's on the east side ..."

"Hey, watch out for security," Al said, walking behind James.

They slowly crept up the pier, moving from behind one group of people to behind another, until they were just on the north side of the restaurant building. They could see security personnel scanning and questioning pier visitors down both sides.

Sticking to the wall like wallpaper, James inched up the building, trying to look nonchalant. A large group of elderly tourists took the east route down the pier and briefly focused all the attentions of security on themselves. James took this opportunity to step away from the wall and get a better view, and spotted an unassuming door with a 'Do Not Enter' sign and, underneath that, another sign indicating that these premises were protecting by 'Storm Security'.

"Hey! Don't move a muscle!" James and Al looked around in unison. Behind them stood five Pharmara Security guards all pointing weapons at them. As instructed, James and Al didn't move a muscle.

Through the gaggle of pensioners walked Gerard, purposeful and with a smile straining at the corners of his mouth. "Well, well, well. We seem to have some Unrecordeds on our hands, unless you can explain why there's no record of you here." Gerard held up a device, the lack of identification causing more of a concern than a lack of a pulse would ever do.

Al put on a ridiculous accent. "No understandi da Inglese. Thank you, please."

James looked around at Al in shock and then slowly back to the guns to see if anyone had even just vaguely bought it.

Gerard cocked his head and five guns cocked their triggers. No such luck.

"OK, OK, yeah, yeah," pleaded James. "We like to … erm … fly under the radar. It seems you've lost what you're looking for. I think we can help you."

"The door you're interested in is standing just in front of us, so I don't think we'll be needing your services anymore."

"Yeah, but do you know how to open it?" James asked.

Gerard examined his questioner's poise and then the door before answering. "You open it and we let you walk away."

"No. We open it and we get Poppy Gold – you can have the other two. Poppy is not important to you, and the other two are not important to us."

Time was of the essence. Gerard couldn't waste anymore. "Do it."

James walked up to the door and then with as much force as possible, raised his right leg and stamped his boot against it. It opened a little easier than James had expected as he fell in after his right leg. He stuck his head out of the doorway and delivered an unsophisticated yet victorious look towards Gerard.

Julius, Amy and Poppy heard the crash from above and looked at each other in the half light of a few bulbs flickering on the old, damp dance floor of a nightclub well past its opening hours.

"We've got to be quick – they're here," Julius said, marching towards a closed metallic door next to the DJ's booth. On the wall beside it was an old fashioned identity lock. Julius bent down so his retina could be scanned. The gears and the cogs of the lock could be heard. Julius swung the heavy door open, urging the others to walk through into yet more darkness. Once in, he slammed the door shut.

In the airlock, the girls could hear more mechanical movements and pumps breathing air into the next room, displacing the sea. The airlock opened, revealing another old and damp nightclub room decorated in a bygone era. Surrounded by tall, reinforced windows curving from one end to the other, this was the end of the old pier. A bar area lay to one side and beyond that lay what was once a large dance floor, but now a crudely constructed hole had been torn into the floor with only the air pressure keeping the sea from rushing in.

Julius walked over to the pool of water and looked in. "They should be here soon."

"Who?" Amy questioned as she gently placed her bag on a rusting table.

"Help."

There was a small rumbling under their feet, and the water in the hole in the floor started bubbling more furiously as the noise grew, until the top of a small submarine, about the size of a truck, broke the surface. The rumbling white water stopped as the submarine shut off its engine. The hatch on top flipped open and an unkempt head of hair popped out.

"*Bon soir, mes amis!*"

"*Bonjour, Jacques-in-the-box! Allez le Non Registre!*" said Julius. "*Ca va?*"

"*Ca va bien. Allez le Non Registre!*" the captain shouted, encouraging everyone aboard with ferocious waving.

The pit of Poppy's stomach was slowly eating her from the inside out. Here she was so close, yet becoming more desperately unhappy the closer she got. What exactly had she achieved? What was she going to achieve on the run, being nothing except a third wheel? She couldn't dissect data or grow plants.

Julius had placed a ladder across the water from the edge of the dance floor to the submarine. As Amy stepped onto the ladder, Poppy noticed a loose hair on the shoulder of her jacket. She surreptitiously picked it up whilst warning Amy to watch her footing. She then turned to Julius. "You're next."

"After you." Julius held out a chivalrous hand.

Poppy used it to effectively slingshot Julius onto the ladder first. "Make sure you get the seeds and data out of here, quick!" Poppy offered him a steadying hand to distract from her other, thieving hand, which stretched into his long jacket pocket and fished out the D 'n' Away sequencer, whilst telling him to hurry up.

The French captain knelt down at one end of the deck, fixing something, but upon seeing the three fugitives standing there, he shouted at Julius, "*Allez!* Go, go Julius! Get ze engines started, we leave now! *Allez!*"

With Julius and Amy across, Poppy could see the French captain urging them all into the submarine so he could initiate their descent into the water. Poppy crouched down, pulling the ladder back across.

"What you do? Come aboard, mademoiselle!"

"Go!" shouted Poppy. "Go! *Allez!* You don't need me! Go!"

The captain, Amy and Julius all continued to plead with Poppy to come aboard. Their ignorance of their own situation and her own pathetic existence only incensed Poppy more. She put down the D 'n' Away sequencer, picked up the lightweight ladder and started stabbing the side of the submarine with it. Harpooning metal with metal, the violence and force of it was intended to scare away any insisting submarine captains. It worked. The captain tossed a French shrug at her, pushing Jul-

ius' head down into the submarine and manhandling Amy inside.

Amy struggled to get free of the captain's grip. "What are
you doing? Get on here now – we've got to go!"

"No! You can get to the Doomsday Vault quicker without
me." Poppy continued her assault on the submarine with vigorous defiance: an act of bravado, a growing pain, a rite of
passage, a teenager taking her first steps out into the world
alone. Permission and curfews finally confined to childhood.

Amy saw her intensity and the stubbornness it fuelled, her
natural poise evaporated with each devastating blow to the
hull.

"Poppy! Get your arse on here now!" Amy screamed.
"You're not being a fucking hero – you're being a bloody idiot!"

"I know!"

Then there was another bang. It echoed strangely around
the dilapidated hall. Poppy dropped the ladder and looked at
the door. It was being forced open by their assailants. Amy
shouted at Poppy to get aboard. Poppy turned her back on the
submarine, taking the hair she'd pinched from Amy and placing it in the D 'n' Away sequencer. Activating it, she turned
towards Amy.

Amy was shouting at her whilst the captain was forcing her
into the submarine.

"She gone crazy. We no wait for crazy girl," he said.

Poppy couldn't hear a thing. The complicated family ties
strangling her wherever she looked were slowly loosening.
Her mind began to free itself from being chained to a mean-
ingless life in a shaded iPatch town. Her conscience indulged

itself in the pleasures of being useful. Finally, she had found a purpose.

The D 'n' Away sequencer beeped to indicate a new solution was ready. Poppy locked eyes with Amy as she sprayed herself all over. Amy continuing to fight the captain from above to remain in eye contact, ignoring Julius' shouts from below.

The door burst open, security men poured in, and the submarine captain kicked Amy into the tin can. "*Allez!*"

Poppy threw the D 'n' Away sequencer into the water before lying on the floor face down with her arms spread to show her submission to the invading security force. Through her wet, tangled hair, Poppy saw the submarine quickly dive, its manoeuvrability and small size allowing it to make a swift getaway. Seconds later, a few bubbles surfaced to wave Wigthorn and Poppy goodbye.

Gerard stepped through the entrance with the two Unrecordeds, James and Al, following behind, keeping an eye on their prize. Gerard walked through his guards to see a girl lying on the floor, wet and motionless. Gerard grabbed a tracking device from a guard and scanned her from a distance and then checked the location of the bugged coat as it sank into the English Channel. It all added up. The security guard verbally confirmed his own conclusion to Gerard. "It's her."

Gerard walked forward a few paces to separate himself from his men. "Miss Amy Jay, I believe you have some illegally obtained information and, forgive me, but were you trying to take it out of the country? Treason is no small matter, young lady."

Poppy slowly got up with her arms stretched out and fingers spread, but kept her head bowed with a veil of wet hair shielding her face from recognition. A measured gracefulness in her rising up also gave the escaping sub more valuable seconds. "The information is already out the country, *you bloody idiot!*" Poppy arose, feeling reborn in her new role as Amy Jay.

Gerard gave the scanning device back to one of his men and placed his hands behind his back to fully concentrate on his latest captive. "The submarine will be destroyed."

Poppy exaggerated a fake laugh, staring at Gerard through her hair. "The sub? The fucking sub?" Poppy especially loved the liberal swearing in Amy Jay's vocabulary. "Nothing's on the sub. The data's been duplicated, copied, uploaded, downloaded, synched and sent out of the country on multiple secret connections already. You think your firewalls are so watertight that the only way to leak information is to download it onto a physical hard drive and actually walk it out?" Poppy laughed again without any fakery. "Don't be so prideful, Gerard! There's nothing you can do. That sub is the least of your worries."

James didn't recognise the voice berating Gerard as the same one that had berated him when rescuing Amy, but those shy eyes behind the hair were no strangers to him, even if they were intensifying with growing vehemence. Something about the woman in front of him didn't add up. He got out his own tracking device to check the merchandise.

Gerard liked playing with the spirited little puppy. "None of its any good without you though, is it? It would take that old man and that stupid little rich girl years to find out what's going on!"

James was uneasy. His pay cheque might be standing in front of him at gun point. Or worse, it may have disappeared under the water. His device was being too slow. He hit it.

Poppy slowly put her right hand behind her back. "Yeah! That stupid little rich girl, she'd never get one over on you, right?"

James didn't need confirmation from his stalling device. "It's not Amy!"

Poppy quickly pulled her right hand back out from behind her, pointing something at Gerard. He ducked as above him flew a hail of bullets, screaming for blood as they sped towards her, using their own inbuilt tracking to home in on their target's DNA signature. Poppy flicked her hair from her face as she swiftly raised her head, revealing her true identity. A new strength grew from her determination to remain standing so they could recognise it was she and not Amy, and see the irreversible error they'd made. Poppy held her head high as bullets filled the gaps in her life with soul-destroying regularity and heartless accuracy. Each piece of lead sought out the numbness of sheltered privilege and bankrupted it, jumpstarting her disused nervous system as the sheer intensity of life briefly flooded her senses. This was living. Death pulled back the veil briefly before bringing down the curtain for good. Clutching a tablet device in her hand, photos of her mother and father rotated on its screen in the half-light of the hall, as though her final thoughts had been downloaded. Her life continuing to flash in front of her, even after she'd gone.

"It's not her!" James screamed again as the gunshots echoed their way out of the hall. He ran to her, wary of slipping on the floor wet with seawater and blood. "Poppy?" he whispered, checking for a pulse but only feeling his own increase. "Look! It's Poppy Gold, you idiot!" James considerately swept away the hair lying across her face. "You've murdered the wrong girl!"

Gerard glanced over his shoulder towards his men before taking a step forward. "You know what I like about you Unrecordeds?"

James looked up.

"No one's going to miss you when you're gone."

The last thing James and Al heard was the loud shock of bullets leaving their chambers.

They heard no echoes.

CHAPTER 20

Duncan hesitantly stirred, aching from an uncomfortable sleep on an unforgiving bed, unwilling to welcome another day of interrogation and accusations. Merciless messengers of pain seared through both his arms, down into his heavily bandaged hands lying limp beside him.

Duncan opened his eyes, blinking at the ceiling of solid artificial light. His bed lay next to the door along one side of the cell. The far wall was a blank canvas capable of displaying projected entertainment. In the opposite corner of the cell was a toilet shielded only by a waist high wall. Opposite the toilet was a small table and chair. Cameras sat in every high corner, occasionally zooming in, zooming out or panning around.

As pain slowly reanimated his senses, Duncan tracked back through his memories in an attempt to discover the reason for this pulsating agony. He went to sleep last night with no pain and no bandages, and now this. Was it even last night? How long had he even been in here? Three weeks? A month? Two months? He had no idea.

This wasn't the first time the morning had greeted him with a new ache or ailment to worry about. He'd had headaches, skin grafts, diarrhoea, nausea, double vision, a hangover, missing teeth and even paralysis from the waist down for three days. All unexplained.

This casino hospitality was gambling with his body, keeping time a mystery, watching his every move, upping the stakes at every hand and not remotely trying to hide the best known secret of all: the house always wins.

As Duncan lifted his head to get a view of his hands, his arms automatically pulled back to try and support his body. Duncan screamed out with intense pain.

There was also an upside-down half dome located at the centre of the ceiling, tiny motors periodically whirring as it adjusted itself for a better view, its laser scanners sweeping over Duncan's body recording every sensory output. Milliseconds later, eager research scientists were hungrily devouring every spike and pattern dancing upon their display.

When the pain had subsided and the sheen of water dried from his eyes, Duncan turned his head carefully to the side and saw a small box on the table with a hand written note attached. Closing his recently damaged right eye, he let his left eye take the strain of reading the note.

'Pills for the pain. Take ten every four hours.'

He'd had no human contact since he'd been captured – nothing. All food, water and medicines were either delivered in between bouts of sleep/unconsciousness or slipped in through a protruding letterbox on the door, whilst all information or contact from the outside world projected via the wall display. This torture by proxy, removing the human touch of the torturer, added to the hopelessness.

As Duncan was planning how he was going to remove himself from the bed and open the box of pills, a message flashed up on the far wall.

Incoming message.

Duncan expected another informational message from his hosts Pharmara: the menu he had no appetite for, the weather he'd never see, company profits he'd never benefit from, new product launches he'd never want – the same as regular TV scheduling. After a lengthy pause of a light grey background, Abby flashed up on the screen, dressed in a ballet outfit in her back garden.

"Is it on, Daddy?"

"Yes."

"Granddad!" she screamed, clapping at her own enthusiasm. "Hiya, Granddad! Hope you're enjoying your holiday in Italy. I've just started ballet classes after school. Here's what I've learnt so far …" Taking a few steps back and shooing the dog away, Abby began her haphazard and unpolished routine.

Duncan looked on, entranced. His eyes welled up and the first smile since his detention crept onto his face. Duncan shuffled in his bed to get a better view, attempting to prop his head up on the headboard.

"Daddy, keep up!"

Dancing and directing – a multi-tasking eight-year-old. Duncan looked on in wonder, pain momentarily unregistering.

"Jerry!" Abby pirouetted, the dog mistiming his own entrance and the two of them ending up on the grass. The dog barked his approval; Abby barked her dissatisfaction.

In the background, Duncan could hear his son and daughter-in-law laughing, but was yet to see them. They weren't close, not like they were with Nicole, yet they had offered help when she passed away. He'd heard his son had even offered to help him now, but Duncan had refused. Their time and money was ill spent on him. They had a much more important investment to make and she was right in front of them all.

"Ta-da!" Abby finished her performance in a pose brimming with pride if not poise and ran to the camera to kiss the lens. "Goodbye, Granddad, see you soon!" She stepped back,

IN A RIGHT STATE · 285

putting her fingers to her lips and twisting an invisible key, unlocking a smile so radiant that if this were Duncan's last view of humanity, that would be just fine.

The camera turned around so Duncan's son could wipe off the smear. Duncan briefly saw his face focused on cleaning the lens before he switched the camera off. Nothing more.

Duncan expected as much. Anymore and he'd have felt even more indebted to his son than he already did.

The blank wall replaced the footage with the words:

If you want more video then tell us the whereabouts of Amy Jay.

Milliseconds later, eager research scientists were swiftly comparing every spike and pattern with the last.

Gerard escorted Mary through the Pharmara Security facility, secure doors sliding open after a DNA scan. This was no tour. Mary was here to get an update from Gerard on how the interrogations were going and to see Duncan for herself so she could report back to Charles.

Mary walked beside Gerard as he led the way through the subterranean building. "Does he know anything?" Mary asked.

"Not really. We've tried sanctioned and non-sanctioned forms of interrogation, dream interpretation, truth serums, emotional blackmail ... We even dug out the old lie detector test but everything points to the same conclusion: he doesn't know where Amy or Julius went or what they intend to do with the data or the seeds."

"Why is he still in the Seriously Indebted section?"

"His son offered to buy him out so Mr Hartley would only be in the Debtors Detention section, but he refused the financial help."

"What about Mr Hartley's assets?"

"They've been seized, and the amount sold at auction will be deducted from his debt to Pharmara." Gerard paused outside an anonymous door. "The sale won't be enough to free him, though."

Mary waited beside him. "Is this his cell?"

"Yes. We want to see if you'll have any luck with extracting the information we need. If not, we have one more approach we can try."

"OK. Let's do it."

Gerard opened the door and let Mary enter first. The lights gently illuminated the room from pitch-blackness to a warm glow. Duncan only stirred when Mary turned around the chair from the table to face the bed.

"Duncan," Mary whispered. "Wake up."

"What are you doing here?"

"Believe it or not, Duncan, I'm here to help you." The pain visible in Duncan's eyes led Mary to closer examine his condition. Her eyes quickly stumbled upon the huge bandages around Duncan's hands.

Mary turned to Gerard in horror. "My God, what the hell have you done to his hands?"

Gerard's expressionless reply told Mary that an explanation probably wasn't best in front of the patient … prisoner. Mary held Duncan's arm just above the bandage. "Are you in pain?"

"There are pills behind you on the desk," Duncan mumbled. "Can you get me one?"

Mary turned round, saw the sealed packet and the glass of water and helped give a couple of tablets to Duncan. "For God's sake! You want a man without the use of his hands to get out of bed and open this by himself?" Mary aimed a stare at Gerard.

"This isn't a holiday camp."

Mary helped Duncan sit up slightly so he could drink and examined the two tablets cradled in her hand. "I don't know what PerFixx is."

Gerard spoke directly to Duncan. "They're harmless, aren't they, Mr Hartley?"

Duncan took his medicine with no expectations. "I sent emails, I made phone calls, and I even tried visiting your constituent office in Wigthorn, but the only way to get a politician to heed their call is when a potential voter is on death's door?"

"I'm here now, Mr Hartley."

"Only because you think I have information."

"Do you?"

"Will you sort out the atrocious recycling collections on Wednesdays? Will you also help the homeless over in East Wigthorn?"

"Is that what you were trying to contact me for?"

"For now. Baby steps, MP."

"And what about the help we require from you?"

Duncan forced a smile. "I have no information. We made no plans. I didn't even know Julius had left The Colonel. Amy, Poppy and Julius made their plans after I was captured. I got what I needed. Good luck to them."

Mary tenderly held Duncan's arm. "Duncan, I'm afraid I have some bad news for you. Poppy and Julius were found dead in an abandoned part of Wigthorn pier. They were apparently shot by an Unrecorded. Luckily, Gerard apprehended the assailant before he could escape."

Had the scanners focused in on Gerard, they would have recorded spikes and patterns commonly found in the guilty.

Duncan rolled his head back, staring at the ceiling and trying to piece together his recent comrade's movements after his own capture. "How did Amy get away from the pier?"

"An unidentified submarine, probably a foreign Unrecorded group, met up with them in the old pier."

Duncan released a blossoming smile under the dark clouds. "Beautiful. I met my wife on the dance floor of the old pier."

Gerard cut in, "Where did Amy go, Mr Hartley?"

Duncan looked up at Gerard, grinning through the pain, knowing it would frustrate him. "You didn't find the data, did you? What about the seeds?"

"What seeds?"

Duncan chuckled dryly. "Good, good. The bullet and the gun left the country together. Brace yourself."

Gerard received orders from his earpiece, informing him Mary's visiting time was up. After escorting Mary out of the room and down the hallway to be led out of the building by a subordinate, he returned to Duncan's cell.

Duncan looked up, his face alight with mischief. "Gerard, you're so kind sending me visitors accompanied with such good news."

"Your friends are dead, Mr Hartley."

"Yes, as I will be soon, no doubt, but the cat's out of the bag, isn't it, my good fellow? Your days are numbered. The countdown has begun."

"No, Mr Hartley, the countdown has just reached zero. It's time for your bandages to come off – but first, you need to eat." Gerard produced a tomato from his pocket – a big red juicy tomato. "You recognise this? We've made some modifications, thanks to seeds left behind at your house and in your wife's stomach. Here, try it."

Gerard offered the tomato. Duncan turned his head away.

"Eat it, old man."

"No."

Gerard stepped forward, gripping Duncan's head with one hand whilst forcing the tomato into his mouth with the other. Duncan offered no defence in his weakened condition. Juice ran down his chin and, amidst coughing and spluttering, Gerard held Duncan's head down by pinching his nose so Duncan had to open his mouth to breathe. Once open, Gerard rammed in more of the tomato until he let go, satisfied he'd fed him enough.

Duncan spat most of it out but still had to swallow bits to clear his mouth and airway. Seconds later his stomach rumbled, upset at the contents. Gerard smiled. Duncan immediately threw his head to the side of the bed, vomiting what little food he'd had within his stomach onto the floor, retching bile and spitting blood. And there, in the detritus, he could see a sprinkling of orangey, yellow seeds.

This had been a natural tomato. The modifications had been performed on Duncan, not the fruit.

"What do you think?" Gerard bent down on his haunches so he was at eye level with Duncan. "We're calling it 'genetic brand loyalty'. Your stomach has been reprogrammed to only accept foods with the Pharmara genetic signature. All other foods are immediately rejected – including patent violations, especially the natural ones. It's for your own good." Gerard, stood back up, cracking his knuckles. "Now let's get those bandages off."

Duncan backed away, retreating in his bed as best he could, but there was nowhere a weak old man could go in a bed backed up against a wall. Gerard, the stronger, younger man, grabbed one bandaged hand and unfastened it before moving onto the other one. With one end of the bandage in each hand, he began to unravel the bandages like a crazed conductor directing a macabre one-man opera, Duncan the lone actor singing the excruciatingly pained falsetto solo.

As abruptly as it had begun, the final length of both bandages escaped their constriction around Duncan's hands, causing Gerard to take a sudden step back. Duncan's arms fell to his side. The room fell to a gradual silence as both conductor and singer awaited a reaction to their performance.

Gerard took a step forward.

Duncan slowly lifted his right arm to view the hand.

It was red, swollen and extremely painful, and it was different. A finger twitched, involuntary. Duncan tried to purposefully move it. He succeeded, somewhat. As the shock and expectation faded, Duncan began to focus in on certain elements. His fingers weren't in pain – it was his wrists. And even though they looked swollen, the fingers seemed thinner, and his nails had grown quite considerably.

Gerard looked on intensely, more interested in Duncan's reaction than the appendages' condition. "Look closer, Mr Hartley."

Duncan lifted his other arm and viewed the similar state of his left hand. Again, it was smaller, but there was a ring on his third finger. He drew the hand closer to examine it further. He recognised the ring. It was strange; why was he wearing his wife's wedding ring?

A million simple memories flooded his brain: holding hands, their wedding day, holding each other, cooking together, watching her play the piano, waking up next to her – Nicole had a hand in all these memories and now that very same hand was staring back at him. Tell-tale moles, scars, colours and shapes were coming recognisably into focus, swamping Duncan's reason and tossing him about in a storm of illogical events, desires satisfied whilst horrors realised. Part of Nicole was still alive. They were together again.

Duncan moved his hand closer to his face, seeing a fantasy within the inhumanity. His eyes shut as he gently stroked his face – a faint smell, a familiar touch.

The cell door slammed shut as Gerard exited, interrupting Duncan's thoughts. The far wall slid upwards, filling with a bright light. Duncan brought up both hands so Nicole could protect him from the intrusion. Blinking from between the fingers, Duncan could just make out someone standing the other side of the glass. Beyond them, a handful of people in suits were sitting in rows on a small transporter, which was manoeuvring them into position in front of Duncan's cell. Duncan could not hear the presentation until it was routed through to the speakers in his cell. Gerard's final act.

"Here in cell 466 we have the first individual to successfully go through a double hand transplant from a donor of the opposite gender, in this case a man receiving the hands of a woman.

"... No, he can't see or hear us ...

"These types of limb transplant procedures are carried out on behalf of clients from societies that do not allow stem cell technology, lack the technological skills for limb transplants, or simply have a social system incapable of producing enough donors for its own needs. We have successfully carried out transplants of hands, ears, fingers and feet, and in the next cell you'll see the recipient of the legs from the same donor as the hands here. The recycling of expired resources can provide solutions for up to twenty separate people, and even though other societies bury or cremate their dead, we can provide you with additional solutions whenever necessary."

As Duncan's eyes adjusted to the light, he lifted his head, attempting to get a better view of his newly acquired audience. They were just sitting there, listening intently to their guide. As soon as Duncan heard that other pieces of his wife were just next door, he made a move to get out of bed and protest his indignity at such experimentation, but his brain and body had already given him away. A clear spray, unseen by the studio audience, burst out from a small nozzle in the wall beside him before he could make any movement.

Duncan was knocked out cold, left lying on his side with his head resting on both hands clasped together in a final prayer.

"The resource here has just completed his transplant and is reacting remarkably well, as you can see. He is sleeping for the moment but will soon be up and about as normal.

"Cross gender limb transplants are vital to improve the availability of products for all people across nations that choose to work with us. We can work with your health and insurance organisations to ensure your citizens get the best

care and are back amongst the work force as quickly and as efficiently as possible.

"The superior quality of the average UK donor, because of the advanced nature of our consumer and citizen tracking systems, means each product is guaranteed to be long-lasting, strong and highly compatible with most patients. The British are very ... malleable and accommodating.

"OK, let's move onto the next cell as I believe our leg transplant patient is up and about, ready to give you quite an amazing demonstration."

Duncan dreamt peacefully of Nicole as his grip on life ebbed away.

Overhead, the satellites continued to harvest the land below for data, gathering up patterns and predictions to be packaged and sold at market. They struggled to detect Duncan's wilting life force; the scanners within the room measured a declining body temperature, and the microchips in his clothing transmitted a dangerously diminished heartbeat. At an altitude of fifteen thousand metres, a drone silently passed over the facility, registering a vacant room. Four hours later, it passed over again, confirming the room was devoid of life. The CCTV camera continued to blindly stare at Duncan's remains in the same way it monitored chairs, coffee mugs or other inanimate objects.

There was no data of value to be exhumed from death, and so Duncan became reclassified by the multi-eyed beast of the state as "unproductive and unyielding". An empty husk in a fallow field.

Databases around the country updated the population of Wigthorn, trends were fine-tuned and patterns were modified. Predictions remained unchanged. Death was a certainty. Twenty-three minutes later, databases sprung into life once more to update Wigthorn's bottom line, as the birth of a baby boy in Wigthorn Hospital restored the balance. Marketing budgets re-adjusted accordingly.

In a hidden corner of the French port of Ouistreham, due south of Wigthorn, under a clear, unmolested, starry sky, three sets of footprints in the silt were gently being eroded by the incoming morning tide.

ABOUT THE AUTHOR

Ben lives in Worthing and writes in his spare time.

@b3n3llis
www.b3n3llis.com

ACKNOWLEDGEMENTS

I want to thank everyone who helped me along the way. My beta readers; Vanessa, Gail, Paul, Damo and Mum & Dad for giving me good feedback, encouragement and saving my blushes for highlighting some egregious errors. I mean, there were some instances of extreme ignorance and moronic incompetence in that third draft.

I also want to thank every agent and publisher that rejected this manuscript because I've really enjoyed self-publishing it. There's too many to list :)

Massive, huge, mega thanks goes to my good friend Emery Greer for designing my cover. Everyone judges books by their cover and my relaxed confidence in this area is totally down to the cover he has created. I love it. Hire his services here www.demographicdesign.com.au.

I also want to shower my editor in a ridiculous outpouring of praise and thanks. I found Sophie Playle after researching editors online (read more here - http://www.b3n3llis.com/2014/01/self-publishing-finding-an-editor/) and she quickly put me at ease. The critique was spot on and the copy-edit makes me appear to be a much better writer than I actually am (this DVD extra stuff was *not* edited by her, look at all the errors!) I was half dreading the editing process but Sophie made it fun, interesting, educational and a valuable experience. I've ended up with an infinitely better novel than when I started. If you need a friendly, thorough, professional, talented editor then I would 110% recommend Sophie. Get in contact with her here www.playle-editorial-services.com.

EASTER EGGS, DODGY NOMENCLATURE & SPURIOUS CONNECTIONS

I've never seen this kind of thing in a book or ebook before but thought it might be an interesting exercise. I could keep quiet about all the little things in the novel and let literary academics throughout the world dissect my work and guess why I named certain things in a certain way, or, I could just come out with it whilst I still remember and then slip back into total obscurity.

If you came here looking for something which hasn't been listed then it was either brainlessly thought up and has absolutely no deeper meaning or I've missed it. If you like this idea or think it spoils some of the mystery then let me know and email me - ben@b3n3llis.com.

Duncan Hartley - the main character was originally called Isaac Miller in the first 5 drafts. I changed it when I stumbled across a breed of Guinea Pig called 'Duncan Hartley' on this page - http://english.stackexchange.com/questions/4806/why-is-guinea-pig-used-as-the-colloquial-term-for-test-subjects - I thought it was perfect as it's a pretty normal bloke's name but also the name of a guinea pig bred especially for laboratory testing.

Rat's milk :: I only thought of this as a joke in a society where nothing goes to waste, land becomes increasingly rare & expensive due to higher sea levels and population growth, and a smaller state means less subsidies. Oops - http://www.telegraph.co.uk/news/uknews/1569871/Drink-rats-milk-says-Heather-Mills.html.

Wigthorn :: Nothing too clever here. It's an anagram of my home town, Worthing. I wanted to set it in Worthing because when was the last time you read a novel set in Worthing? Never, right? It was easier for me to imagine a fictional situation in a fictional town so I changed the name.

Below is a page from my notebook detailing the extensive cerebral work involved in this task.

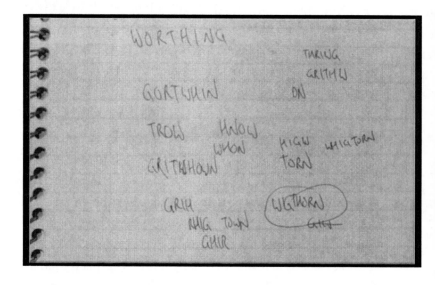

Pharmara :: I needed a name for a pharmaceutical company and I stumbled across Mara, an Egyptian God or princess or someone like that. I could stick 'pharm' in front of it and it sounded alright. That's all I remember. I never said this bit would be mind-blowing!

Wind turbines :: I originally finished the 1st draft at the end of 2008 and then this happened a few years later - http://en.wikipedia.org/wiki/Rampion_Wind_Farm. A wind farm off the coast of Worthing. Unfortunately, I can't predict lottery numbers, football matches or horse racing results.

CBID (Constant Broadcast Identification) :: Is just a progression of the RFID tags currently being used http://electronics.howstuffworks.com/gadgets/high-tech-gadgets/rfid.htm.

C.I.C.S.I. (Centrally Integrated Computer Systems Intelligence) :: Its fun making acronyms that can be shortened and bastardised into another, completely unrelated word. Governments spend millions doing it. Call me.

Mordinges Drive ::

1086 Worthing itself appears in the Domesday Book as the tiny hamlets of Ordinges and Mordinges.

Quoted from - http://www.worthing.net/history.shtml.

Mozart's 'La Finta Giardiniera' :: I just wanted a garden themed piece of classical music. I've never actually heard it, hang on, that sounds so bad *goes off to YouTube* https://www.youtube.com/watch?v=eW__mySMcd0. Yeah, I'm sure tomato plants would love that.

Percy :: The underground garden computer is named after Percy Thrower, the old Blue Peter gardener - http://en.wikipedia.org/wiki/Percy_Thrower.

Marks & Waitadsco :: I'm sure British readers will have spotted this. In a future where businesses are merging and getting taken over with hardly any government to protect against monopolies then eventually monopolies will happen. So this is an amalgamation of some of the main supermarkets in Britain; Marks & Spencer's, Waitrose, ASDA and Tesco's.

Solar Car/PMP :: I've written more about this here back in 2009 - http://www.b3n3llis.com/2009/09/self-sustainable-and-carbon-neutral-car-travel/. Recently I stumbled on this YouTube video from SolarRoadways.com - https://www.youtube.com/watch?v=qlTA3rnpgzU - well worth a watch.

And there's a sensible, boring, total bummer, fact-filled retort video here - http://www.youtube.com/watch?v=Mzzz5DdzyWY. Boo!

Doomsday Vault :: It's a real place - http://www.croptrust.org/content/svalbard-global-seed-vault.

The Florida Isles :: This is imagining Florida as a series of islands after the sea level has risen quite dramatically. You can see for yourself here - http://geology.com/sea-level-rise/florida.shtml.

Billy Gold :: When I lived in Miami I went to an electrical store to buy a toaster and kettle. The sales assistant was called Billy Gold. I thought it was the best name I'd ever heard (this was before Leroy Merlin came into my life). The real Billy Gold asked me, "Are you from Barbados?" 'Fraid not Billy.

Prospero X4 :: One of the 5 huge corporations running the UK along with Pharmara. The Prospero X3 was the first British satellite launched by a British rocket in 1971 - http://en.wikipedia.org/wiki/Prospero_(satellite). You live and learn.

The 'Big Five' corporations :: Pharmara, Prospero X4 and then three others that don't get mentioned but I think I did name them in my notes somewhere.

Whale Café :: This doesn't exist in Worthing. But it should.

Leroy Merlin :: This is a French chain of DIY superstores. I remember driving past one and thinking what a wicked name it is. If this ebook does well in France I'll probably get the merde sued out of me.

Sonjitsonic :: Another amalgamation. Sony, Fujitsu and Panasonic. I told you, making up acronyms and amalgamations are a valuable source of procrastination and fun.

C.O.V.E.R.T. :: This one was my favourite acronym to make up. I had my head in a thesaurus for ages.

Googazonbay :: I have no shame.

Only Dad's Office in Adder Towers :: I'm taking this too far, right? This is a mash-up of some of the most iconic moments from some of the most popular comedies in the UK;

Only Fools & Horses, Dad's Army, The Office, Blackadder and Faulty Towers.

One-seven-bravo :: My old flat number, 17b.

Millyla :: The names of my two Goddaughters; Milly and Lyla.

Charles Sand :: A bit of an injoke amongst some friends. Whilst being 'proper mashed up' in the early 90's we watched a film called 'The Eyes of Charles Sand' and it done our boxes in. https://www.youtube.com/watch?v=Gq0LzSE26rg - for God's sake Raymond, just bloody answer her!

Black Star :: The only other pharmaceutical company along with Pharmara. Named after the Radiohead song - https://www.youtube.com/watch?v=EmNuMrbV6nU.

Mossyface Wood :: Right, you're not going to believe this but I'm related to Captain W.E. Johns...yeah, the guy who wrote Biggles! I'm related to him by my great, great 2nd cousin removed (or something) marrying him, meaning there's no Biggles blood running through these veins. His first Biggles book, 'The Camels Are Coming' is great but his first ever published novel was 'Mossyface Wood' - http://www.wejohns.com/Adult/Mossyface/. I've never read it as it's as rare as chicken's teeth, so if you can lend me a copy that would be spiffing!

Monkey Riding a Dog :: It happens - https://www.youtube.com/watch?v=IolGVHkv1vQ.

Railroaded :: 'Railroaded' was the original title for this novel for the first 5 drafts but was deemed a little archaic and maybe a little confusing. I much prefer the new title now anyway.

The Passion Fruit Café :: A real cafe in Worthing. I worked near it for a year and became addicted to the toasted bacon, cheese and avocado sandwiches with a healthy dash of chilli oil.

East Neighbourdale Street and Away :: A mash-up of British and Australian soap opera's. This has gone on long enough, right?

The Baggy Trouser Brothers :: I have actually written a rough outline of this children's story which is meant to be a political allegory. Two boys don't want the Nanny to fix their trousers...yeah, not sure how profound it is that's why I only give it a cursory mention.

New Aquarena swimming pool :: In the time it took from the first draft to self-publishing this, the council proposed, planned and built a new swimming pool to replace the original Aquarena in Worthing. They called it Splash Point swimming pool though - http://www.worthingleisure.co.uk/splashpoint/. My prophecy skills have weakened...but I knew that was going to happen.

YOU!

Yes, YOU!

Thank YOU for buying my novel. Thanks for taking the plunge and buying the self-published, debut novel of an unknown author. I hope you enjoyed it. If so, there's a couple of things you can do on various sites to help spread the word. You could even '*talk*' to someone about it! Radical!

Any positive vibes would be very much appreciated. You feed authors you like with positive vibes, they're inspired to write more, you have a wider range of quality books to read, editors can afford a microwave meal, designers can pay for deodorant and a writer might pause to step out into the sunshine and get some vitamin D. It's a vicious circle...I mean, virtuous circle.

Here's some 'Vibe Boosters' I prepared earlier because you're probably relaxing in bed or lazing on a sunlounger right now. I'm slaving away here!

Amazon :: If you left a review and a rating on Amazon, that would be amazing!
UK - http://www.amazon.co.uk/gp/product/B00LET3E8Q
US - http://www.amazon.com/dp/B00LET3E8Q
Canada - http://www.amazon.ca/gp/product/B00LET3E8Q
Australia - https://www.amazon.com.au/dp/B00LET3E8Q

Goodreads :: Friend me on Goodreads here - https://www.goodreads.com/author/show/8344637.Ben_Ellis

Review 'In A Right State' here - https://www.goodreads.com/book/show/22610750-in-a-right-state

Twitter :: Follow me on Twitter @b3n3llis.

#ivereadinarightstate - Write a tweet with this hashtag. Ask a question, leave feedback, comment, talk with other readers, anything!

B3n3llis.com :: Come and visit me on my site where I talk more about this novel and another two that are at various stages. Sign up for the mailing list to stay updated.

CPSIA information can be obtained at www.ICGtesting.com
Printed in the USA
LVOW10s0410230716

497472LV00013B/268/P